THE SILENT MIDWINTER

Jamie-Lee Brooke

To Lynn

Thank you!

Jamie-Lee Brooke

ISBN: 9798-3771-8857-5

For my mum and dad x

CHAPTER ONE

The first photo is easy. That one must be filed; there's no question, doubt or maybe. It's clearly explicit, with a close-up shot of Anna West performing a sex act with a vibrator. But for some reason, that photo isn't stirring the same uncomfortable feeling that the second photo seems to. I find this photo more intimate. Full breasts cupped by a lacy bra with a delicate red ribbon at its centre. I'm not sure why I find this one more intimate. I think it's because I know that he can have this one. It's not explicit. It doesn't need filing. He can have it; it's the rules. I push the feeling aside, stuff the photo back into the envelope with its letter and go to file the explicit one and then I stop. I take the photo back out of the envelope and file them both. I'm keeping his photo.

'Ooh, let's take a squiz then,' Mala bursts back into the post room. 'I can smell a juicy picture a mile off.'

I hand her the pictures. 'It's Anna, Jason Sawyer's girlfriend.'

'And you were just gonna stuff these away and not share? Holy moly, this woman's got it all on show. Cooee.' Mala whistles, examining the more explicit photo from different angles. 'You know he can keep this one, right?' She hands the photo of the breasts back to me.

'Just wasn't sure. I was on the fence with it.' I don't think I'm lying. Mala just raises her eyebrows at me.

'So, Phil said that tensions are high on B wing still. Nasty business that was, never known it so close to a riot. If Phil hadn't… are you okay?'

Mala's voice trails off. There he is, on the lower walkway, taking the bins out. Jason Sawyer. He stops momentarily and looks in this direction. My heart stops. I guess he can't really see me, but I feel like he knows. He knows I was going to hide his photo from him. It's ridiculous to feel this guilty. It wouldn't have been that much of a crime. He would have received it on his release. Some years away yet, but he would have got it eventually. It's not like stealing. Why do I feel bothered? I don't have a crush on Jason. I can't. I wouldn't. Not with a dangerous criminal – a murderer. I refuse to believe that I'm feeling jealous over him receiving pictures from his girlfriend. Then why do I feel guilty? It's a small thing. Does he ever feel guilty over what he did? Something on a whole different scale to hiding a stupid photo.

'Yo, Kate.' Mala's words suddenly break through.

'Sorry, I'm just not with it.' Again, I don't feel

like I'm lying.

'You having problems at home still?'

'Yeah, it's Felicity… and it's Harper. It's all just full-on with them.' My eyes well up which takes me by surprise.

'Looks like more than that to me.' Mala gives me a stern look.

'I think Jon is having an affair.'

'Whoa, sister, you serious? Here, you don't go getting upset in here.' Mala hands me a tissue. 'I tell you what. You, me, cocktails tonight at Red's. You can tell me all then.'

'I don't know. I can't; it's Felicity. It's not that simple.'

'You need a break. Put your foot down, girl. C'mon, it's Friday, Friday, Friday,' she sings, swaying her hips.

I laugh. Mala always makes me laugh. She has that natural vibrant energy. 'I'll text you when I'm home. I need to check with Jon first.'

Mala carries on jigging away over to the other end of the post room. I look through the window again and Jason has gone. A small number of other prisoners pass by, helping with the bins. I turn back to my desk and continue processing Jason's post. He will get his letter and his photo.

The next letter that I open has a sweet, sickly scent, noticeable instantly. I imagine the sender lightly spritzing the floral notepaper before sealing the envelope. Then I picture her spluttering from the taste as she licks the seal.

Who said romance was dead? It's a shame, though, that her efforts are wasted as I place the letter inside the photocopier. Inmates only receive a copy of the original. Perhaps it's to redeem myself for almost hiding away one of Jason's photos, but I take the perfume-soaked notepaper and rub it against the photocopy. Perhaps not the same but it gives me a small sense of goodwill.

Mala clocks what I'm doing and shakes her head. 'You are way too good to these criminals, woman. And whoa, that perfume is nasty.' She mocks a gag and carries on typing up her e-mails.

I carry on processing and logging the remaining few items of mail. I don't think that I'm too good to the inmates. It's the families and loved ones that I think more about. That I'm curious about. Day after day, I read the prisoners' love letters from home. How they are yearned for, how they are missed. It doesn't matter what some of these inmates have done; there is still someone out there that loves them regardless. I don't get it. The photos, the passion. What sort of woman is Anna West? I'm back to thinking about her, then I catch sight of my reflection in the PC monitor, and I tuck a stray strand of hair back into my bobble. I'm lost for a moment as I think about how cold Jon was with me this morning – how cold he has been now for weeks. *Where does the passion go?*

Mala looks at me and mouths the word,

'Cocktails.'

'Yes, yes okay.' I grin back at her, defeated. She looks back at her screen with a smug expression of victory.

A night out would be perfect. It really would. I've turned down Mala too many times lately. Jon would have to let me have a night out. He goes out whenever he likes, after all. I push away the sinking feeling in the depths of my stomach and gather up the final batch of mail.

'Right, I'm just going to hand this lot over to Phil and I'll be back shortly.' I leave Mala singing to herself and push the mail trolley out of the office.

There is something about the sound of the trolley clattering along the lower walkway that I enjoy; it's rhythmic and soothing. The inmates on this side of the wing are quiet at the moment so the rattling is magnified. As I pass through the doors onto the next walkway, my heart just about stops. I pass inmates all the time. They don't bother me. When I first started here at Standington Prison, I did feel intimidated by them, but not so much now. I have little to do with the prisoners, only in passing and they take no notice of me. But the sight of Jason Sawyer in front of me halts my breath.

He is leaning against the wall with a mop and bucket in hand. The pungent smell of the disinfectant wafting from it. Even in his tracksuit and handling cleaning equipment, he still looks like he has just stepped off a Hawaiian beach with his tanned complexion, floppy black hair, stubble and rich chocolate brown eyes.

I'm now passing him, and he speaks. 'Could you unlock the staff toilets, please? I need to clean them.'

The toilets sit adjacent to the prison guard's office, which was just ahead and where I was taking the mail. It's not unusual for an inmate to ask me to unlock that door but rarely do they say please. This murderer has manners. There is a presence about Jason Sawyer, something mysterious, dangerous. I want to see the appeal but he's a murderer. He's killed a person in cold blood. So what kind of woman is Anna West, to not care about that? I think about the photos and hope that I'm not blushing. I agree to unlock the toilets and as I speak, I can taste the fumes from the disinfectant. I feel a tickle in my nose and I suppress a sneeze.

Jason follows me to the door and watches as I select the key I need. I can feel my nose now filling with a cool fluid and I fear the worst. I quickly unlock the door and allow Jason to pass by inside. It's no good, my nose drips red despite my attempts to suppress the blood. Of all the times to get another nosebleed.

'Are you okay?' Jason asks me.

I nod, brush past him into the toilets, and grab a handful of tissues, pressing the bundle against my nose.

'Keep your head down,' Jason advised. 'I used to think it was hold your head up but it's down.'

'I know the drill, I get them I lot,' I say, realising how I must sound whilst pinching my nostrils together.

Jason hands me more tissues. 'Looks like a heavy one. Do you want me to call someone for you?'

I shake my head. It dawns on me that I'm alone in the toilets with one of the prisoners so I turn on my heels and head out. Not that I felt threatened at that moment. Far from it. For a dangerous murderer, he was kind and polite. I step over to the guard's office and Phil is quick to take the mail from me and sit me down. I ask him to make sure that the toilets are locked up once Jason finishes.

Fortunately, the bleeding ceases quickly. I thank Phil and scoot off back up to the post room. I don't know why I'm cringing to myself. It doesn't matter what a killer must think of me. It doesn't matter at all. I'm a frumpy mess who gets nosebleeds. I'm fine with that. Mala's face is a picture when I re-enter the post room. She jumps up and inspects the collar of my shirt. There is blood splatter. Of course there is.

'What on earth have you been up to, missy? You only had to deliver the mail.' Mala laughs.

'Another nosebleed,' I smile. I could see she was trying to formulate a witty scenario of what could've happened.

'Well, that ain't gonna stop you drinkin' some cocktails and busting some moves tonight, sister.'

I sit back at my desk and chuckle to myself watching Mala shimmy around her swivel chair. Any embarrassment is now forgotten. Yes, I need a night out. I have the urge to feel like the old me, the fun me. Surely Jon will allow me a bit of me time. It's not too much to ask after all that I do. It's not just him I have to convince though. It's Felicity. Without me there, she won't talk to her dad or her sister. She won't talk to anyone. She only talks to me. My beautiful seven-year-old stepdaughter has me trapped.

CHAPTER TWO

The town centre of Bracknell was already looking lively on my drive home. It would be though, wouldn't it on a beautiful Friday evening in May. It was only five-thirty and there were groups of people glammed up gathering outside of the local pubs. With any luck, I'll soon be one of them. In a couple of hours, that could be me, in a dress, hair in curls, laughing and drinking with Mala in Red's beer garden. Pulling up on my driveway, I suddenly don't fancy my chances.

I'm in time to witness Harper storming out of the front door and slamming it behind her. She glares at me, arms folded as she strides past. *Here we go again.* I think about opening the car door and shouting after her, but I know it won't do any good. As I go to though, the front door opens, and Jon appears. He shouts after Harper, but she carries on. If she's not going to listen to him, then she sure as hell won't listen to me.

Jon rubs his face as I approach him. 'What's happened?' I ask.

'Harper's in trouble for fighting at school. Apparently, she punched another girl, Mrs Davis said. She's been suspended for a couple of days next week.'

'What? Why?'

'I've tried to get to the bottom of it, but she yelled that I never listen anyway, and she's stormed off.'

We head inside the house, and I have a sinking feeling I know what the real reason is, and I'm sure Jon knows it too. I try to approach the subject, but I'm interrupted by Felicity. She skips over to me and wraps her arms around my waist, burying her head into my stomach.

'How was your day Fizzy?' I ask her, flattening down her blonde curls.

'Okay,' she replies in her usual small voice.

Without looking up at either me or her dad, she lets me go and skips back out of the kitchen.

'Don't you think she's getting too old to be called Fizzy now?' Jon almost snaps as he fills the kettle.

'No, I don't think seven is too old. She likes it.'

'Of course, you're the only one that knows what she bloody well likes.'

His words sting. I've literally just walked through the door and all I can do is imagine a scenario whereby my husband greets me home from work with a hug and asks me how my day was. My reality now though, is a desperate need to get out of here. I need my best friend and I need to get drunk.

'Mala has invited me to Red's tonight. I was hoping it'd be okay as I haven't had a night out in ages.'

Jon drags his hands down his face. 'You have therapy with Felicity tomorrow morning.'

'I know. I won't have a lot to drink. I'll be fine.'

'It's not good timing is it. Harper has created an atmosphere, Felicity will be anxious; she's going to need you tonight.'

So, one minute, I'm being scolded for being the only one that Fizzy opens up to and the next I'm being begged to stay in with her as I'm the only one she opens up to.

'She seems fine at the moment,' I push it. 'Work has been stressful and I'd really like a night out. It'd do me good.'

Jon doesn't get a chance to respond as Harper bursts back into the house.

'It's her fault,' Harper all but screams at me.

I knew it. I knew this would escalate and be about me.

'You need to tell us what's happened.' Her dad's voice remains calm.

Harper looks at me with hatred in her dark eyes. Her dyed black hair clinging around her sweaty, pale face.

'Lexi Keggans started it. She kept calling me a "Snitch Bitch" because my stepmom is a screw. She was done for smoking by the tennis courts, but I didn't tell. I didn't. Everyone hates me because of her job.'

Harper stabs her finger towards me and bolts from the kitchen. I throw my hands up in defeat.

'I'm not a prison officer. I just open the mail.

We need to go into that school together and sort out this bullying. It's getting worse, and look, she hates me.'

'Her first GCSE exam is just a few weeks away, we can't let all of this ruin her chances.' Jon all but slams down two mugs from the cupboard. 'You know, I've never been comfortable with you working at Standington. I think it's time you reconsider finding something different.'

'I like my job.'

'You said it's stressful.'

'I'm not leaving my job. We'll go into school first thing Monday and put a stop to it.' I feel myself start to shake. It's not so much that we are having this disagreement, but it's the tone of Jon's voice – that sarcastic tone. Lately, I feel like an idiot every time he talks to me with his snapping and sniping. I turn the oven on and busy myself rummaging in the freezer for something for dinner.

'Shall we have these pizzas?' I say holding up a box.

'Just go to Red's tonight with your mate. You and Harper need some space,' Jon sighs and strides out of the kitchen.

My eyes sting, I guess what he actually means is 'Just go out, but don't you dare.' It doesn't matter; it's not space from Harper I need. It's from him, my husband. I take out all the pizzas and finish off making my own coffee. Taking my mobile from my bag, I text Mala. *I'll meet you outside of Red's at 7.30x.* I'm not going to let all this ruin my night. It'll blow over. I'll talk to Harper tomorrow when she's calmed down. My thoughts turn to what I'm going to wear tonight, realising that it's been so long since I've been out that I don't think I have any nice going out clothes. My thoughts are broken as I feel arms wrap around my waist from behind almost making me jump. I hadn't heard Fizzy sneak up behind me.

'Miss Fizz, you made me jump!' I smile down at her.

'What's for dinner?' She softly speaks.

'Pizza, is that okay?'

Felicity nods greedily and I hand her one of the pizza boxes. 'Will you help me unwrap them?'

'Yes,' she gleams, and rips away at the packaging.

'I'm going out with a friend after dinner. Is that okay with you?'

'Will you wear a pretty dress?'

'If I can find one in my wardrobe that fits,' I laugh.

Felicity chuckles covering her mouth with her hand. 'Cheese and tomato is my favourite pizza. Yes, you can go out to play, Kate.'

I smile affectionately at her and we continue to prepare the pizzas. This special girl never ceases to amaze me and I find myself having second thoughts: that I should stay in with her tonight. No. I'm going out and that's that. I'm going to let my hair down and after the weekend, not only am I going to get to the bottom of Harper's problems, I'm also going to get to the bottom of my husband's too. I've seen his bank statement; I know that he's lied. I want to know who he's cheating on me with. No more treading on eggshells. It's time that I confronted him.

CHAPTER THREE

Mala throws her arms around me and plants a smacker of a kiss on my cheek. 'Whoa, sister, you're looking hot.'

I'm not, I know I'm not and I know Mala knows I'm not. I am wearing a knee-length black skirt and a conservative cream top. It does have a section of lacy detail, but overall, I'm feeling very plain next to my best friend in her skimpy low-cut dress and devil red lipstick – lipstick which I'm now trying to scrub from my cheek. Now that's how I'd like to be greeted by my husband when I return home from work. Eyes lit up, happy to see me, telling me I look nice. In the early few months, I'm sure that used to happen. I don't know exactly when the opposite to that started to happen but gradually it did. My friends never cease to show me love and affection – never. Why is that?

Mala links my arm and within minutes she has marched us inside to the bar, ordered us two cocktails each, and found us a table in the garden.

'Two drinks?' I laugh at my friend.

'Happy hour is nearly up, and it saves queuing again. C'mon you know the drill; you've not been out in way too long.'

'You know it's difficult for me with Fizz. Oh,

and don't go getting me too drunk. We have a therapy session in the morning.'

Mala raises disapproving eyebrows at me. 'I get that Fizz relies on you but don't let Jon take you for granted. So, what's this about an affair? Who do I need to put a hit out on?'

I laugh at Mala pursing her full lips in an attempt to look aggressive. 'Right, okay, I don't know for sure but Jon was meant to be working away last weekend, as you know he does. He told me that he was staying at the Premier Inn in Docklands. I didn't intentionally snoop. I had no cause to, but he'd left his bank statement open on the laptop and I was drawn to quickly looking at it and I saw a payment to *The Moors Country Hotel* —'

'And where's that?' Mala butts in, taking a big sip of her Porn Star martini.

'I googled it and it's in bloody Dartmoor, practically in the middle of nowhere. A far cry from bloody Docklands. I've never known him to do business in Devon.'

'Did you ask him about it?'

'No... don't look at me like that. I'm going to though. I have to be careful. Jon has been cold with me lately and Harper is on the war path and hates me and I can't risk unsettling Fizz.'

'With what you do for his kids, he should be treating you as a goddamn queen. Don't let him take advantage. Look at you, you're beautiful and worth so much more. Perhaps it's something innocent. Don't do your head in over it until you know the score.' Mala takes my hand and squeezes it.

'I think we need two more drinks, don't you?' I say before we've even finished the ones that we have. 'Back in a mo. Same again?'

Mala nods and I make my way back into the bar which is filling up fast. The atmosphere is rowdy and I'm sure they have turned the music up. The décor is dated inside Red's and the carpeted area feels sticky underfoot but there is rarely trouble in the bar, unlike The Duke over the road. The beer garden here is at least spacious and attractive. I squeeze my way past a group of guys to get to the bar and find a gap to wait to be served. At the end of the bar, I can't help but notice a young-looking couple practically eating each other. Young love, I smile to myself. Where does that passion go? It's something that just keeps creeping into my mind. It's not something I even want anymore, at least, I don't think it is. Snogging in crowded pubs makes me cringe. It's for other people, not me, not for someone in their forties. I try to ignore the twinge in my gut and dismiss that it might actually be a twinge of jealousy and then she pops into my head again. Anna West. I wonder what she looks like. I've only seen a few pics of her naked body. Not her face. Not yet. I imagine that she's a looker to attract Jason Sawyer. How does a cold-blooded killer find love and passion and all I can manage is a few grunts when I arrive home from work?

I'm aware I may be blushing now that I'm thinking back to Anna's intimate pictures. I try to be pleasing in the bedroom but perhaps it's not enough anymore. Not that Jon comes near me much lately to even try. I feel sad that it's not something we talk about. We should be comfortable enough to, shouldn't we? *Who is Anna West?* Is she more than just sexy underwear and a high sex drive?

I realise that the bartender is waving at me to get my attention. I apologise and ask for two more Porn Star Martinis and two Mojitos. A few minutes later and the drinks are lined up in front of me and I haven't planned on how I was going to carry them back outside. I'm about to wave to the barman for a tray but the guy standing next to me leans into me and shouts above the music, 'I'll help with those. Lead the way.' He takes two of the glasses without waiting for me to agree. I just smile and take the lead. He follows me out into the garden and Mala's face is a picture.

'You return with drinks and a man. I'm impressed, sister.' Mala winks at both me and the guy.

The man laughs and says that he was happy to help, 'Looks like you ladies are in for a good night.' He continues eyeing up the collection of cocktails on the table.

'You betcha.' Mala winks again.

'Have a good one.' The guy winks back and

makes his way back into the bar.

'You're incorrigible.' I laugh and shake my head at my friend.

'Whoa, you're the one picking up men from the bar here.' She raises her hands in protest with that wicked smirk of hers.

'Hardly,' I say, taking a large gulp of Mojito. 'Oh that is good. Anyway, I didn't quiz you more on what Phil was saying about a near riot on the B wing. So, all is okay now?'

I was keen to get off the subject of men. Mala is single and loves to flirt and probably has a lot to do with why Jon is reluctant for me to go out drinking with her. She goes on to tell how one of the officers, Nigel, was accused by an inmate, Ben, of stealing his cash. It's not been proven yet, but I had heard about that. After all, the cash usually comes to our office first in the mail so that we can load it onto their accounts. We had no record of receiving this payment unless Nigel somehow intercepted it. Why Ben has accused him, we don't know yet, but there has been a history of trouble between the two men – complaints being thrown back and forth.

Mala proceeds with her gossip in her usual animated way, 'So, Ben is shouting and mouthing off, his mates are getting all riled up and they're mouthing off. Turns out Ben owes Harrison money; you know, the one with that nasty scar. The kinda guy you don't wanna be owing money to. So Harrison and his guys are threatening Ben and you've got his lot going off at Nigel. Stuff is getting thrown. Right, get this… then Jason Sawyer swans over to Ben, whispers something in his ear, then has words with Harrison. There's almost a scuffle but Harrison backs off and calls his guys off. Within no time, everyone just chills it out.' Mala sits back in her chair looking satisfied.

'Didn't know Jason had that much influence in there,' I say.

'That's what makes these assholes dangerous, you never know them,' Mala scoffs and I have to agree. 'Anyway, enough about bloody work. Let's get these down our necks,' Mala raises her Porn Star Martini and we clink glasses.

I clock Mala's eyes raising mischievously and I turn around. Approaching us is the guy that helped carry our drinks and he's with his mate who's carrying a tray holding a wine bottle and glasses. 'Can we join you, ladies?' The guy smiles.

'Pull up a chair.' Mala doesn't hesitate.

Oh well. I did say that I wanted the old me back, the fun me. I decide to relax and enjoy the company. For one night I can just be me.

CHAPTER FOUR
Harper

Harper hears the front door open. She mutes her TV and checks the time. It's just after two a.m. She decides that a night of binge watching *The Vampire Diaries* is needed to help relax her. She can't sleep; she has too much whirring around her mind. Her GCSEs, her best friend Callum whom she has now grown stronger feelings for, that cow Lexi Keggans, and Kate – her stepmom. Everything is all getting too much, there is no release, no escape. Everything feels against her.

She creeps over to her bedroom door to listen to Kate shuffling around downstairs. *What was she doing out so late?* she wonders. Her stepmom never goes out this late. She hears a creak from across the landing. Her dad is awake and she can hear him now making his way downstairs. Raised voices can be heard but she can't make out the words. 'Ha.' The teenager breathes out loud to herself. *Hopefully, Dad is cross with her enough to throw her out.* She strains to listen harder, but it's gone quiet. She holds her breath as she hears footsteps coming back up the stairs. If her dad knew she was awake he wouldn't be pleased. Even though it was the weekend, he'd think that two a.m. is a bit too late to be up watching TV.

She could only hear one set of footsteps though. *Perhaps that dragon is being made to sleep on the sofa?* Harper has been waiting for something like this to happen. For Kate to do something bad enough so she gets thrown out. Maybe then Lexi and her gang would leave her alone. It felt good to lay that bully out, to blast Lexi in the face but it's left her feeling sick. She knows that her life won't be worth living when she returns to school. It had already been bad enough. She had tried showing the hateful texts to the school's pastoral team and tried to open up about being poked fun at during every break time. She even braved grassing Lexi up for the time that she pushed her over and took photos up her skirt.

None of that was easy to do and it turned out that none of it mattered. "Can't you two just be friends?" Mrs Davis would just say. It was Harper's word against Lexi's and there was no proof apart from a few text messages that were sent to her out of school, which apparently is not the school's responsibility. The next best advice from Mrs Davis was, "Can't you just ignore her?" Lexi has had it in for her even more since branding her the 'Snitch Bitch' and all because of Kate – the embarrassing stepmother from hell. It was all so unfair, and she wishes that Kate was more like Callum's mum, who works as a hairdresser.

Callum is the only person in the world who

listens to her and allows her to cry on his shoulder. She could be herself around him and he made everything better. He only saw her as a mate, but she couldn't bear to be without him. Her world is crashing in on her, crushing her soul. Nobody understands. Harper slides down onto the floor and brings her knees up to her chest, hugging herself tightly. She wipes away a tear, never feeling so alone. She couldn't even talk to her younger sister. *Why wouldn't Felicity talk to her? Why Kate and not her?* Harper wishes that her real mum had never died and curses how terrible everything has become since. Kate has ruined everything and now she must pay.

CHAPTER FIVE

Ten minutes left of today's session and for once I couldn't be more desperate to get back home. Suppressing the overwhelming nausea is taking its toll on me and the paracetamol is wearing off. I rub my forehead. Felicity is finishing off a pattern finding task whilst the therapist is going over old ground with me. There are still no answers as to why Felicity will only talk to me, has only ever talked to me, since I met her dad. I could drive myself crazy wondering what it is about me that she likes; that she feels comfortable with. I say again that it's not like I have experience with kids. I'm not a mother, I've never worked with them. 'What's so special about you?' Harper has shouted at me on more than one occasion.

We have ruled out that it's not because I look like her mother. I don't at all. Felicity was three when her mum died suddenly. She witnessed her mother knocked down by a chance thief snatching her handbag. He didn't intentionally kill her, but she lost her footing, cracking her head on the corner of a wall. It was enough to kill her. The trauma of losing her mum must have triggered her condition – her selective mutism. Before then she was reaching all the standard milestones when it came to speech development and then she just stopped. That is, until she met me.

Felicity raises her hand to signal that she has finished her activity. The therapist takes her workbook.

'Excellent work, young lady,' the therapist smiles proudly, 'all correct.' She then turns to me and shows me her work. 'You know, Felicity's incredible aptitude for problem solving and pattern finding will take her far. These are the skills that engineers possess, for example.

'Yes, well, academically she's continuing to do well all round. She absorbs everything.' I beam at Fizzy, 'You're as bright as a button aren't you?' Fizz sits next to me and places her arm across my stomach looking tired. I try not to heave from the pressure. Whatever it is about me, I may never know, but right now I know that I'm not winning any Stepmother Of The Year awards. All I can taste is stale alcohol and I have blurry images of stumbling home. *How did it get so late?* Jon hardly said two words to me this morning. I guess he'll find plenty to say to me later.

'That's it for today then,' the therapist says.

Felicity realises that she hasn't put her shoes back on. She'd taken them off when she had time in the ball pit in the garden. She skips over to the other side of the room to collect them.

The therapist continues, 'I know I've said it numerous times, but Felicity isn't textbook selective mutism. It's a little more unusual for a child with her condition to clam up and be unable to communicate with her close family members. We have a long road ahead of us. I want to schedule some sessions with her dad and include her sister in with some too. Some team-building exercises. Try something different.'

'That sounds great. Jon will be up for that, I'm sure of it.'

Fizz returns with her shoes back on and takes my hand. 'Come on then, let's get us home.' I thank the therapist and agree to see her again in a fortnight.

'Can I have an ice cream treat please?' Fizz looks up at me as we make our way to the car. I had promised her at our next visit that we would try out the new ice cream and shakes parlour that had opened along the high street. The thought of ice cream churns its way inside my gut, but I couldn't refuse. I can do one more stop; I can do it for Fizzy. Peace, quiet and my darkened bedroom can wait a short while longer.

We pull up in the park's car park so that we can bring the ice cream back and sit on a bench to enjoy a bit of the morning sun. We hurry across the road to the high street and before long Fizz is clutching a double scoop of Rocky Road. My phone rings. It's Mala. I hesitantly answer it, unsure of what revelations will be revealed from last night. I have hold of Fizz with my free hand as we make our way back across the street.

'How's your head?' Mala sounds irritatingly cheerful for a morning after.

'Not good, not good at all,' I can barely speak up as the sight of Fizz's ice cream is creating bile in my throat.

'Sign of a good night, sister. Man, you were on fire on that dance floor.'

And so the flashbacks begin. Mala continues to laugh down the phone at my efforts to grind to the floor. *Oh God, did I do that?* The twinging in my hips is suddenly starting to make sense. I join Mala in fits of giggles but my head pounding forces me to take a breath. And then I remember that guy.

'You left with that guy, didn't you?' I screech down the phone.

'Nothing happened. We shared a taxi back and he carried on to his. You know I ain't that type of woman.'

I laugh, 'I'm not saying anything.' I joke, but I know for all of Mala's flirting, she does have standards.

'I did get his number though, oh yes.'

'So, you going to call him?'

'Hang on a minute sister, what about you more importantly. His mate. Can't even remember his name... We left you with him. Well?'

I struggle to grasp at hazy memories. The guy. I think I slow danced with him. Nothing happened. It nearly did. I'm sure I went to kiss him. Did I? He pulled away. Or was it the other way round? Or was it nothing? The main thing is that nothing happened. *Oh God.*

'Look, I've got to go. Felicity is with me. We'll talk later. Love you.'

'Okay but you're going to tell all on Monday. Love you.'

Fizz and I find our bench and take a seat. It's our bench because this is where we met. Where this five-year-old little girl sat beside me and asked me what book I was reading. Two years on and me and her dad married. I could never have foreseen that happening. The shocked look on Jon's face alarmed me that day, the first day we met. I thought I'd done something wrong, that I was some monster talking to a young child. Far from it though, he was choked up, listening to his precious girl chatting away to me about what books she likes. I told him that most weekends I would sit in the park and read for a bit of time out and the following week, they found me there again and Fizz chatted away to me some more.

It's hard to resist someone who makes you feel so special, so wanted. Sadness washes through me. What am I to Jon now? Was I always just being used as his daughter's carer? My previous husband left me as I couldn't give him children. One failed IVF attempt and he was out the door and off with someone else. Yes, that hurt. And once more I find myself not feeling loved for me. Wallowing in a hangover of self-pity is not helping. I need to talk to him – and I will. As soon as I feel less like vomiting.

'C'mon Fizzy. Let's get home.'

CHAPTER SIX
Gregg

Damn it, she's freakishly strong, Gregg wrestles with the seventeen-year-old, trying to pin her arms behind her back. She's slippery though and manages to release an arm, spin around and boot him in the shin. She loses her footing and stumbles backwards. Gregg strikes her head, forcing her down. He seizes the upper hand now to pin her down, pushing her face into the dirt. With the other hand, he whips out his knife and holds it to her face. He didn't think he'd need the knife. He underestimated the fight in a young woman. It's not a story to retell the others.

She lay still for a moment, sobbing to be let go. Gregg quickly checks out his surroundings. No one around. It's a quiet lay-by just off the main car park to the woods, but it's the middle of the day. There could be a sodding dog walker at any time, he panics. It should have just been a quick grab and run. Grooming and luring them to a location was easier. They came to him. Easy. But that takes time, and he was pushed for it. He forces the girl up and marches her to the back of the van, pulling the door open, maintaining a firm grip on her. She screams. Gregg forces his gloved hand around her mouth and bundles her inside the van. He releases the pressure from her mouth so he can grab the rope. The girl clamps her teeth into his wrist, biting hard. Gregg yelps out, pulling the teen's head back with force. She screams again. Gregg punches her in the face and gets his knife to her throat. He's got her cornered now and gets the rope around her wrists. He then tapes up her mouth.

Falling back on his bum for a moment with relief at the restrained young woman, he inspects the blood seeping from the teeth marks. 'Damn it,' he curses. He took a last look at the wide-eyed girl and slips out from the back of the van. He slams the doors shut and checks his surroundings again. Quiet. He looks carefully. Definitely no one around. He jumps into the driver's side and starts the ignition. He's about to pull away but his phone rings. It's Riley.

'Riley, what's up?'

'Word's in that Jason Sawyer has been granted his appeal.'

'You don't need to worry about that.'

'He can't get out. Do you hear me?'

'He won't. The evidence was stacked against him.'

'But he's been granted his damn appeal.'

'What can I do?'

'We'll talk. But one way or another, he's not coming out. Oh, and Gregg… the girl?'

'I have her with me right now.'

'Good. We have an order for another so sort it.'

'I gotta get movin'. Talk later.'

Gregg hangs up and inspects his hand again. "*Sort it,*" he mimics. *Where's the please and the thanks*? He thumps the steering wheel before pulling away. He prays that he wasn't seen and no one heard the brat scream. Next time he'll do it his way.

CHAPTER SEVEN

Jon greets me when I get home with a smile and a peck on the cheek. This takes me by surprise, he can't be too cross with me then.

'How was the session?' he asks, giving Felicity a big hug.

'It went well. The therapist is going to arrange a family team building activity for us,' I say.

'Sounds good,' he says as he lets Fizz go and watches as she skips from the kitchen.

I pour myself a glass of water, willing my headache to leave me. I'm ready to crawl back to bed.

'Hangover?' Jon asks with some tone of sarcasm.

I merely nod, waiting for the lecture.

'You were funny last night.' He winks at me. 'Starting to strip and offering to have me on the couch, whilst falling over was quite something.'

Oh God I did. I threw myself at my husband. Which should've been fine, but he sat me on the sofa and went off to bed. I think within minutes, I had curled up and passed out. At some point I had made it upstairs to bed though.

Jon puts his arms around me and I place my heavy head against his chest.

'We should make more time for each other, but

perhaps not in the middle of the night and not when you're half-cut.' Jon quietly speaks in my ear.

It's like my hangover has just melted away. My stomach flutters for the first time in a long time. Perhaps he does still think of me in that way after all. Perhaps he does still love me. I shouldn't doubt him. He works hard, he has a high-pressured job, and two daughters who present different challenges. I admit that perhaps I don't make enough effort with him either. After all, when was the last time that I suggested making love to my husband or got dressed up for him or suggested we go out somewhere just the two of us? It shouldn't wait until all my insecurities bubble over after a cocktail-infused night out.

Jon kisses the top of my head and suggests that I go for a lie-down and he'll bring me up a coffee. This is music to my ears and I gladly agree.

'Dad, I know wh–' Harper bursts into the kitchen and freezes at the sight of us hugging. She turns to leave.

'Harper wait. Well, what is it?' her dad asks.

She holds back in the doorway, 'I know what I'd like as a treat for finishing my exams.'

'Go on then, how much will it cost me?' Jon laughs.

'I want my lip pierced.'

Jon mocks looking horrified but then laughs. 'Yes, you can have your lip done. You're already starting to look like the undead. You may as well.'

Harper looks insulted but then grins and hurries back to her room. No doubt she'll be straight on the phone to Callum to tell him the good news, I smile. Jon is in a good mood this morning which I couldn't feel more thankful for right now, especially with a hangover from hell. We all need a weekend of peace. That will have certainly put a smile on Harper's face anyway. But then I remember. The hotel. He spent the night in a country hotel in Devon when he said he was on business in London. I need to ask him, but I don't want to ruin the moment. Funny, isn't it, how he's the one that has lied yet I'm the one that doesn't want to rock the boat? No, I'm not going to bring it up now; I'm going to enjoy the relaxed atmosphere, get rid of this hangover and broach the subject later.

'Oh, by the way, I'm out for dinner this evening.' Jon pipes up just as I'm about to finally get back to bed.

'What? Since when?'

'Last minute thing, a business dinner, as Alan wants to go over strategies.'

'On a Saturday night? But we were having a takeaway night.'

'You can still do that. Have a girls' night without me.'

'Fine, it's okay. I need to have lie down. I'll help sort lunch in an hour.'

I head upstairs, my head feeling heavier suddenly. Is this why he's in a good mood? What is he really doing? I stop outside Fizz's bedroom and listen in. She's chatting away to herself – probably acting out something with her dolls and horses set. I don't tire of listening in on her when she's alone in her room. It's the only time she feels uninhibited. I really would do anything for that special girl. I look up with a start as Harper opens her bedroom door. She sees me and retreats into her room, closing the door with force. I rub my forehead and shut myself away in my own sanctuary. *Girls' night.* Somehow, I think our girls' night will consist of us shutting ourselves away in our rooms.

My bed embraces me as I press my head into the pillow. Just an hour, I just need an hour. My body aches with fatigue from head to foot. I'm sure that there was a time I could party all night and then manage a day's work with none of my joints hurting. Mala has a lot to answer for. Never again. I reach for my phone and scroll through Facebook, my eyes feeling heavy. A few minutes of this and I'll be out like a baby. But my eyes are now wide open. I've stopped on a news post with a picture of Jason Sawyer. His appeal has been approved. I read on with interest. Jason has always maintained his innocence after being accused of stabbing a man called Michael Bennet to death. He admitted to stabbing the man in the upper shoulder in self-defence before fleeing the scene and calling the police. He stabbed the man once, yet when the police arrived the victim had numerous stab wounds and was dead at the scene. Forensics found the knife which was used and only Jason's prints were on the weapon. However, forensics brought to light that the majority of the stab wounds were made with a different knife. The jury were not convinced at the trial and Jason was sent down for life. Jason has now won the right to appeal and for the evidence to be re-evaluated.

I sit up and read it all again. What if he is innocent? I'm unnerved at how much I hope that he is. What should it matter to me? I refuse to believe that I have a crush on an inmate. I don't. It's definitely not that. Perhaps that's why Anna West still loves him, because she believes that he is innocent. Makes sense, right? She's standing by her man because he hasn't killed anyone. But he did have a knife on him and was capable of stabbing Michael at least once. He must have been involved in something dodgy. Anna has put in her letters to Jason enough times that she'll never give up on him. Anna is filling my thoughts again now with her intimate pictures. I don't want to but I have to admit it to myself. It's not Jason that's making me feel uncomfortable. It's Anna West. I'm curious about her and I feel like I can't let it go. She's there all the time. I have to know who she is.

CHAPTER EIGHT

'But we had pizza yesterday.' I mock a frown at Felicity whose eyes are sparkling. 'What do you fancy Harper?' I raise my voice a notch to be heard through the teenager's earphones. She just shrugs.

'Answer Kate.' Jon snaps, removing Harper's earphones for her.

'Hey.' She snaps back.

'Fizz wants pizza. That okay with you?' I try to keep my cool.

'Yes,' Harper replies curtly putting her earphones back in place.

'I'll get the usual then shall I,' now feeling like I'm talking to no one in particular. Jon pecks me on the cheek and says he won't be in late.

'Where is it you're going?'

'The Castle Inn. Nothing fancy, just a quick business meeting with Alan over some pub grub.' With that, he swipes up his keys and says that he won't be back late again and off he goes.

I sit down at the table opposite Harper and pull the pizza menu up on my phone and start selecting items. Harper scrapes her chair back and heads out of the kitchen. I sigh but I'm not surprised. The image of a girls' night in where we're all giggling over pizza and watching a movie together was never going to be one that was going to materialise. Fizz looks over my shoulder and asks if she can have one of those squidgy chocolate chip cookies. I add it to the basket with a smile. I have Fizzy at least.

'Shall we paint our nails tonight?' I ask her.

She nods, twirls around a few times in a circle, and skips from the room. I complete the order and watch the little timer pop up, telling me that our order will be with us in thirty minutes. I still can't say I'm very hungry. It really will be the last time that I drink that much. It was a bit inconsiderate of me when I had to be out of the house so early with Fizz. It's rare though that I don't put everyone else's needs first. That I chose to have some fun for me, yet Jon does it without batting an eyelid. He just comes and goes as he pleases without feeling any weight of responsibility, so it seems.

It is unusual for Jon to need to dash out for a business dinner on a Saturday night. I can't think of a time that's happened before. His good mood this morning felt unusual too. I would doubt him though, wouldn't I, after discovering he has lied? This is why I should just ask him about the hotel. If there was a good explanation, then I wouldn't be sitting here doubting his every move and mood. But that doesn't help my paranoia now though, does it? Has he really gone out with Alan? I pick up my phone again and without thinking it through I call Mala.

'Hey what's up?' she chirps.

'Are you free? Just for half an hour or so?'

'Yeah just about. I'm meeting Tom at eight. Why?'

'The guy from last night?'

'This girl doesn't waste time, you know that,' Mala laughs.

'Look anyway, I'm sorry to ask this but could you come pick me up, take me to The Castle Inn. I just want to see if Jon is in there. It won't take long… please?'

'Sure, but why do you need me for that? You've lost me.'

'I don't want to risk Jon seeing my car. I don't want him to know I'm spying on him. Could you go inside and see if he's there with Alan like he should be?'

'A secret mission? Hell yes, count me in sister. I'll be with you ASAP.'

I hang up and take a breath. This won't take long and then I can relax for the evening. I'm sure that he'll be there with Alan and then I'll talk to him tomorrow about the hotel and then I can stop feeling like this suspicious wife. It's not something that I'm enjoying. I head upstairs and cautiously knock on Harper's bedroom door. She throws the door open, her rock music blaring out. She has put on dark plum lipstick and thick lines of eyeliner. It actually looks quite striking on her pale complexion. She is a beauty even though she hates to be told so.

'I need to pop out just for ten mins. I said I'd help Mala with a quick job. Can you just watch Fizz and open the door to the pizza guy? I honestly won't be long.' It's not something that I ask Harper to do much of – babysitting. With Felicity unable to communicate with others, it's a worry should there ever be an emergency. It's a big responsibility for a sixteen-year-old who has emotional issues of her own at the best of times.

'Yeah sure,' she nods and closes the door.

I knock on the door again, 'You'll need to turn the music down so you can hear the front door.'

I'm surprised that the music actually turns off so I'm feeling less on edge. I really won't be gone long. I have to do this for my own sanity. I run down the stairs and slip on my shoes. I poke my head around the living room door and explain to Fizz that I'm popping out and that I'll be back to paint our nails very soon. She looks happy watching *Frozen*, which must be for the millionth time. I hear the beep of a horn and rush out to meet Mala.

'I really can't be long,' I gasp, breathless from just jogging from the front door to the end of the driveway.

'Buckle up sister.' Mala grins. 'So have you not asked him about the hotel?'

'Not yet. I can't. I don't want to risk an argument and upset Fizz and not to mention Harper is on the warpath. I'm waiting for the right time.'

'How many times! You are everything to those girls. Don't let him take you for granted. Just have it out with him. You have to consider your own feelings and needs too.'

'I know. I hate all of this suspicion... I mean, look at me now. Look at what we're doing.'

'It's cool, you gotta do what you gotta do.'

'Anyway so... Hot date tonight huh?'

'If he's lucky it'll be scorchin' hot.'

We both laugh, and I relax. A couple of minutes later, we are pulling into The Castle Inn car park. I duck down like some criminal on the run, hiding from the law. Mala simply shakes her head at me and steps out of the car, saying she'll be back shortly. I sit up a little and look around the car park. I can't see his car. He would be here by now; he had a good head start. Even if he was picking Alan up on the way, he'd be here by now. I duck down again, my heart beating that bit faster. It seems to be taking too long. *Hurry up Mala.* She should have just walked in, seen him straight away and walked out. What if he's stopped her to chat? I can only hope that she's come up with a good reason to be there on her own. We hadn't discussed this scenario. I trust Mala. I know she'll be quick thinking.

The driver's door opening makes me jump. Mala slides in.

'He ain't there.'

'What?'

'I looked around the whole pub and did a

second lap to be sure. I checked in the smoking area outside too. He ain't there.'

I'm speechless. Despite my doubts, I was sure I'd be wrong. I needed to be wrong. My eyes sting.

'Okay,' Mala says sternly. 'Don't go freakin' out yet. They may have decided to go elsewhere last-minute.'

'But they booked a table.'

'Plans can still change. Just talk to him yeah.'

I nod through the bile rising in my throat. Mala leans over and hugs me. I'm grateful for it. I don't know what I'd do without her. She starts the car up. Now I have to get back and push it out of my head and try and enjoy the rest of the night with Fizzy. I'm trying to think rationally but it's no good. He's having an affair; I know he is.

CHAPTER NINE
Harper

Just be ten minutes. Yeah right, Harper scoffs to herself as she closes the door to the pizza delivery man. She calls Felicity to the kitchen and starts to unpack the boxes.

'Margherita for you,' she says, sliding the pizza over to her younger sister. 'Double pepperoni for me.'

Harper inhales the meaty and cheese aroma. She moves her stepmum's BBQ chicken over to the side. She doesn't care if it goes cold – serves her right. So much for a family takeaway night. Sitting opposite her sister at the table, she asks her if her pizza tastes good. Felicity nods, licking her lips.

'So, you're watching *Frozen* again?' Harper quizzes her.

Felicity nods again.

'Did Kate tell you where she was really going?'

Her sister says nothing and takes a big bite of her Margherita, leaving a stringy trail of cheese.

'She could tell you anything and you wouldn't tell. She uses you, you know. I bet you know all her secrets.'

Felicity puts her pizza slice down and stares at the floor. Harper spots her hand starting to tremble.

'I'm sorry. I didn't mean it like that. I'm just worried about Kate. She said she'd be ten minutes, but it's been at least half an hour.' She gets up and wraps her arms around her little sister. 'I can take care of you, you know. Shall we eat the rest in front of the TV and finish watching *Frozen* together?'

Felicity smiles and, picking up her pizza box, she slides from her chair.

'And I've got the squidgy cookies.' Harper sings.

Harper remembers when her sister was born; the first day she was brought home. Despite the nine year age gap, she couldn't wait to share sisterly moments together – dressing up, playing together, and doing everything else that sisters do. She was determined to be the best big sister ever. She promised her mum every day that she would be. They sit close to each other on the sofa and Felicity resumes play on the film. Her little sister suddenly grins and leaps from the sofa and twirls around the room to the song, pretending to be Elsa. Harper laughs and jumps up to join her. Together they wave their arms around and prance about dramatically, miming the words.

Harper was giggling away to her sister but then she froze. She could hear Kate. She's back.

'Sorry it took a bit longer Fizzy. Have you picked your nail polish…?' Kate bursts into the room as she's finishing her sentence. 'Oh, carry on having fun girls. I'll go grab my food and join you.'

'It's probably cold by now,' Harper snaps and leaves the room.

She darts upstairs and slams her bedroom door shut. Throwing herself onto her bed, she swipes her phone up from her bedside unit and calls Callum.

'Hey Harps. What's up?'

'Everything.'

'Right, I'm sitting down. I'm all yours. Cue the moaning.'

Harper giggles down the phone to her friend. 'I'm sorry about the other day. What I said. We haven't spoken much since, have we? Wasn't sure if I'd screwed up our friendship.'

'Harps, it's okay. I know how desirable I am. You can't help it.'

'You're a jerk.'

'Ah, but a desirable one. We're mates though, aren't we? I like what we have. Just kinda don't wanna spoil it, you know.'

'So, we can still be mates? Good. I need my partner in crime.' Harper was keen to move the subject on. She felt her cheeks begin to flush.

'Is it that Lexi?' Callum's tone changes, starting to take the conversation more seriously.

'Don't get me started on her. Can you believe I'm suspended and she gets nothing each time she does something to me?'

'What you did was class though. She had it

comin'.'

'Anyway, no. I think Kate is having an affair.'

'Shit.'

Harper sneaks over to her door and peers out, just to make sure no one is in earshot. 'Yeah. Last night, she was out until all hours and earlier she sneaked out for over half an hour, whilst my dad is out for dinner.'

'And you think she hooked up with some guy in half an hour?'

'Yes I do. She seems on edge. She's just grabbing opportunities whilst my dad's back is turned. I know it.'

'Could you ask her?'

'No, I need more proof. My dad and Kate were all loved up this morning. He won't believe me. I know he won't. Can't believe it after she'd been out half the night.'

'Sounds like you're jumping to conclusions a bit, Harps.'

'Whose side you on? Something's not right. Next time she goes out, I'm gonna follow her and you're coming with me.'

'Okay, okay, if it'll put your mind at rest.'

'You're a good mate.'

'And a sexy one.'

'You're also a jerk. Look, I gotta go. Check in with you soon.'

Harper hangs up and flops back onto her pillow. Relief washes over her that Callum wasn't being off with her. She was relieved that they could laugh it off. She felt a twinge of pain that he didn't want to be more than mates, but as long as she had him in her life it was all that mattered. He was the only person that she could tell everything to. Everything was going to be okay. She will get proof that Kate is up to no good, her dad will divorce her and everything will go back to normal. Perhaps Felicity will start speaking to her. Surely she'd want her big sister more without their stepmum around? A knock at the door makes her jump. She opens it to Kate.

'Thought you might like a cookie before Fizz eats them all.' Kate offers her a plate with a large chocolate chip cookie on it.

Harper takes the offering and looks into her stepmum's eyes and smiles sweetly. 'Thank you. I'll come downstairs and eat it with you.'

Well, you know what they say, Harper thinks to herself: *Keep your enemies close.*

CHAPTER TEN

I arrive at work just over an hour late. Jon and I were able to catch Mrs Davis at the school for a chat. I expected that we'd be fobbed off, that she'd be busy with it being first thing on a Monday morning, but to our surprise, she was happy to give us her time. Mala greets me with a smile but looks apprehensive.

'What did Jon say about Saturday night? And how did it go at the school?' she asks.

Where do I start? Mala is so much more confident than me and not one for being messed around. She's good at demanding her rights and is by no means a pushover. I don't find it that simple. I start with news about the school to help explain the Jon bit, because I didn't challenge him over Saturday night and I know Mala will roll her eyes at me.

'Well, both of us questioned Mrs Davis as to why Harper has been suspended and that Lexi didn't get so much as a detention for assaulting Harper that time. We got the usual response of no evidence. Lexi had alibis. Harper could've made it up for some kind of revenge for some of the horrible things that Lexi has admittedly said to her.'

'That's shocking! So they reckon Harper just

invented the fact that Lexi and her minions pushed her to the ground and took a photo up her skirt? And they wonder why kids don't speak up about bullying.'

'I know, I know. Oh, but Mala, I feel like I've failed her. This happened about a week ago and I just accepted the outcome, you know. Like that was that. It's not that I didn't believe Harper, but Lexi got away with it. I could've pushed more, fought her corner. The whole thing has pushed her too far and it's escalated. She's had no support so she's flipped, resulting in punching her one.'

'Whoa, don't be hard on yourself. Remember she has her dad to look out for her too. Don't lay everything at your own feet. Sounds like there wasn't much else you could do?'

'I don't know. Anyway, we told Mrs Davis that Lexi's sniping at Harper about my job has got to stop. We made sure we insisted that Lexi be pulled up on it. It's affecting our relationship, her upcoming exams, everything. Turns out Lexi's dad is currently doing time for something, not here though.'

'Sounds like they're using that "tough home life" excuse.'

'Yeah, it did sound like that but for goodness sake, she has to stop. Look at me. I just open the freakin' mail. It shouldn't make a difference anyway. Lexi needs educating and to show more respect. She needs to leave Harper the hell alone.' I can feel my temperature rising and start organising my desk and paperwork as I talk. 'Anyway, as you know Harper has been frosty with me lately. Well, we've had a lovely weekend. She's been chatty. We've watched TV together and eaten together. I didn't want to challenge Jon and spoil things.'

'Yes but—'

'I know what you're going to say, but it's not that simple. What if it's all innocent like you say and he takes offence at me and we argue because I don't trust him? You know Fizz has a severe anxiety disorder and Harper was in such a good mood that I didn't want to spoil the weekend. It almost felt like Harper liked me again and the last thing she wants is for me to accuse her dad of cheating. It'd give her ammo to hate me more. I'd do anything for those girls.'

Mala gives me a sympathetic nod, but I guess that she's really thinking that I'm a wuss.

'I'll say no more then. You know what you're doing,' she says brightly, returning to her computer screen.

I set to processing the mail – read, scan, input, repeat. Nothing out of the ordinary; same old generic updates from home. Even though I'd come into work late, I feel that the rest of the day is going to drag. I pick up a bulkier package and wonder how interesting this is going to get. Tearing it open, I pull out a box of chocolates. Score! I wave them to Mala. Her eyes widen and she snatches them from me. She opens them without hesitation. It's been a while since we had a food item to raid. We still get the odd treats sent in from those that clearly don't understand the rules or just ignore them. Anything like boxes of chocolates just get confiscated and binned. Their stupidity is our gain. Mala pops a strawberry cream into her mouth with a look of pure pleasure.

'Well, that's brightened up a Monday morning,' she says.

I've clocked that my friend isn't quick to offer me one so I attempt to take the box from her, but she hugs them to her tight. I tickle her under the arm and she gives in and hands me the box. It works every time. We laugh after she's called me something obscene. I couldn't get through the day without working with my best friend and there have to be some perks to the job.

We settle back into our chairs and I spot Mala putting two chocolates into her mouth at the same time. She glances at me as if to say "What?" She turns her attention to her screen and a moment later with her mouth still full she mumbles, 'Check this out.'

She's processing the incoming e-mails to the inmates. I step closer to check over her shoulder and she muffles an e-mail to Jason Sawyer as she's trying to swallow the treats. I scan the words:

Hi gorgeous. I can't tell you how overwhelmed I

am that you've won your chance to appeal. Now we have hope. I know you'll say not to get our hopes up, but how can I not? I can't bear you being in that place. There will be justice. I have to believe it; you have to believe it. I need you home where you belong. I love you and I'm here for you waiting. Always. Hang on in there. You can do this. All my love, A x

'I had seen on the news online that he's appealing,' I say, still taking in the words. So much affection, passion and belief. Anna sounds like she's in love, that they are a couple who are completely in love. But her pictures suggest lust – something that's just physical. I'm not sure why my brain can't compute that perhaps you can have both. I don't have a wide circle of friends, but with the few that I have, I know that things are no longer that exciting in the bedroom department – including myself. It's probably because Jason and Anna don't have kids. I've not seen any mention of them in any letters or anything that I've read online about Jason. I'm sure I used to wear sexy underwear before I became a stepmother. Did I?

Sex used to be all about getting pregnant when I was with my ex-husband. The desperation to conceive kind of killed the passion. Well, it did for us. I know that Chris was desperate, but then so was I. Yet he moved on and I was left with ovaries that won't play ball. My womb stopped aching though when Harper and Felicity came into my life. Sex with Jon was awkward at first;

the loss of his wife only two years previous felt uncomfortable. But then it was all new and exciting – and then we married. And then it changed. I'm not sure when I stopped bothering with matching underwear and only buying the big knickers. It must have been when Jon stopped coming near me.

Here I go again. I was feeling positive and now I've allowed my mood to plummet. I pile together this batch of mail and inform Mala I'm off to take it to Phil. I'm suddenly grateful for the distraction and the chance to stretch my legs. It's just me, my clattering trolley and the confines of a prison. Oh, and Jason Sawyer, because there he is. The same place as before but carrying a waste bin.

'Was your nosebleed okay?' he asks as I pass him.

I'm confused, just for a moment. His question throws me. I wasn't expecting it.

'Friday, you had a bad nosebleed,' he continues.

Now he's looking at me confused, wondering if he has the right person, 'Yes, sorry, yes. It was fine,' I quickly say. 'It's just the time of year, bad hay fever and all that.' I go to carry on, but then I halt and turn back to him. 'Thank you,' I say. He simply nods and carries on in the opposite direction with his bin. I carry on to the guard's office. It's hot under my collar and I'm feeling lightheaded all of a sudden. I replay our exchange of words over and over to reassure my anxiety. *Did I sound like an idiot*? Why am I caring if I sound like an idiot? I wipe my brow and wonder if the air-conditioning is faulty.

Phil greets me at the office door, 'What did Jason have to say for himself, then?' he asks.

I hadn't realised he was watching our exchange. 'Oh nothing. Just saying hello, asking how I am.'

'I don't trust that one.'

'Well, they are criminals in here. I wouldn't either,' I say cheekily. 'But I heard that he helped defuse a riot in here last week. That's a good thing isn't it?' I ask more seriously.

'I had it handled,' Phil says puffing up his chest. 'I reckon he has a lot of connections. I don't trust those with connections. He is appealing and I'd hate for the scum to get off because of connections.'

'It sounds to me like there are plausible reasons for his appeal though. Sounds like the evidence is rightly in question?'

'Don't you be fooled by his pretty-boy face. I'm telling you he's dangerous. I'm telling you he has —'

'Connections. Yes, I know, I get it.' I smile and reassure him that I believe his instincts. I have to get back so say goodbye to him. It's not ideal to leave Mala working on her own for long – because it's busy and for safety reasons, but mostly because there won't be any chocolates left and there is still an hour or so until lunchtime. I skipped breakfast and my stomach is growling. As much as I'd like to gossip a bit more about Jason Sawyer, I'm conscious not to sound too keen. I don't have a crush on him. I absolutely don't. I'm facing up to it now. There is something seriously lacking in my home life if I'm so curious about someone else's life, because I am. I'm just going to accept that fact. I'm curious. I'm a people watcher and I'm interested in behaviour. It's kind of what drew me to prison work. See, it's okay. It's normal to be fascinated by other people's lives; there's no harm in it. I feel myself relaxing and not in conflict with myself for having obsessive thoughts about Jason Sawyer and Anna West. As I rattle back along the walkway, a thought pops into my head – an idea. Could I? What would be the harm? It could mean me losing my career if I get caught but not if I'm careful. It'd be easy, wouldn't it – with a bit of careful thought? I quicken my pace. Yes, I'm going to do it. I need a bit of excitement.

CHAPTER ELEVEN
Gregg

Gregg shows Brian his phone. 'Missing Holly Stevens, not seen since Saturday morning.'

Brian smirks and slaps the drowsy seventeen-year-old's face. 'See, love, they've only just noticed you're not around. It's now bloody Monday, love. Dear, oh dear, no one cares for you, do they?' He grips her cheeks roughly and shakes her head. 'Christ, Gregg, how much did you give her? She best be with it for tonight. There are a bunch of people that'll want to care for her later,' he laughs, elbowing Gregg.

'Trust me, this bitch needs sedating, she's an animal.' Gregg checks that the cuffs chaining the girl to the bed were secure.

'What's this?' Brian grabs Gregg's wrist, clocking the wound. 'Bite ya, did she?'

Gregg pulls his wrist back. 'Just watch her, yeah? Make sure she don't wet herself. We need to keep the bed tidy, yeah?'

Brian mocks a salute.

Gregg looks around the basic room – the floral bedspread, the mustard curtains, the grubby carpet. It's about time they became more upmarket, targeted high-end business. *Not this bollocks.* It was the last time he was going to hold a girl at his place, too, until it was time to move them to the house. Why he just couldn't bring the bitches straight here, he couldn't understand. It was more risk for him, and he was sick of it. He marches from the room and jogs down the stairs.

At least the fridge was full of beers. Gregg knew they were for the guests but swipes one out, using his teeth to rip the top off. He necks half of the bottle without taking a breath. Brian was lucky not to get blasted in the face for commenting on his wrist. He doesn't get his hands dirty enough to pass remarks. Michael was the only one that was his equal, that he could trust. But he's dead. That prick, Jason, knifed him down. Gregg downs the rest of his beer and slams the bottle down. Where was Michael's protection? Too many risks and no brains from above. His phone rings.

'Riley, 'sup?'

'Is the girl in place?'

'Yeah.'

'Good. I want you on the door tonight, cash upfront. Brian can clean up. You did a good job. You'll get your fair share when the night's out. It's a fortnight for the next one. Can you do it?'

'It'll be done.'

'Music to my ears... Oh, and Gregg, don't touch the beer.'

The line goes dead. Gregg smirks to himself. He knows he did a great job. He wants more than his fair share though. He wants it all. At least that prick Brian will be cleaning up tonight. It's how it should be. If Michael was still here, they'd be running the show by now and Brian would be on his arse. He hopes for Jason's sake that he stays locked up because the urge to want to gut that son-of-a-bitch was growing. He has no contacts on the inside so he can't get to him. Riley will need to sort this one. Failing that, Gregg would be waiting for him, if he got out. He'd be ready and waiting. He slams his palm into the fridge door and then swings it open to swipe another beer.

CHAPTER TWELVE

I slump into my car seat and leave the door open to allow some of the cool breeze in. It's a hot day and the slight breeze is welcome. The staff room might have been cooler, but I need to call Harper. First, though, I take a big bite out of my sandwich. It's a wilting cheese and tomato sandwich, but I'm too hungry to care that it's warm and limp. I make a mental note to invest in one of those cool lunch bags. Feeling more satisfied, I grab my phone out of the glove compartment and switch it on.

I check my Facebook notifications first. I'm aware that I'm delaying phoning Harper. Her reaction to hearing how the meeting went with Mrs Davis this morning could go either way. I scroll through my newsfeed for a moment and a news report grabs my attention. A missing seventeen-year-old named Holly Stevens from the Tilehurst area of Reading has not been seen since Saturday morning. Friends say she was last seen heading into Lousehill Copse for a walk.

I shudder at the thought and hope that she is found well. She's at the age where she probably wants to run off and do her own thing. Then I recall a teenager had gone missing from Reading a few weeks ago. She was found dumped at the side of the road. She had been attacked and raped. She claimed to have been kidnapped but I don't recall any arrests being made. I do a quick Google search out of curiosity, but don't come up with any answers. It's frightening to think that someone could do that to a young girl and get away with it. Reading is so close to home and Harper is a similar age. I smooth my goosebumps and tell myself to not over-imagine things.

I'm suddenly keen to hear her voice and dial her number.

'Hey Harper.'

'What did Dopey Davis say then?'

I let that slide in an attempt to minimise any further confrontation. Harper feels let down, so she will take it out on her teacher but calling her teacher names won't earn her much respect.

'Your dad hasn't filled you in yet, then?' I was hoping he had, so if there was any verbal backlash, he'd get the initial brunt of it. But I guess it's down to me again. 'Your suspension still stands, but she has promised to pull Lexi in and insist that she leaves you alone in the future. I've told her we're not tolerating any more or I'll be up the school every day until it stops.'

The line is quiet for a moment.

'Okay.'

Is that it?

'Look Harps, I just want to say I'm sorry again for not fighting your corner more before with what Lexi and her friends did to you.

Being in that office this morning made me more determined to ensure you're okay. We won't let you down again. I just want you to know that.'

'Okay.' Her voice is quiet.

I can tell I'm not going to get much out of her. 'So have you completed any of the work you've been set yet?'

'Yeah, some.'

'Great, alright then. I'll leave you to it. I best get back to the office. Love you.'

'See ya.'

I switch my phone back off and shove it back in the glove compartment. I don't know what's more infuriating – when she snaps and shouts at me or when she goes quiet. Harper was fourteen when I met her. I've only known her as a headstrong teen who enjoys challenging everything. For the first few months, we seemed to gel; we bonded quickly. I thought that at her age she'd take an instant disliking to me for trying to fill her mother's shoes. I helped to support her through her first period and bought her first bras. She'd never admit it now but I knew she was grateful to have me around.

I sigh, my chest feeling heavy. I rub my clammy neck underneath my collar. The heat is getting a bit much. My bottled water doesn't offer much relief as that's gone warm. Yes, I'm going to treat myself to lunch containers that keep my food and drinks cool. The rest of the family has them. I make sure that they are catered for; I never think of me though.

A sparrow dives inches away from my windscreen in a blur of brown feathers and for a second my heart stops and then I feel ridiculous. It's time to get back inside so I lock up the car and head back towards the main security gates. It takes a lunch break just to navigate the security passes, the key collections and the gauntlet of locked doorways before reaching the post room. They should allow an extra half an hour on your break, just for this.

Mala greets me and pulls her chair out for me. It's my turn to check the e-mails. We rotate the jobs around a bit so that we don't get bored.

'I've just read about another teenager that's gone missing in Reading. Remember that one from before and then she was found dumped on the roadside?' I say.

Mala nods looking serious, 'Yes, someone mentioned it over lunch. Let's hope it's nothing like that again. It's a scary world with some nutters out there.' Mala gently smirks. 'Well, we should know. Look at where we are.'

I smile in acknowledgement. It suddenly feels good again to be contributing in some way to keeping the bad guys off the streets. Jon might not like me working here but I'm not giving it up. I'm proud of what I do. It might be a small role in comparison to the prison officers but it's a vital role. I'm needed and important. I start processing the e-mails on my screen.

I print off and log a number of incoming e-mails to the inmates and then I start on the outgoing ones. The inmates handwrite them and we type them up. My heart quickens. At the top of the pile is one from Jason to Anna. I read the note carefully, taking in the words. He has beautiful handwriting for a murderer. It's suitable to send so I type it up.

Dear Love, you know when I told you over the phone that things got heated in here last week? I need to make good on my word. I need you to send over some cash to Harrison and Ben. A couple of hundred each. I need to keep the peace until my appeal. I'll do anything to get out of this shithole and to be back with you. Love you, gorgeous. Sort it for me okay? Speak soon x

I wonder if it's money that he actually owes those guys or whether he is being bullied. Phil did say that Jason had a word with both of them when all hell was breaking loose and it settled everything down. Did he just bribe them with cash? Did he offer them money to shut them up because he didn't want to get caught up in any trouble which might harm his appeal?

It's not uncommon for this stuff to go down in here. None of it usually bothers me. I read the messages. I process them. I send them. Move on to the next. But again, I find myself overthinking what's going on with Jason. I'm asking questions. I'm curious and basically, I'm bothered. The plan I allowed myself to come up with creeps back into my mind. I did push it away but now it's back. Can Anna West just stump up all of that money to pay off a couple of low lives? Will she do it without question and just for the love of her man? Where do they live? What's their house like? As I told myself before, it's okay to take an interest in other people's lives.

Mala is focused on her work, so I sort through the file to find one of Jason's letters off Anna. They are kept for seven days before being shredded, so I know that there will be one in here. I come across one and pull it out. As always, the address is scribbled on the top right corner of the letter. I'm not sure why Anna puts their address on the letters. I guess that she is just attempting to follow the rules; to meet the criteria for the inmate to receive the letter. But then again, she's not exactly careful with what photos she sends in.

Mala is still busy typing away. I quickly snatch a piece of scrap paper and scribble down the address. I stuff it into my pocket and file the letter back in its place and then settle back into my chair. Mala still isn't looking over at me. I put the backs of my hands against my cheeks, they are starting to burn.

'It's getting hotter in here isn't it?' I pant the words.

Mala raises her eyebrows, gesturing over to the fan behind me.

'I know, I'll turn the fan on.'

Mala laughs and carries on working. Good, she doesn't suspect me. She wouldn't approve and she'd talk me out of it. I know it's wrong, of course I do, but it's harmless. I tell Mala everything but it's good to have my own interests, my own personal curiosities that I have to satisfy. Call it research, an investigation into how the other half of a murderer lives. What kind of woman loves a killer and stands by him? All I need is a glimpse of the house, a glimpse of her, a glimpse into their life. I just need a day when I can get away and I'll take a trip. I'll go and find Anna West.

CHAPTER THIRTEEN
Harper

Harper gives her tear-stained pillow one last squeeze before throwing it back down. She looks into her mirror and inspects her smudged mascara. Her sandwich is still sitting on her bedside table, uneaten. She couldn't stomach it, not after speaking to her stepmum. She wanted to throw up. Lexi is going to be dragged into Mrs Davis's office and ordered to leave her alone. She keeps playing Kate's words around in her head, over and over. This doesn't help. The only thing that this does is make it worse. She can see Lexi's nasty little face now sneering, "Snitch Bitch, Snitch Bitch." Harper was dreading returning to school after her suspension, but now she feels paralysed. She's convinced it's going to turn ugly and she scrunches her eyes shut and wishes that Kate had just kept her mouth shut. In fact, she wishes that Kate would just disappear. Forever.

Feeling emotionally exhausted, she snatches her black nail polish and starts to paint her fingernails with shaky hands. She may as well make the most of not being at school for a couple of days. No one can yell at her for her black nails. She couldn't be more desperate to finish school, to get her stupid exams over with. She'll have her lip pierced and her nose. She'll get a tattoo, she'll get to be free, to be who she wants to be, away from those nasty bitches and Mrs Dopey Davis. She feels her lower lip quiver again, so she quickly asks her entertainment system to play Slipknot, turning the sound up loud.

She lets the music cloud her senses, whilst blowing on her wet nail polish. It's no good though. She slams her hand into her mirror but not enough to crack it. It was Kate that kept insisting on sorting things out at the school. Her dad would have left alone if it was just up to him; she was sure of it. If only Lexi had been expelled for what she did, but she wasn't. Kate's interfering is making it worse. She doesn't get it. Harper storms from her room and stomps into her dad's and Kate's room. *There must be something in here, anything.* She rummages through her stepmum's underwear drawer. She goes through any pockets that she finds from clothes hanging up in the closet. She leafs through some paperwork, through her jewellery box, everything that's hers. She's not sure what she's looking for, just anything that proves she's up to something – an affair. Evidence that she can show her dad.

She slumps on the queen size bed, rubbing her forehead. Kate would be too clever to hide anything in plain sight. If anyone is going to hide her secrets, it's Felicity. She runs across the landing to her little sister's room and again starts to look through her drawers and her toy boxes. She works quickly and carefully, not wishing to mess up her sister's stuff. She pulls a decorative floral storage box from underneath her bed and lifts the lid. There are a few pictures that Felicity had drawn back in preschool, a dance certificate and trophy engraved with *little movers champion,* more preschool stuff and underneath that a small bottle of perfume. Harper catches her breath for a moment. A flashback. A memory of her mum. She picks up the distinctive star-shaped bottle with small stars cut into the glass. *Reach for the stars.* Her mum's favourite perfume.

She wonders why Felicity has it hidden away under her bed. Perhaps she took it without their dad knowing so that's why it's hidden. The tears fall again. Harper slumps to the floor. She'd do anything to share memories with her sister, to talk. She wonders if her sister remembers playing dress-ups and their mum spritzing them all with the perfume and saying that just like the name on the bottle, we should always reach for the stars.

That's a joke. Harper shoves it back in the box and slides it back underneath the bed. *How can you reach for anything, when everything is against you?* Picking herself up off the floor, Harper heads downstairs. She won't find anything to suggest that Kate is having an affair. She probably isn't and there's nothing she can do. She doesn't know how she's going to face school and she doesn't know how to make anyone listen. She opens the fridge and takes out an opened bottle of wine and pours herself a large measure into a mug. She takes it up to her room and slams the door shut. Taking a large gulp, she grimaces and lets the fuzziness wash over her. She climbs back into bed and allows fresh tears to soak her pillow.

CHAPTER FOURTEEN

The rest of the afternoon goes quickly. It takes me by surprise to see the time says four-fifty p.m.

'You've hardly said a word all afternoon, you okay?'

Mala interrupts me stretching. The thought of being nosey and going to seek out Anna West has zapped my brainpower; the anxiety, the excitement, and the nerves have drained me. I stand rubbing my lower back.

'I'm fine, honestly. Just a lot on my mind with Harper and the school and all of that. She was quiet on the phone earlier. I'm worried about her.'

'You know what's good for stress?' Mala puts her hands together as if to pray. 'Yoga. It'll do your back good too.'

Mala has been trying to get me to go to yoga with her for weeks now. I'm not sure I even own any kind of gym wear.

'When is it?'

'Tomorrow evening at seven. It's every Tuesday. Just come along; it'll do you good. You're all uptight and stuff.'

'You know I can't, Fizz needs—'

'Whoa, stop right there, sister. Stop using the excuse that Fizz needs you. You can take a break.

It's an hour's fitness class. You need you time. How many Goddamn times do I have to repeat myself. Stop letting Jon take you for granted.'

It's hard to explain to her that it really isn't that simple. She's single, she has no kids, no dependents. I love my best friend, but I sometimes wonder if she really understands what it's like for me. But then I guess she's right. It is only an hour out of my evening once a week. It gives me plenty of time for Felicity to have her after-school chats with me and to help her with her homework. As I rub my back again, I think that it would be nice to feel less stiff and a bit more flexible. Perhaps I'll tone up. Perhaps Jon will find me attractive again.

'Go on then. But I do need to check with Jon first.'

'No checking, just tell him.' Mala tucks her chair under her desk. 'Right let's get the hell out of here.'

There's no hanging about. We make our way through the numerous locked doorways until we're out into the open. It's still warm and bright.

Mala breathes in deeply. 'The inmates see more of the outside than we do. I'm gonna have me a cold shower, then a large pink gin in the garden, I reckon.'

'On a school night? You bad woman.'

'You know it.' Mala winks at me and catwalks over to her car.

I laugh at her and struggle to remember what

it's like to be so carefree. I have an opened bottle of wine in the fridge at home. Perhaps I'll live a little and also enjoy a drink in the garden. I wind all of the windows down inside my Skoda before pulling away. The heat is suffocating. I put my foot down driving to the other end of Bracknell. I do pride myself on being a careful driver but the cool breeze feels too nice to care right now. I'm soon pulling up outside of the school to collect Felicity from the after-school club.

I'm only waiting at the gate for a minute before I see Fizzy skipping up the path with Clare, her support worker, striding behind trying to keep up.

'We've had a great afternoon,' Clare says, almost out of breath.

Fizz smiles up at me and then gets herself into the car.

Clare continues but lowers her voice a little. 'Felicity said a few words to me.'

I hold my breath for a second, as if the sound of my own breathing would drown out Clare's words.

'She was playing this fun beginner coding game and she was chatting away to herself like she usually does. I look at what she's doing over her shoulder, and I was so impressed with how quickly she'd picked it up that I praised her. I don't think she realised that I was standing behind her. She turned around and, in her excitement, said, "I did it, didn't I? Look! I made the shapes move."

'Oh my goodness,' I gasp, realising that I still hadn't taken a breath.

'I wanted to make you aware that in my surprise, I told her again how amazing it was. I don't know if it's because I sounded overexcited or too loud, but it's like she suddenly realised that she'd said something and she clamped her hand over her mouth and hunched herself over. She completely withdrew. I hope that I didn't upset her.'

'I shouldn't worry.' I look over at Fizz hanging her head out of the car window. It looks like she's smiling. 'It's wonderful she said that to you. Yes, over-excitement can escalate her anxiety. Her therapist recommends not making a big fuss whenever she speaks to someone. To let it be natural and normal. But honestly, this is normal for her. Thank you so much for today.'

Clare waves goodbye to Fizz, thanks me, and walks away. It's been a while since Fizz has spoken a few words to someone other than me. Jon will be so happy when I tell him. I climb into the driver's side and turn to Fizzy. 'So, you're a future engineer and a coding mastermind. Put it there, brain box,' I say, holding my hand up for a high five.

I drive the five minutes home more carefully now that I have Felicity in the car. I make a mental note that my next car must have aircon that actually works. Fizz tells me how hot she's been today, and we both agree that iced drinks in the garden are a good idea. We pull up onto the driveway. Jon isn't home yet; he must be working that bit later today. He usually gets in just before I make it home.

'Let me quickly get changed and I'll fix us an icy glass of lemonade each, okay?' I say to Fizz as we get out of the car. 'And you change out of your uniform.' She skips ahead of me through the front door and races upstairs.

I was going to hit the wine but lemonade with Fizzy now sounds more appealing. I swing the fridge door open and, to my surprise, the bottle of wine isn't there. I saw it there this morning; I know I did. Jon isn't home yet, so he couldn't have had it. I have a sinking feeling and head upstairs. I gently knock on Harper's bedroom door, but there is no answer, so I slowly open it. Harper is curled up on top of her bed; she looks fast asleep. Sure enough, the empty bottle of wine is lying on the floor below her. She must have had a good two large glasses out of it. It would have been enough to knock out a teenager not used to drinking alcohol.

I take a closer look at my stepdaughter and see that her eyes look puffy and her mascara is smudged. I watch her breathing, steadily in and out, her eyelids flickering. A wave of sadness washes over me. She was quiet on the phone earlier. Did I mistake her for being okay when she was really putting on a brave face and struggling emotionally? She has been through a lot and with her exams looming. I can't recall a time when Harper has ever shown an interest in drinking, not even jokingly. Even through all of her rebellious phases, she has never taken to booze.

I'm unsure how to handle this. She can't think that this is okay, that she can just day drink when she should be doing her schoolwork. She can't just get into the habit of hitting the bottle when things get a bit tough. Her dad and I have done all that we can to be supportive, to give her all that she needs. I've promised her that things will get better with Lexi at school and I won't stop until that bully leaves her alone. If I lecture her though, she'll only rebel more and hate me more. Perhaps if I keep it quiet, not tell Jon, she'll be thankful to me. I'll earn some of her respect. Just this once. Just one little cover-up. I do need to make sure she's okay though.

I gently shake her shoulder and whisper, 'Harper.'

She stirs and slowly opens her eyes. It takes her a moment to focus on my face, and when she does, she pulls her pillow over her head and mumbles for me to go away.

'Harper, look, I don't know what's gotten into you but I'm going to take this empty bottle and I'm going to tell your dad that I drank it. You know he'll hit the roof.'

Harper peeks out from under her pillow, and

I wave the empty bottle for her to see. She cautiously sits up, curling her legs underneath her and pulls her pillow around to hug tightly.

'Are you okay, love?' I ask her.

'I just wanted to try it; I got bored,' she says, with a croaky voice.

'I get it. I'm not a dinosaur like you might think, you know. Just don't let this be a habit. I won't tell your dad. Just get yourself up. I'll make you a cup of tea. You feeling okay?'

She simply nods and whispers, 'Thank you.' I leave her to sort herself out. I'm not convinced that she drank it just because she was bored. I wasn't going to push her though. If she was upset, then hopefully she'll open up about it later. This never knowing how to handle a teenager doesn't get any easier. I take the empty bottle to my room and I can hear Fizzy singing to herself as I pass by her door. It never fails to make me smile, even when I'm surrounded by teenage angst.

It's a relief to strip off my uniform. I stand for a moment in my underwear. Something feels uneasy. A prickle of goose pimples raises on my arms despite the heat. It's strange but I feel like someone is watching me or someone has been in my room. I look around but nothing is out of place. I think that I'm just feeling anxious over Harper and the prospect of lying to her dad. Perhaps I should tell him about the wine. No, I won't go back on my word to Harper. Still, the uneasy feeling in the pit of my stomach remains.

I quickly pull on some shorts and a vest. I can hear Fizz calling my name. I meet her on the landing.

'We need lemonade,' she beams.

'Yes, I've not forgotten.'

Moments later, we are sitting in the garden listening to the tinkling of ice cubes against our glasses.

'Can I grow some vegetables?' Fizz asks me.

I giggle at her randomness. 'Yes, why not? We could probably have a little vegetable patch in that corner, just for you.'

'And for you too,' she says back as a matter of fact.

Her blue eyes sparkle and everything feels good again. My heart could burst. At least Fizzy loves me even if Harper and Jon don't. Because that's how it feels, and as if on cue, I hear Jon calling out to me. A second later, he has joined us on the patio.

'Tough day?' he mocks, waving the empty bottle of wine at me.

I can only think to shrug it off. I curse myself for not putting it straight into the recycling bin.

'At least you've had it with lemonade,' he continues, checking out my glass. 'We don't need a repeat of the weekend do we?' he winks.

I decide to change the subject, 'Mala's invited me to go try out her yoga class tomorrow night. Is that okay? At seven... just for an hour.'

'Yes, sure. There are worse things that Mala could be getting you to do.'

He walks off and says he'll put the oven on. I watch him walk away and spot Harper standing by the back door.

'You didn't drink the wine,' Fizz says to me, defensively.

'It doesn't matter, Fizzy. Right, so what veg are we gonna grow?'

I watch Harper go back inside as I listen to Fizz list vegetables that I don't think I've ever even heard of. I can only admit to the fact that unusual vegetables would fit in perfectly with my little family.

CHAPTER FIFTEEN
Gregg

Gregg pulls up in the lay-by just off the Lousehill Copse. He figures that he may as well put the girl back where he had taken her from. At least at nearly four in the morning, there is less chance to be seen. He had started to doubt that someone had not witnessed or heard anything. After seeing the appeal online, he reckons that he has got away with it. No one mentioned anything about the sighting of a van or hearing a girl scream. He smirked to himself, admitting that he had some balls.

He jumps from the van and scouts around. Silence. No lights or noise from anywhere and the road was quiet. He wasn't going to take any more risks; he'd get this done quickly. He pulls open the rear doors and clambers in. The girl is just about conscious. The interior light illuminates the bruising across the left side of her face. *Animals,* he sneers to himself. He's seen worse. He knows that some of the customers like it a bit rough. *Animals.* When he runs the show, it'll be more upmarket than this crap. Every time a bruise or injury is inflicted on the girls, it is an extra forensics nightmare. There have to be rules, standards, a bit of class. If these degenerates are so ready with their cash for a bit of sex then how much would the elite shell out? All men want to shag a firm young lady; doesn't matter who they are. They all want it. Not too young, that is. He's repulsed at the thought. He wasn't a dirty nonce.

He drags the girl to the opening of the van. She whimpers through the gag. Gregg unties her wrists and pulls her out, shoving her to the ground. 'Ain't got the energy to fight back now, have ya,' he spat.

The teenager curls into the foetal position, trembling. Gregg looks down at her and swiftly rips away the tape from her mouth. 'Scream all you want, love. I'm out of here.'

He jumps back into the van leaving the girl sobbing hysterically on the gravel. He put his foot down. Still no one around. Good. Another night's work was done and dusted. He reckons Brian is still cleaning up back at the house, the waster. One customer vomited in the bathtub; couldn't hold his beer. Pathetic. He smirks, betting that the loser couldn't have got his dick hard at his turn. He needs to head back to the house to check that Brian has disposed of the sheets, the mess, the vomit and that all evidence has been removed before he can collect his takings and then go home for a kip. The adrenaline is wearing off – and the coke. Yes, he is ready for bed. He'd turn his phone off and spend the day sleeping. Riley could kiss his ass and leave him alone for the day.

'What the hell,' he curses out of the window as he pulls up outside of the house. One of the night's customers is staggering out of the house. Brian is standing in the doorway. Gregg jumps from the van and shoves the man to the side. 'Get outta here,' he growls. The man regains his balance and continues to stagger away and up the street.

'What the f—! Sun's comin' up. He should've been gone. People will be waking up. You wanna draw more attention to us?' Gregg shoves Brian in through the door.

'You need to chill, man,' Brian raises his hands. 'It's all sweet. He was passed out in the bathroom. Took a while to get him movin'. You got rid of the girl without being seen?'

Gregg clenches his fists. As if he should be questioned over his part. He didn't need to explain himself; he didn't have to answer to anyone, especially to scum like Brian. He curls his top lip and jogs up the stairs. Brian follows. Gregg is relieved to see that at least the idiot seems to have done a good job clearing away. The bathroom smells strongly of bleach. Not a speck of sick left.

'I don't know why we just don't finish off the girls. Just smother them. Eliminate the risks,' Brian says.

'Jesus, we're not savages. Stick to the precautions. That's all we gotta do. I'm the one risking my ass bringing the girls in.'

'How are your bite marks?' Brian laughs.

Gregg grabs him by the throat and punches him with a right hook to the head. He falls back, the bathtub breaking his fall. He regains his composure, lunging at Gregg. Gregg knees him in the groin and throws him over.

'Bastard.' Brian sits up against the bath panel, clutching his groin area.

'I don't put my ass on the line for a prick like you to take the piss. I'm the one bringing the cash in. Got it?'

Brian grimaces and gets to his feet. 'I'll get us a beer.'

Gregg tells him to stick it and orders him to lock up. He needs to sleep. He wants to turn his phone off and sleep all day. He doesn't have to answer to Riley or to anyone. He is his own boss and it's time to shake things up.

CHAPTER SIXTEEN

I'm relieved to see that the missing teenager, Holly Stevens, has been found. There isn't any other information other than that she was found by a dog walker early this morning in Lousehill Copse, the area she was thought to be last seen, and a request for any witnesses to anything unusual to come forward. I can't help but wonder where she had been and what happened to her. I guess because Harper is so close in age to her that my heart goes out to the poor girl. I wonder if she's troubled at all. It didn't escape my notice that she had gone missing on Saturday but reports about her being missing didn't appear until Monday. I'm pretty certain that the moment my daughter, or stepdaughter even, didn't return home for the night, I'd be out looking immediately. Everyone would know about it. Where were her parents? Who was looking out for her? I suppose I shouldn't judge. I don't know the facts.

'That smells delicious.' Fizzy skips into the kitchen. I wish that I had her energy this early in the morning.

'Good, it's nearly ready. Do you want ketchup on yours?' I ask her.

She nods greedily.

'Bacon sandwiches?' Jon sounds surprised, entering the kitchen.

'Yes. I thought I'd make Tuesday more exciting, cook us breakfast to set us up for the day.'

Jon inhales the aroma over my shoulder before planting a kiss on my cheek. 'Sorry. love,' he says. 'I'm dashing off this morning. I have a meeting over breakfast to attend. I'll see you tonight.' He grabs his car keys.

'Don't forget I have yoga this evening,' I shout after him.

'Not forgotten, see you later, love you.'

I stand watching the door that he's just gone through, temporarily confused. He said, "I love you." He kissed me on the cheek. He had a spring in his step. I can't figure him out, he's been so distant, so cold. It doesn't feel right.

'Kate, the bacon,' Fizz says, tugging on my nightshirt.

I quickly remove the frying pan from the heat, the bacon now crispier than I intended. I look up to see Harper in the doorway.

'Good, you're up. Want one?'

Harper nods.

'How are you feeling this morning?' I dare to ask her.

'Okay,' she says, looking down a little sheepishly.

'Have you got much homework to finish before going back to school tomorrow?' I feel like I'm already pushing the boundaries by overloading a teenager with questions.

'A fair bit but I'll get it done,' she says quietly.

I'm relieved not to be snapped at and decide to leave the questioning at that. I continue to butter some bread and assemble the sandwiches, making sure that Fizz gets a decent dollop of ketchup. The three of us sit around the table in silence whilst we tuck in. It's small moments like this that I treasure.

'Thank you for last night,' Harper finally says. 'You know, for not telling—'

I just wave my hand to dismiss her and smile warmly. 'Let's just forget it.'

'Do you want me to put your hair up in a ponytail today?' Harper asks her little sister.

Felicity nods.

'Okay. Go get dressed and I'll do it for you.'

Her little sister stuffs the remaining sandwich in her mouth and skips from the room.

'Are you sure you're okay?' I ask Harper. 'You do look a little pale. Are you worrying about school tomorrow?'

'I'm fine,' Harper snaps. She stands up, roughly tucking her chair under the table. 'And I hate school,' she shouts, storming from the room.

And there it is; the nice moment having breakfast together, gone. At least Harper's behaviour is consistent, unlike her father's. He's left for work a good hour and a half earlier than usual. *A breakfast meeting?* He could be telling the truth. I have known this to happen. I realise that I'm scraping leftover crusts of bread into the sink rather than the bin. I clear everything up and head upstairs to get a quick shower and get dressed. I have a quick rummage in my wardrobe and drawers for something remotely suitable as gym wear for later. I find some black leggings. Those and a T-shirt will do. I'll just add gym wear to the list of things that I need to treat myself to.

Once dressed for work, I set about scooping up Jon's clothes that he has left screwed up on the floor. This wouldn't be a problem if it was a couple of items but it's not. It's a few days' worth of stuff and not to mention that the washing basket is right there in the ensuite, literally about five paces away. I continue to Fizz's room where Harper is fixing up her sister's hair. I scoop up Fizz's clothes from the floor. I don't even ask if Harper wants anything washing. I'm not even going to go into her room to look.

'I'm just going to stick these in the machine and then we'll be ready to go. Okay Fizzy?'

She nods and I can feel Harper's eyes burning into me as I leave the room. So much for keeping her secret and making her bacon sandwiches. I know it's a slow process but I'm here for her and I'll do what it takes to strengthen our relationship. I remind myself that's why I won't rock the boat with her dad just yet. I will learn the truth if he's having an affair, but until I'm certain I'm not going to risk pushing Harper away or Fizz for that matter. I love them like my own and no matter what, I can't change that now. As I load the machine, I can't help but have a quick rummage through Jon's pockets but there's nothing there. Not that I know what I'm expecting to find. I even inspect his collar for lipstick marks. Ridiculous and cliched, I know, but I do it anyway.

I call up to ask if Fizz is ready. She comes skipping down followed by her big sister. Harper gives her a big hug goodbye.

'Are you okay, Fizzy?' I ask her.

'Of course she's okay,' Harper snaps.

'I didn't mean…' but it's no good. Harper has gone back upstairs.

Fizzy shrugs her narrow shoulders up at me and picks up her rucksack. I shout goodbye to Harper and I'm unsurprised to get no response.

*****

I don't recognise him at first. His face looks darker. Not the sun-kissed tanned tone, but darker. So I didn't notice right away until I got closer. I'm approaching my office and he's standing there with his mop and bucket. It took a second glance to see that it's Jason Sawyer. His face is battered black and blue – a swollen eye and a bulging upper lip. I realise that I'm staring and snap out of it. My jaw drops and I go to say something but the words don't come. He turns and walks back along the lower walkway.

'What happened to Jason?' I ask Mala.

She spins around in her chair to face me. 'And good morning to you, honey.' She over-exaggerates the sarcasm.

I ignore her. 'So what's the goss? His face is a mess.'

'I've been in the office for five minutes. Give me chance to get the goss,' she laughs.

'That's usually plenty of time for you,' I reply. 'Should he even be working? What if he's got concussion or something?'

Mala raises her newly shaped brows at me. 'Stop fussing after the cold-blooded killers. Leave that to the medics. I'm sure they've checked him out.'

'But what if he's not a killer? There is evidence that might prove he didn't kill him. Two different knives were used. Hence his appeal.'

Mala pulls out my chair and gestures me to sit down. She leans into me and I'm bracing myself for an interrogation. 'You don't have a crush on Mr Sawyer do you? You've mentioned him a number of times lately. Don't you be one of those wacko women who fall for murderers. Now I know you and Jon ain't been—'

I laugh and gently push her away. 'I am no wacko and I'm insulted,' I pout. 'I'm just nosey that's all. It's hard not to be in this job.'

'Then I suggest that you get your ass through this pile of mail, take it to Phil and get all of the juicy details.' Mala gives me a knowing wink.

I shake my head and chuckle, settling into work mode. She's right though, sort of. I have been fixating a little too much on Jason and Mala can see straight through me. Of course she does, she's been my best friend since forever. But I don't have a crush on Jason, I'm not that stupid. I'm just fascinated by what his life might be like on the outside, what his girlfriend is like, what his house is like. I'm aware that these things do sound like I have a crush and that's why I can't explain that to Mala. I decide to be more careful how often I bring up his name.

The first letter that I open reveals an explicit photo. It's vulgar and I feel my bacon sandwich repeating on me. I pass it over to Mala. I don't see why I have to be the only one to see it.

My best friend suppresses a gag and she asks who the lucky guy is that it's meant for. I tell her that it's for Peter The Wife Beater. We have our little nicknames for some of them. She hands it back.

'And still women will do this shit for him,' she grimaces.

It's odd but I don't see Anna West as any different to this woman – putting everything on show for a dangerous lowlife. Yet nothing about this stirs up the same interest in me as Jason and Anna do. I process the photo and file it away. Peter The Wife Beater can't have it anyway. Access denied. The next several letters, I process quietly in order to get through them quickly.

'Right, I'm just going to take these up to the office,' I say.

'Come back with some juicy gossip, okay.'

I salute my best friend and wheel the trolley out. There are several inmates bustling around but I don't see Jason, but when I reach the office, there he is. He's stood talking to Phil. My heart quickens. I'm still unnerved as to why it does. I have Jason's address and intend on going to snoop at his house and check out what Anna looks like. These are good reasons why my nerves are on edge. He's looking at me with those chocolate eyes, straight into my thoughts, like he knows. I make the decision there and then not to do it. It's a stupid idea and I'm not cut out for this snooping stuff; my nerves can't take it.

Jason greets me and I try not to stare at him. His face looks even worse up close.

'Any mail for me, Miss?' he asks, looking at my trolley.

'Not this morning, I don't think.' I don't want to sound like I'm certain there's no mail for him. Like I know him well and have been savouring each and every letter he gets. There I go again; I can't stop thinking about it. About them.

'Go on then, off you go,' Phil says to Jason. 'Remember what I said, yes?'

Jason saunters off, head low.

'What happened to him?' I ask Phil, not wasting any time. We step inside the office.

'He's not giving much away but it was Dan and

Ryan who jumped him last night.'

'Do you know why?'

'Nah, he's not saying. The boys aren't talking yet. They've been segregated for now.'

'In an e-mail to his girlfriend, he asked if she could transfer money to Harrison and Ben. This was after they were all kicking off. It said it was money owed but I wondered if there was more to it.'

'Don't know about that. I got the impression that Jason is doing everything to keep his nose clean because of his appeal. He's probably paying these dicks off to keep trouble away. Perhaps Dan and Ryan wanted in on some cash? It's a thought.'

I had already wondered the same.

Phil continues, 'He never even fought back. He just took the kicking. Not a scratch on the other two. Seems we could be right. Jason will do anything to not harm his appeal.'

I imagine him for a moment, lying there taking the beating. His thoughts were probably of Anna. She kept him going. I imagine the phone call that she received, giving her the news on what had happened and how helpless she'd be feeling. I shake my head. *I actually don't know what's wrong with me.* I'm turning this reality of a killer in prison into some romantic fantasy.

CHAPTER SEVENTEEN
Harper

Harper hops off the bus and is relieved to see Callum waiting for her as he should be.

'You owe me big time for this,' he greets her. 'So, what's the plan?'

'Yoga starts at seven so we have an hour to kill. Hang on, I just gotta text Dad. Let him know I got to your house okay.'

'I'm surprised he didn't insist on driving you.' Callum says.

'He knows he can't wrap me up in cotton wool anymore. It's taken him a long time after mum died. Don't think he'll ever stop imagining the worst happening to me but as long as I keep texting him, I have some independence.'

The roads throughout the town centre are still busy from the rush hour traffic. Harper jumps at the sound of a car horn blaring. The island just ahead is well known for drivers not getting in the correct lane. Harper has seen enough angry posts on Facebook about drivers getting cut up and all of the near misses.

'So?' Callum asks again.

Harper looks around, 'We can go over there to the burger joint and grab something to eat whilst we wait. I have some cash.'

'I've had my dinner.'

'Well, I haven't. My dad and Kate think that I'm at yours for dinner, don't they?'

'Who am I kidding? Of course I've got room for a burger.'

Harper playfully tickles his ribs and she leads him to the crossing. Once inside, they both settle into a booth by the window with their burgers and shakes. The gym is adjacent to the burger joint but just out of eyesight, which Harper thought was a bit annoying. She made a mental note to keep an eye closely on the time, to make sure that they were out there ready.

'Harps, do you really honestly think that Kate is having an affair? Do you not think that she is just going to yoga with Mala?'

'I dunno, do I? That's what I'm trying to find out. I'm telling you, she's hiding something.'

'What are you going to do if she doesn't show for yoga then?' Callum asks with a mouthful of burger.

Harper shrugs and takes a glug of her chocolate shake.

'It's not like you can tell your dad, is it? How would you explain you were spying on Kate when you should be at mine having dinner?'

Harper shrugs again, 'Perhaps we were getting dinner from here. Your parents brought us here for dinner and that's when I noticed Mala go into the gym without Kate... Oh, I should have just said that to start with.' Harper could visualise the lies snowballing and kicks herself for not making a better plan.

'I think you're crazy.' Callum shakes his head.

Harper looks injured. Laughter erupts from the booth opposite them. She looks over at the family. A young girl has chocolate ice cream smeared all around her face and her older sister is taking photos whilst the parents are laughing. The younger girl is repeating the words, 'Do I have something on my face?' The banter between the siblings continues.

'You okay?' Callum breaks her thoughts. 'You haven't said if you're looking forward to school tomorrow?'

'Well that goes without saying… err no.'

'You know I have your back, right?'

Harper feigns a smile and puts her remaining burger down. Suddenly she's no longer hungry. 'We should go. We have to make sure we are outside the gym in enough time in case Kate and Mala arrive a bit early.'

Callum shoves the last bite into his mouth and takes a mouthful of his shake at the same time.

'You're disgusting.' Harper laughs.

Callum clutches his full stomach and they both head outside.

'How we gonna do this without being seen?' Callum asks.

Harper suggests that they cross over the road and watch the entrance to the gym from the opposite side of the road. As long as they both spot Mala and Kate first, they can duck and hide or run off or something. Callum mutters that he is thankful that the weather is at least warm and that he feels like an idiot. Harper reassures him that twenty-five minutes isn't long to wait. They stand in comfortable silence and Harper thinks again how lucky she is to have him in her life. Her only friend, the only person to love her for who she is – just not in the way she wants. She glances at his lips and blushes, thinking what it'd be like to kiss him. She imagines this too much. She always thought that her first kiss would be with him but she's certain now it'll never happen – he told her as much.

'That's Mala, isn't it?' Callum blurts out, tapping Harper on the shoulder.

Mala is unmistakable with her tall, shapely figure. Even in gym wear she looks striking with her mass of black curls scraped up.

'Is Kate with her?' Callum asks.

Kate was unnoticeable at first. A couple was walking in front of her, blocking her as she was bent over tying her laces. She was there.

'See, she's not having an affair,' Callum says gently.

Harper quickly grabs his arm and turns him away from facing Kate's direction. She hurries him along up the road before they risk being seen.

'Okay, so she's gone to yoga, but this means nothing. She's a snake and I will prove it eventually.'

Callum puts his hands up in surrender and they continue to the bus stop. Harper thinks that Callum doesn't believe her at all but at least he's helping her, unlike anything her stepmum would ever do. Everyone hates her at school because of Kate. The words 'Snitch Bitch' ring around her head. She doesn't know how much more she can take. The bus home is approaching, and Callum asks her a few times if she's sure she'll be okay. Harper reassures him that she can manage ten minutes on the bus and to stop acting like her dad.

'See ya at school tomorrow. I'll find you at break, okay?' Callum says as the bus pulls up.

Harper nods to him and boards the bus. Taking her seat, she wishes that they were in the same classes. At least then she wouldn't feel so alone. She takes out her phone to text her dad to say that she's on her way home. The Snapchat icon shows a notification. She opens it up and almost drops her phone. She knows exactly what that picture is. A bit of leg flesh and a flash of knickers. Hers. The photo that Lexi snapped after knocking her to the ground. The words said, *see you tomorrow,* with a laughing face emoji. She didn't recognise the sender's name but it was there and now it was gone. How many people had seen that photo? She feels lightheaded. This is exactly what she feared. Lexi is going to make her life hell.

CHAPTER EIGHTEEN

The hour went quickly and I must admit that I'm feeling suitably relaxed and stretched. The dimmed lights in the fitness room brighten and the yoga class is now a bustle of chatter.

'Well?' Mala asks. 'Have I converted you?'

'I found some of the floor work a bit tricky. I kept cricking my neck, looking at everyone else to see if I was doing it right.' I laugh. 'Yes, I feel good.'

Therese joins us. I was briefly introduced to her at the start of the class. She asks Mala if they are still heading over to the pub. Mala hadn't mentioned that they had plans to go for a drink afterwards.

'Yes, indeed,' Mala answers her.

'Are you joining us?' Therese asks me.

I shake my head. 'No, I best get home.'

Therese links Mala's arm and she laughs about how good wine tastes after a hard workout.

'How about Red's again this Saturday night?' Mala asks me. 'Therese hasn't been yet. She hasn't experienced life in Bracknell until she's experienced Red's.'

'My expectations are high now.' Therese laughs.

'I can't,' I say. 'I'm needed at home. Anyway, I

have to dash. See you tomorrow.' I say to Mala, without giving her much chance to reply. I hurry out of the gym and into the fresh evening air.

I feel a bit silly for feeling a twinge of jealousy. Of course it's okay for Mala to have other friends, and she does, but she and Therese seem close and Mala hadn't mentioned her before. I suppose she is fairly new to the area. Mala is single; she likes to go out. It's not something I can do all of the time. I have responsibilities at home. I'm needed. But then sadness washes over me. Jon doesn't feel like he's needed, does he? He's having an affair; he's moving on to someone else. Mala is now moving on to a new best friend. Am I really so boring? No one needs me anymore. Just two troubled kids. I inhale deeply as I feel my eyes sting. I'm not sure if I'm being ridiculous. Fizzy and Harper are enough for me anyway.

I spot that the shop across the road is still open and I decide to pop over and grab some cupcakes. I'll put one in Harper's lunch bag tomorrow. It'll be a little treat for her first day back after her suspension. She must be dreading going in so it might help brighten her day. I tell myself to stop being silly and to focus on the girls. I hurry straight to the bakery aisle and select a box of triple chocolate cupcakes.

'They look good, don't they?' an attractive blonde woman says, reaching past me to grab herself a box of the same cupcakes. She pops them in the basket under her baby's pram.

I smile and agree and spend a moment to coo over her baby.

'Thought I'd find you at the cakes.' A man suddenly appears at her side. I glance up at him and my heart misses a beat.

I stare at him and he stares at me. I'm looking into the face of Chris, my ex-husband.

'Oh, hi.' I manage to spit the words out.

He looks awkward, but only for a moment. 'Hi. Good to see you,' he smiles.

'I heard you moved out of Bracknell,' I say.

The blonde woman is looking a little perplexed, so Chris quickly introduces us. She doesn't look fazed at all by being introduced to his ex-wife.

'We did,' he says, 'but we came back to be nearer family for when our Maisy was born.' He nods to their baby.

Maisy gurgles a cry and her mum strokes her cheek and tells her she knows it's very late but they'll be home soon.

'She's lovely,' I say, my voice almost faltering. 'Good to see you. I'll let you get on,' I quickly say and walk away.

The cashier couldn't scan the cupcakes fast enough. I will her to hurry up so I can get as far away as possible. So Chris had got what he wanted; it's what he left me for. I couldn't give him his dream of being a father, so he sought it elsewhere. He moved on from me. Just like Jon is doing, just like Mala is now doing. I get outside and steady my breathing, walking at pace to the car park. Sliding myself into my car, I scold myself for being ridiculous again. I'm not sure where all of this feeling of self-pity is coming from, all of this insecurity. Chris didn't hang about though, did he? He only walked out on me a couple of years ago. It's still so fresh, so raw. But then I moved on quickly too, didn't I? My whirlwind romance with Jon. My heart felt full for the first time when Felicity and Harper came into my life. It still feels full. They're all I need and they're all that matters. I drive away and hope that I don't start bumping into Chris all over the place now he's back in town.

Jon is in the kitchen when I get home. I breeze in and greet him with a kiss on the cheek, but he flinches and pulls away.

'Sorry love, you startled me,' he says. 'How was yoga?'

I know damn well he saw me approach him. When did I become so repulsive to him? I can't keep up with him blowing hot and cold. I say yoga was good but leave out the rest of the evening's details. I just tell him I'm off for a shower. Fizz is in bed fast asleep. I poke my head around her door and blow her a kiss. I can hear Harper's TV on so knock on her door and poke my head inside.

'Are you going to sleep soon, Harps?' I ask her. She's curled up on her bed still dressed and hugging her pillow. She ignores me.

'Right, well, you do have school so…'

'I'm not going,' she mutters into her pillow but loud enough for me to hear.

I approach her bed and crouch to her level.

'You will be fine, you'll see. It's just the thought of it but once you're there—'

'I'm not going to that fucking hell hole.'

Her voice is venomous and throws me off guard. Of course I've heard her slip out the odd swear word but this startles me.

'I can imagine how you're feeling but you have to face it. You've got your exams—'

Harper rolls over, turning her back on me, placing her pillow tightly over her head. I can feel my blood pressure rising. I don't know how to get through to her anymore. I've done everything I can to keep her happy, to make things right at the school, to make her feel supported. I'm being pushed away by her dad, I'm being pushed away by my best friend and now her.

'Right, give me your phone,' I snap. I snatch it from her bedside table and grab the remote, turning off her TV. 'Get to sleep and stop being so bloody ungrateful.'

I march from her room with her phone in my hand. Harper sits up and throws her pillow with force at the door just as I pass through it. I shut the door on her and hear her scream followed by the words, 'I hate you.'

Of course this is going to be my fault. Jon comes dashing up the stairs raising his voice, asking me why I'm shouting at his daughter.

'She's refusing to go to school tomorrow. You deal with it,' I bite back.

He glares at me and goes in to see Harper. My cheeks are burning. I stomp into my bedroom and turn the ensuite shower on full. My clothes are thrown to the floor and I let the hot water blast down on me. I slide down to the floor of the shower and hug my knees up to my chest. The water is soothing and I start reflecting that I could have handled that better. It's hard though to keep treading on eggshells, to keep worrying whether whatever I'm going to say is going to annoy her and have her jump down my throat. All I get is backchat and sarcastic retorts. I'm nice, I get snapped at; I'm firm, I get snapped at. I make excuses that she's a teen but Jon is no better. All I am is an irritant to them. One minute I'm being led into a false sense of security when they show a small token of affection and the next it's forgotten and I'm back to being their punchbag.

Do I have to be some dangerous criminal to earn their love and respect? Do I have to become a cold-blooded killer? Being a loving, decent citizen and a good wife is getting me nowhere. How do these prisoners get so much love and adoration in their letters from home and I get treated like something scraped off one of Harper's trainers? What the bloody hell does Anna West have that I don't? I'm working myself up so I inhale some deep breaths to relax my stiffened frame. No, Harper is nervous and scared and I shouldn't have raised my voice. You don't shout at scared people, right? I overreacted. I'll tell her I'm sorry and that I just want what's best for her, with her exams approaching. It's only because I care. I'll leave her be for tonight and see her in the morning.

I know I should stop comparing myself to some woman that I've never met, this Anna West. I imagine that she's beautiful, glamorous and confident, and full of passion. I can't be that – I can't force myself to be that. But other people's relationships are fascinating and I'm still going to pay her address a visit. It's for a kind of research, some domestic psychological interest thing. Yes, people study criminal minds; it's the same sort of thing. I'm interested, that's all.

Jon is waiting for me as I step from the ensuite wrapped in my bathrobe.

'She's calmed down,' he says. He picks up her phone that I had left on our bed. 'I'm handing this back to her. You need to stop treating her like a kid.'

'But I don't know how to talk to her. She keeps biting my head off no matter what I do.'

'Give the girl some space. She's under a lot of pressure. When have we got this family team-building day with Felicity's therapist? Perhaps that will do us all good.'

I'm grateful that Jon's tone is now calm and

he's thinking logically about what we can do to get help as a family.

'I'm not sure. I could ring her tomorrow and chase it up?'

'Perhaps we should look at a holiday too. For when Harper finishes her exams, something to look forward to. We haven't been away for a while have we?'

My heart could burst, and I suddenly feel bad for feeling negative. Perhaps I've been escalating things inside my head unnecessarily. He does love me; we just need to talk more.

'I'd love that,' I say, feeling my eyes shine.

'Start having a look at locations. I'll go make us a cuppa.'

We haven't had many holidays as a family due to Fizz's anxiety and her struggles communicating. Jon never wanted to unsettle her. But she has me. If she's unhappy or homesick, she can tell me. At least she's one person who won't snipe at me every time I try to help. I've got her little back. Harper will also be less stressed once she's left school. She'll be a different person. She just needs to get through these last couple of months. A family holiday will bring us closer together again. I push the niggling thoughts aside that I'm sure Jon is having an affair. I don't want to think about it, not now. Despite my outbursts, I'm not losing my family for anything.

CHAPTER NINETEEN
Harper

Harper sits inside Mrs Davis's office for her return to school meeting. She fidgets in her chair, thinking how ridiculous it is that she needs a back-to-school meeting when she's only been off for two days.

'Your welfare is our priority, Harper, so this is just a quick chat to make sure that you have no issues, worries or concerns following the incident you were involved in. Lexi accepted your written apology, and she is happy to make amends and move on. Is there anything you'd like to add to that?'

Harper wants to scream. Where was her written apology when Lexi attacked her? She wanted to scream that she sent her the photo, that it does exist and loads of people have probably seen it. She wasn't listened to in the first place and she won't be listened to now. She didn't believe for a second that Lexi had forgiven her. Not a chance. Not after sending her that photo. Telling anyone would only make it even worse anyway so she quietly says no.

Mrs Davis relaxes her hands on the desk and her face softens. 'Now, I've had a good chat with Lexi regarding some of the names she's been calling you. Your mum... your stepmum has expressed her concerns that you're being bullied. You know that Lexi's dad is in prison and she's admitted that she struggles with her temper and feels angry at the situation. I've helped to make her realise that she can't use that as an excuse to say nasty things to you just because of your stepmum's job position...'

Mrs Davis continues to talk but Harper stops hearing the words. Lexi hasn't realised anything; she's not going to be sorry for anything. Why couldn't Kate just stay out of it? The whole thing is bullshit.

'Now, I know you and Lexi are in the same sets for Maths and English. Your teachers will be keeping an eye out for both of you during those lessons and you can sit further apart if you feel more comfortable.'

Harper is looking down to her lap and twisting the cuffs of her blazer.

Mrs Davis continues, 'Harper, my door is always open for you. We do have counselling available for anything that you may feel you need. The loss of your mum was traumatic and I'm aware of your sister's difficulties. How are things at home?'

'Everything is fine,' Harper says defensively. 'I take care of my sister. We're close. She is fine.'

Mrs Davis gives her a sympathetic smile. 'Well, the offer is there if you need any support with anything.'

Harper feels her chest tighten. What she wants is to be listened to; it's a joke. All of these offers of support but nobody actually listens. Everything just gets dismissed or she gets told to just ignore Lexi. It solves nothing. Mrs Davis shows her to the door and adds, 'Enjoy your day.'

The first lesson has already started – Maths. Harper looks up and down the empty corridor and to the exit signs. The urge to run is overwhelming. Perhaps she could at least just hide in the toilets until Maths is over. How is sending her into her first lesson back with Lexi helpful? She's rooted to the spot until she hears footsteps. They spur her on to move. She hurries over to the toilets and sinks to the cubicle floor. She's sure it's disgusting but she doesn't care. Her Maths teacher will assume that she's been in her meeting the whole time. She has her rucksack with her and pulls out her lunch bag. She pulls out a triple chocolate cupcake – no doubt it was Kate's way of making her day back at school nicer. Things can't just be fixed with chocolate cake or simply ignoring things. When will people listen? However, a sugar fix wouldn't hurt so she bit into the frosting.

Twenty minutes later and the bell signals the end of the first lesson. Harper jumps, brushing away the cake crumbs. She figures that it will be okay now to blend in with the crowds and make her way to Humanities. She opens the cubicle door to be met with Lexi Keggans. Lexi looks equally startled looking back at her.

'Welcome back, Snitch Bitch.' Lexi grins wickedly.

Her friends, Jody and Amy, burst in laughing.

'Hey, you didn't wait up—' Jody says to Lexi, but she shot Amy a knowing look when they both realise who Lexi was with.

The three girls closed in around Harper.

'What are you doing in here, skank? Eating your own shit?' Lexi spits.

Harper wipes her mouth and realises there is chocolate on her lips. She tries to walk around them; she doesn't even try to speak but Lexi grabs her elbow.

'My dad was beaten up by a screw over the weekend. All screws are bent, do you hear me?'

Harper pulls away, 'Kate isn't a screw; she just reads the mail. We've got nothing to do with what's happened to your dad. Leave me alone.'

'Run along then, you little skank.' Lexi steps aside. 'Keep your mouth shut or you'll find your windows bricked in.'

Harper pushes past a couple of girls entering the toilets. One of them curses her to watch it.

So much for avoiding Lexi. Harper's eyes fill with tears as she hurries along with her head down. Mrs Davis has fallen for that cow's sorry act. She knew that there was no way Lexi was willing to move on. All she wanted to do was go back into the toilets and smash Lexi's head against the wall but she'd only be the one in trouble again. She didn't want to give Lexi the satisfaction. That and her hands were shaking at the thought. She knew she didn't have it in her. She looks at the exit sign again and this time she follows it. She leaves the building and heads up the path and out of the gates without looking back.

CHAPTER TWENTY

It's nearly lunchtime and my stomach is growling. I ought to go to my car and check my phone, see if the school has left any messages. Hopefully, Harper has settled in fine and there aren't any issues so no reason for them to call. She did leave for school okay this morning despite her outburst last night. Jon must have done a good job in talking her round. I can't argue that she is daddy's girl. It crosses my mind whether it had always been the case when her mum was alive or did they grow closer when she passed away? It's not something we discuss. Jon does talk about Marie and shares some memories but sometimes he shuts down like it's too painful.

'Is that your stomach?' Mala interrupts my thoughts.

I laugh. 'Yes, I'm starving.'

'I've got time to get this morning's mail over to Phil before we break for lunch.' Mala gathers what she needs and says she'll be back in a jiffy.

The e-mails this morning have been uneventful. I work my way through the last few before lunch but then one does get my attention. It's to Jason Sawyer from his sister, Melissa.

Hey Jase, the police have requested that I take

Chloe in for another chat. Don't know if you heard about that teenager that went missing the weekend and then found Tuesday morning. She'd been beaten and raped. That's a few of them now in this area. They're following all leads and want to see if Chloe can shed any more light, I guess. They should've been focusing more on the bastards that took Chloe, not sending you down for murder. Let me know if they question you again too. Mel x

I print it off and log the details. So that poor girl was beaten and raped and just dumped in the road. A shiver runs up my spine. I don't know how that young girl is going to get over something like that. I try and push away the dark thoughts, imagining what she must have gone through.

'You're looking serious,' Mala says, coming back into the office.

'You were quick.'

'I'm hungry.'

'Look at this,' I hand Mala the e-mail.

She scans the page and her eyes widen. 'That's what's-her-face… Holly, who was on the news. Poor thing. Bet Phil will have the goss on how Jason is involved in all of this. You coming to the staff area? Phil's just said he's taking his break too.'

I think that I should go to my car and check my phone but perhaps I shouldn't worry so much. The school can get hold of Jon if they need to. It'll be good to gossip over lunch for once instead of sitting in the car park on my own. Who am I trying to kid? It's gossip about Jason and I can't resist. We grab our lunch and head to the staff area.

Mala doesn't waste time filling Phil in on the e-mail. He's biting into a crusty ham and cheese roll and chews for what seems like an age. When he finally swallows, he tells us what he knows.

'Jason has admitted to dealing in weed. We're talking small-time stuff here. He claims it's all he's guilty of. Michael, the guy he stabbed, was the guy who was supplying him with the plants. Now, this guy made some sleazy comments or something to his niece, Chloe. When she didn't turn up for school the next day, Jason went with his gut instinct and headed over to this Michael's house. The whole family was out looking for her, the police were called and all that. Jason claimed he was just trying everything to find her. He entered the house through an open window and found Chloe tied up on the sofa. This Michael jumps him, they fight. Jason pulls out a knife and stabs him in the shoulder. The guy falls back and Jason grabs his niece and they run. He calls the police when they're at a safe distance.'

'So, if he's telling the truth,' I say, 'then who could blame him for stabbing that guy if he was saving his niece. Look what happened to this Holly and the others. Who knows what would've happened to Chloe? I know what I'd do if it was Harper or Felicity. Good job he followed his gut.'

'Maybe so, but he was dealing with some dodgy people, and he was carrying a knife. Who's to say Jason wasn't in on his niece's abduction? He knew where she was. People are capable of all sorts for money.'

'So, no other leads on Chloe's abduction?' Mala asks. 'Because other girls have gone missing since her kidnapper was killed. Could he have been part of a gang?'

'There's nothing that I know of. Like Jason claims, he only stabbed him once in the shoulder, but the guy had multiple stab wounds. Neither he nor Chloe saw anyone else at any time in or around the house.' Phil took another bite of his roll.

I was so engrossed that I'd forgotten to start my own lunch. I tuck into my own sandwich and mull it all over. It was interesting to hear more details about what happened. It all seems to make more sense to me. Jason doesn't seem like a cold-blooded killer the few times that I've spoken to him. He's polite – warm almost. And he took that beating. Would he have just laid down if he was a violent criminal? I won't share my thoughts on this. I know Mala already thinks that I have a soft spot for him, and Phil will always counter argue everything.

I unwrap my triple chocolate cupcake and my thoughts turn back to Harper. If her day is not going so well then hopefully at least her cupcake will make her smile. I know she hates school, but she just needs to hang on a few more weeks. I bite into the chocolate sponge and the gooey centre dribbles onto my chin. Mala laughs at me and hands me a napkin. At least I didn't get it on my white collar. Simon, one of the younger new recruits, calls Phil over for his help. Phil shakes his head and gathers his lunch wrappers together.

'One day I may get a full lunch break,' he grunts.

Phil is part of the prison furniture, and he just has a way with the inmates. He gains their trust, and not to mention he's a strapping guy with a lot of muscle behind him. It does mean that he's called on a lot to settle disputes and to break up fights. There are other officers sitting around but it's always Phil that gets called. Mala always says that if he just had a bit more hair on top then she'd be in there. I always remind her that it's not a good idea to mix work with pleasure anyway and she always says, 'But we are best friends working together. It's the same thing.' Then I remind her he has a wife anyway and then she reminds me that none of it matters because he needs more hair on top for her taste. I love these familiar and repetitive conversations with my best friend. They never get boring to us and we laugh every time.

'Are you sure I can't talk you into Red's this Saturday?' Mala asks me.

I shake my head. 'No, I can't. Not two

weekends on the trot. Maybe next time though. How's it going with that guy you met?'

'It's not. We text a few times since hooking up but there's no spark. He's not my type.'

I don't actually think Mala has a type. If she wasn't so fussy, she wouldn't still be single and I tell her that all of the time too and she doesn't disagree. Then I remember Chris.

'I saw Chris in the shop last night after yoga.'

Mala's eyes widen. 'What's that arsehole doing back in town then?'

'He's had a baby with his new wife. They're back to be closer to family.'

Mala doesn't have to say anymore. She leans over and gives me a squeeze. She's the only person who knew how devastated I was when he walked out on me. I scold myself again for feeling jealous about Mala's new friend. Our friendship bond is tight and it's just my stupid insecurities talking.

'We're not dwelling on the past. C'mon, let's get back to the post room,' Mala says, taking my rubbish and hers to the bin. I follow her out.

On the way back, I spot Jason chatting to another prisoner by the exit to the garden area. I grimace at his face; it looks so sore. He looks over and I quickly look away. I wonder how he'd feel if he knew we were just gossiping about him over our lunch break. I wonder how he'd feel if he knew that I still have his home address tucked away safely. I feel naughty and it excites me a little even though I'm trying not to admit it to myself too much. This weekend, I'll try and escape for a couple of hours to go and nose at his house, his neighbourhood. His girlfriend. I just need to work out some story to tell Jon. I don't feel guilty. After all, he has lied to me.

When we reach the post room, the internal phone is ringing. Mala picks it up and hands the receiver to me, 'It's for you,' she says. The switchboard lady says it's Jon on the line and he says it's urgent. The operator puts him through.

'Jon, is everything okay?' I ask.

'I know I'm not meant to call you at work but the school phoned and said Harper is missing. She was there for her meeting with Mrs Davis and no one has seen her since. Has she tried calling you at all? I've tried her mobile, she's not picking up. I did try you on your mobile. Did you not check your phone at lunch?'

'Okay, slow down. No I didn't. It's fine though. I'll go to my car now and double-check. If she's not picking up to you then I doubt she will to me, but I'll try. I'll call you straight back, okay.' I hang up.

Mala gives me a concerned look.

'I'm sorry, mind if I dash out for a few mins? Harper's gone AWOL.'

'Yes, go.' She shoos me out of the post room.

I curse Harper all the way to the car. She couldn't just stay in school for the day and see it through. She always has to create drama. This'll mean another suspension for her. I reach my car and fumble in the glove box for my phone and impatiently wait for it to turn on. The phone beeps to signal missed calls and voicemails from the school and Jon. I try Harper's phone first and it just rings out. I try again and leave her a message. I reassure her she's not in trouble but to call her dad ASAP. I call Jon.

'No, I've tried her, she's not answering,' I sigh. 'I have a missed call from the school.'

'Yes, they couldn't get hold of me straight away so the receptionist said she tried your phone too. But obviously, I've spoken to them now. She didn't turn up for her morning lessons. What's she playing at?'

'Has she just gone home? Have you been back yet?'

'No, I'm up to my neck in it at work but I called my mum to swing by the house and she said she's not there or just not answering the door.'

I think rationally. 'Harper isn't going to go far. She'll be home by the time we get in from work. Just keep trying her phone. I can't have my phone on me, can I? You watch, she'll be shut in her bedroom with the music blaring come home time. It's a bit early to start worrying.'

Jon agrees and mutters something about killing her before hanging up. I rub my face in my hands. I feel bad that I didn't check my phone earlier but there's nothing I can do right now anyway. Despite my rational words, I can't help a wave of fear wash over me. The news of what happened to Holly Stevens and the other teenagers is unnerving. It might have happened in Reading but it's still too close to home. I couldn't bear it if anything happened to her.

CHAPTER TWENTY-ONE

I pull up outside of Fizz's school to fetch her from her after-school club. I call Jon the moment I stop and he says that he's just got home but there's no sign of Harper. I hang up and pace back and forth by the school gate, willing Fizz to hurry up. I see her emerge from the double doors and head this way with Clare.

'She's been fine this afternoon,' Clare says. 'A bit quiet but fine…'

Her voice trails off when she realises what she's just said. We look at each other a bit awkward but I don't remark on it. Slips of the tongue happen. I briskly thank her and bundle Fizz into the car. We need to get home.

I start the engine. 'Fizz, did Harper say anything to you about any plans she had today? Did she tell you she was going anywhere?'

Fizz looks thoughtful. 'No, she was just going to school. Why?'

'She's a bit late home, that's all.'

'I bet she's kissing her boyfriend, Callum,' Fizz giggles.

I hadn't thought of Callum. I'll try calling him as soon as we're back, see if he knows where she is. Perhaps they've bunked off together. I put my foot down.

Jon greets me on the driveway. She's still not home. I tell him I'm calling Callum. I have his mobile stored on my phone and hit call.

'Hey Callum, is Harper with you?'

'No, I didn't see her at school today. She alright?'

'She bunked off. Are you sure you haven't seen her? Did she say anything? Do you know where she might be?' I realise I'm raising my voice.

'I don't know anything. I know she wasn't looking forward to going to school but I said I'd look out for her. I'll try calling her.'

'Please let me know straight away if you hear from her.'

He hangs up. I just shrug my shoulders at Jon.

'Should we call the police?' he says.

'I don't know if it's a bit early for that. Let's give her a bit longer, shall we? See if Callum can get hold of her. If it starts getting dark, perhaps we will then...' I don't really know what to do for the best. I don't want to overreact, but I don't want to waste time finding Harper either. Jon nods in agreement and we set about prepping dinner. We try to remain calm so as not to frighten Fizz. It's approaching six p.m. and this is definitely out of character for Harper. She should be here.

My phone buzzes signalling a text message. My heart races. It's from Callum.

Harps isn't answering my calls. Sorry. I'll keep trying. Cal.

Jon looks at me, his jaw set firm. Fizz wraps

her arms around his legs and he picks her up and softly swings her from side to side before releasing her again.

'Can I help cook?' She looks at me, turning her back on her dad.

Jon strides from the room. It's times like this that Jon is resentful, I'm sure of it. He's spent years now, trying to understand Fizz's condition but there are times when he gets frustrated with her and himself. I pass Fizz the pasta for her to weigh out.

'The twisty ones are my favourite.' She smacks her lips together as she pours them into a bowl.

'She's back,' Jon shouts from the lounge.

He rushes into the kitchen and, seconds later, Harper is entering through the back door.

'Where the bloody hell have you been?' He raises his voice.

'Oh, you're in trouble.' Fizz says.

It's enough to stun us into silence. Harper's jaw drops and Jon does a double-take at Fizz. He's lost for his next words. Fizz drops to the floor, crouching behind my legs and then a second later she bolts from the kitchen.

Harper bursts into tears, 'I'm sorry. I just couldn't...'

Her dad steps forwards and hugs her and tells her it's okay. He lets go.

'Have you eaten? Are you hungry?' I ask her.

She nods.

'We were worried sick,' I say calmly.

'Well that makes a change,' she snaps, her tears turning angry.

'That's not fair. I've done everything to try and help you. If you just talked to me... to us then we'd know what to do.'

'You think a fucking cupcake is trying to help me?' Harper throws her bag to the floor.

'Don't speak to Kate like that,' Jon tries to reason. 'Love, just tell me where you've been? I'm going to make you a cuppa. We're not angry.'

Harper looks at me with pure venom and Jon gives me a warning look.

'I'm going to check on Fizz. She needs me,' I say in defeat and I leave them to it. I fight back the tears. I should be used to this now but I don't know where I'm going so badly wrong. And it's times like this that I understand Jon's frustrations. *Where am I going wrong*?

I let myself into Fizz's room and I join her sitting on the floor. She edges close to me and I stroke her silky hair. Her arms are shaking so I shuffle round to sit facing her and I demonstrate a breathing technique. Breathing slowly in and slowly out. Fizzy copies me.

'There, it's all fine,' I softly say. 'You haven't done anything wrong. Feel better?'

She looks at me with those sparkly blue eyes and she nods.

'I'm going to finish dinner; do you still want to help?'

She shakes her head.

I'm not going to push her. I'll leave her be. I can hear Harper stomping past to her room, so I feel like the coast is clear to go back downstairs. I'm rapidly losing my appetite though. I enter back into the kitchen and Jon has already got the bolognese and pasta bubbling away.

'Felicity alright?' he asks.

'Yes,' I nod. 'And Harper? What did she say?'

'I've told her to stop shouting and swearing at you. I don't know why she's so hostile.'

'She's safe, so where was she?'

'She said Lexi started on her and she walked out of school. She's been wandering around the town and the park. She reckons she was going to try and be in by five before we all got home but she lost track of time and it was a longer walk than she thought.'

'That name again, Lexi. Right, I'm going straight to see Mrs Davis—'

'Harper doesn't want us to make things worse. We need to think this through and give her a chance to calm down. I'm letting her have the day off tomorrow. Calm things down and take it from there.'

I agree with Jon. I don't know to handle things anymore. I can't seem to do right from wrong. At least if she's off school then she won't feel the need to run again. At least we'll know where she is. I'm keen to get out of my uniform so leave Jon stirring the bolognese. I hear talking in Fizz's bedroom and listen in. Harper is in there with her. I put my ear closer to the door.

'Are we good now?' Harper says. 'I'm scared you're frightened of me. I'm so sorry that you can't speak to me. I don't know what I've done... I love you, little sis, and I'm not leaving you, okay. I'll always come back for you.'

I allow a few moments pause and then I open the door. 'Dinner will be ready in ten mins, okay?' I say and then walk away.

Now would not be a good time to remind Harper not to put any emotional pressure on Fizz. She's frustrated though just like her dad is. He wonders what he's doing wrong and so does she. I go to my room and pull on some comfy joggers and a T-shirt. I text Mala to let her know that Harper is home safe and sound. She replies,

That's a relief. You'll never guess who I'm hooking up for dinner with tomorrow night. I'll tell all tomorrow. Love you x

I can't think who she's on about. It can't be the guy from Red's because she'd only said earlier today that there was no spark and she wasn't interested. I smile and welcome the distraction to puzzle over something more light-hearted. Before I go down for dinner, I open my underwear drawer and dig out a pair of Christmas-themed socks buried at the back. I unravel the sock bundle and fish out the crumpled piece of paper with an address on it. Jason and Anna's address. The urge to get out of the house for a drive is overwhelming.

I trot downstairs just as Jon shouts up for the girls to come and get their dinner. I help dish up as the girls join us. Jon suggests that we all sit together to eat and to my surprise, Harper agrees. After a few minutes of eating in silence I say, 'Mala's just text me. She could do with a hand with something. Do you mind if I pop out for an hour?'

'Popping out again with Mala? She's demanding a lot of your time this week, isn't she?' Jon says.

I can't tell if he's joking. 'I'd hardly say demanding. She needs a hand that's all.'

'What with?'

I'm already irritated by his questions. Why can't he just say yes? 'Just to shift some furniture around before she has her walls done tomorrow.' It's a small lie. Mala is having her lounge walls papered but not until the weekend.

Jon looks like he's thinking. Fizz is slurping up a mouthful of spaghetti and Harper is toying with hers.

'Yes, sure,' Jon finally says, 'But don't make plans for Saturday night. I'm out for another business dinner.'

So, Jon just says he's out and that's that and I have to just accept it? He doesn't ask, he doesn't check, he just declares it as fact. I say I'm off out and I get the third degree. Once more though, I bite my tongue so as not to cause an argument, so as not to upset Harper and not stress Fizz out.

I finish my food and slip my trainers on. I say I won't be long. Fizz is the only one to say goodbye to me. I blow her a kiss. It comes to something when this is the only excitement that I get. I slide into my car and fish out the address from my pocket. I punch the postcode into the satnav. Nelder Street in Whitley – approximately twenty minutes away. Not far but enough for me to enjoy some peace and a drive out on my own. It'll just be a quick look at the house and then back home. Where's the harm in that?

CHAPTER TWENTY-TWO
Gregg

The art gallery is already buzzing with animated young ladies, showing off their artwork to their families. Excited young faces, feeling their five minutes of fame. Gregg stands in a quiet spot at the far end of the gallery away from the display. He pretends to study a painting, occasionally scoping out the students. He doesn't care much for the girls' stuffy dark green uniforms. He didn't expect any less though from a private girls' high school. The open evening for the display from this local school was even busier than Gregg imagined it would be. So many young ladies ripe for the picking.

He is upping the game and he feels smug. No more trash, no more dropouts, no more girls with no class. This open event was too good an opportunity. Bright, fresh young ladies. Well-kept and well-groomed. Wealth breeds wealth. Men will pay more for a bit more elegance with virginity intact. This is the start of something big. Gregg prides himself in his online grooming. His talents have served him well over the years. He doesn't know what kids get taught in school anymore, but he's never failed. If a troubled teen wants attention, then they aren't going to listen to reason from any teacher or parent. It's too easy. Every time. This is a different game though. It's time for his skills to evolve.

He walks over to the crowd and methodically looks around the school's display, pretending to take an interest in each painting. He gets into small talk with a few of the girls, keen to show him what they've painted. He doesn't want to waste much time though. He knows exactly what he's interested in; however, he doesn't want to be too hasty. He has to look realistic; he has to look the part. His body tingles when he finally moves onto his target. He stops and studies an abstract painting of an elephant. The colours are bold and the elephant's disjointed body is surrounded by misshapen trees.

'Do you like it? I'm the artist.'

Bingo. Gregg looks at the blonde who is smiling sweetly at him. She is the one who stood out most to him whilst he was checking out the stock. 'It's breathtaking,' he says. 'What was your inspiration?'

The girl looks like she could burst. 'I wanted to show the destruction of nature. I painted this for my GCSE mock exam. I got a distinction.'

'I'm not surprised. You have quite the talent. It's very thought-provoking.'

'We're incredibly proud,' a woman says, appearing with a man by her side. The parents.

Gregg greets them both and pulls out a black leather cardholder. He produces a card and hands it to the girl's father. 'I'm here especially on a talent hunt. I offer representation to young upcoming artists. I get their work showcased in the big London galleries. It's an initiative to boost new talent into the industry.'

The man studies the card for a moment with his wife looking over his shoulder at it.

'Are you offering my daughter representation?' the father asks.

'Absolutely. She has just the style that I can work with. I can only take on a few clients at a time in order to give each artist my full attention. Of course, there are no costs involved. It's a community scheme.'

'It's something we can think about, isn't it?' the mother says.

'I can't believe you think my work is good enough,' the girl says.

'Do you have a portfolio of work?' Gregg asks the girl.

She nods enthusiastically.

'Well then...' Gregg looks at the placard beneath the painting, 'Sophie Banks, if you're interested, check out my website, get your parents to give me a call, and we can have a meeting. Bring your portfolio and we can take things from there.'

The father shakes Gregg's hand and thanks him. 'We'll think about it and be in touch,' he says.

'Wow, imagine your work all over London,

Sophie.' Her mother clasps her hands together.

'I shall look forward to hearing from you,' Gregg says, and bids them farewell.

Gregg steps outside and grins. He smooths down his trouser suit and straightens his cuffs. It didn't take him long to get a website knocked up. It looks the business. Either they fall for it or they don't, but dangle fame in front of people and the blinkers come on. Gregg is counting on it. It's like fruit picking and he's picked the juiciest.

CHAPTER TWENTY-THREE

I'm glad for the light evening. I don't think I could've attempted this in the winter, in the dark. I've pulled into the street but I can't see many house numbers. I'm crawling along but I'm wary that I look suspicious, and this would look worse in the dark. I decide to pull up into a parking bay. I think that casually walking along might be less conspicuous. My first impression of the street is fairly unremarkable and not too dissimilar to where I live, with rows of detached houses that are standard looking with three or four bedrooms. I don't really know what I was expecting so I'm unsure why I'm feeling disappointed. Perhaps I wanted different.

I need number fifteen. I can now see that it's odd numbers on one side and even on the other, so I cross over and straight in front of me is number thirteen and to the left of that is number fifteen. There it is. There's no car on the driveway and the windows look dark, I see no movement but I'm trying not to stare too obviously. The driveway is lined with small conifers and the garden isn't sparse of flowers. It's beautiful. I've convinced myself that no one's home, therefore no one can see me, so I look a bit longer than I should. There aren't any weeds. Not one. The topiary is individually shaped and the borders are bursting with colour. The front door is white with three decorative windows: diamond-cut shapes catching the light. It's pretty. The whole frontage is pretty.

I didn't take Anna West to have green fingers and it's hard to imagine that Jason Sawyer knows his chrysanthemums from his geraniums. I turn and cross back over the road, walking back to my car. I still can't work out why I feel deflated. Was I expecting a lavish house or something more shabby? It's a bit of an anti-climax. It may not be a high-end neighbourhood but it's pleasant and looks respectable. I bet the news of living on the same street as a killer still rocked the residents. I can hear them saying that you never know what goes on behind closed doors and nothing like that ever happens around here. I wonder if the curtains twitch every time Anna comes and goes. I realise the irony of my thoughts. What am I doing if not being nosey? I can't judge.

I unlock the car, but something is stopping me from getting in. I'm honest with myself and realise that I don't want to go home yet. I can't face going back to the drama, back to being scowled at. As weird as I feel being out and doing this, it does feel good. I'm out on my own, having some me time and it's such a lovely evening to be outside. I wonder what the back of the house looks like. That's if I can see anything from the back. The street is quiet and I forget about whether I look conspicuous or not. I head back to the property. I head to the end of the row and take the path leading around to the back. The pathway leads directly behind the houses with bushes and trees lining the opposite side. It looks fairly secluded and not overlooked.

I count four houses along and stop at its back gate. This is the rear of Jason and Anna's house. I can see that the upper windows are closed. On a warm evening like tonight, you'd think they would be open. The neighbours have theirs open. There must be no one home. The fence has a couple of holes in the panels. I look around and there is still no one to be seen. I step towards the fence and peek through one of the bigger holes. From what I can see the back garden is as attractive as the front and a decent size too. Because it's so quiet here, I start to relax about being so nosey but at the same time, I don't want to push my luck so I move on. A cat bolts out from the bushes scaring me half to death. It's a black cat and it bolts across in front of me and leaps up one of the garden fences. It's a good job that I'm not superstitious, although I'm never certain if it's good luck or bad luck when a black cat crosses your path.

I feel more satisfied now that I've seen around the whole house but what I really want is to see Anna West. I have played out many scenes in my head and the different reasons why I could knock on the door and say hi. I could pretend to be a salesperson or someone spreading the word of God. But each scenario that I play out doesn't end well. I'm nosey, not a great liar. I couldn't carry on the act if Anna wanted to buy something that I was pretending to sell and so on. Perhaps because I've convinced myself that there's no one home, I find myself walking up to the front door instead of past it. I'm just going to say that I've got the wrong house if the door opens. But as there's no one home, it'll be fine. I knock on the door. I wait. Nothing. My stomach is in knots. From feeling brave to ridiculous in a heartbeat, I turn and hurry off the property.

'Can I help you with anything?'

I look up, startled at the elderly lady who's appeared from the house next door. I'm cursing myself for being spotted.

'No, I'm fine. Just... my friend's not home, that's all,' I stutter.

'Didn't think they had any friends left,' the lady scowls.

I don't comment. I just walk on. How rude, I think. I'm a complete stranger and some old busy body thinks that they can just insult my friends. Who aren't my friends, I correct myself. I was right about the curtain-twitching in the area, then, and them being unpopular with the neighbours. This time, I don't hesitate to get into the car. That's enough snooping around for one night. If the close neighbours dislike Anna West, then they aren't likely to tell her that they saw me hanging around. I could pop back at the weekend and try again. It seems easy now. When she answers the door, I'll just say I have the wrong house and walk away. Easy.

The drive back to Bracknell is peaceful. The roads are fairly quiet at this time. I'm hoping all has calmed down at home. I hope Fizz is relaxed too. That's twice this week she has blurted words out to someone other than me. I wonder what her therapist will make of it. Bang. My heart jumps into my throat as a car smashes into mine. It's cut me up and I slam on the brakes. A series of horns sound out as the few cars on the island come to a standstill. The driver of the car that's hit me has put their hazard lights on and is beckoning me to follow him. He slowly pulls away and I crawl along. We take the nearest exit and pull up at the side of the road, where it's safer. He gets out of his car and first inspects the rear side of his car where he hit the front end of mine. *Shit.* He hits the roof of his car and I can hear him growl.

I hold my breath and step out of my car. I'm certain he's going to yell at me. But he doesn't.

'I'm so sorry. I was in the wrong lane, wasn't I?' he pleads. 'I thought I had enough space to slide in front of you. Too much on my mind, I guess.'

He looks at the front of my car and above the driver's side headlight is a reasonable dent. *Shit.* I think I'm in shock. I'm struggling to get my words out.

'Blast it,' he says. 'I really am sorry. I'll give you my details and I'll make sure it's sorted.'

It dawns on me that I shouldn't be driving near the town centre; I should be at Mala's house. There was no need for me to be driving around that stupid island. How am I going to explain this one to Jon? It'll all go through the insurance, where it happened, how it happened. What do I say? I can't say, 'Well actually, I was stalking a prisoner's home', can I? Even saying that to myself, I feel ridiculous.

'Any damage to your car?' I say.

He shakes his head. 'Not a scratch but look at yours.'

'It's not so bad. That island is terrible for accidents. The lanes are confusing, aren't they?' I reason. My mind is racing. I can't think of a lie to tell Jon fast enough to explain why I'm driving through the town centre. 'Look, let's just leave it. I can get the dent fixed by a friend for next to nothing.'

'No way, I insist on sorting it out—'

'No, I insist, it's fine. It's no bother. These things happen.' I go to get back into my car. I have to get away and think.

'Okay, if you're sure, but here's my number if you change your mind. I take full responsibility.' He hands me a business card.

I thank him for his honesty and reassure him again that I wish to leave it. I drive away, the steering wheel supporting my shaking hands. I'll just tell Jon that a car pulled out on me at a junction near Mala's and didn't stop. Nothing I could do. Nobody saw it and no witnesses. I'll pay for the damage. That seems the easiest thing to say. Yes, I'll go with that. All I can hope is that the lies don't snowball.

I reach home to find Jon and Harper watching TV. Jon tells me that Fizz has gone to bed fine. It's nice to see Harper spending time with her dad. I suddenly feel like an intruder, an outsider in my own home. Everyone is relaxed and happy when I'm not around, it seems.

'Jon, I need to show you the car. Someone's hit it. There's a dent.'

Jon jumps up, 'Bloody hell, love. Are you okay? What happened?'

Harper follows us to the driveway and I fill them in on everything. I stick with my story that a car pulled out on me and didn't stop.

'We should contact the police,' Jon says. 'There could be CCTV near that road. Might be able to get a reg.'

'I'm not sure we should bother the police over this,' I say a bit too desperately, so I take a breath. 'It's not that bad. I'll pay for the dent. I don't want the stress of it. Hopefully Karma will catch up with the idiot who did it.' I bite my lip. The man that hit me was polite and honest. *I'm a terrible person.*

'We'll talk about it tomorrow. You must be shaken up?' Jon puts his arm around me.

Harper walks away quietly and I say that I would love a cuppa. I pray that Jon doesn't insist on calling the police. I never thought of that. It's getting out of hand. I should have just said something else; that I was in town to pop to the shop. Anything. And now I've made things worse.

CHAPTER TWENTY-FOUR
Harper

Harper jumps onto her bed and uncurls her fist to reveal the scrap piece of paper that she'd lifted from her stepmum's back pocket. Kate was so busy leaning over and inspecting the damage to the front of the car with her dad that she didn't feel the note being taken. It was poking out and Harper couldn't resist. It didn't matter if it was just a receipt or a shopping list; she had to see it.

The unfolded paper reveals an address. No name, just the address: 15 Nelder Street, Whitley, Reading. She's trying to think who they know that lives in Reading, but she can't. She wonders if that's where she really went this evening, but why? She's still convinced that she's up to something. That she's having an affair or something. If Kate isn't happy then she should just leave. Harper hugs her pillow to her middle. Things will be so much better if she did. She thought about her little sister and the words she spoke earlier, "Oh, you're in trouble." She'd give anything for annoying banter like that off her sister all of the time. It's hard for her not to think that without Kate around, Felicity might be tempted to speak to her and her dad more. Even though her sister has had selective mutism since their mum was killed, she is sure that she would start talking eventually. But then Kate turned up into their lives and Felicity attached herself to her, almost like a replacement for her mum, so now she doesn't feel the need to talk to anyone else.

If Kate went then her little sister might start seeing her as the only female figure to look up to instead, and not to mention how Kate has made her life at school miserable. The altercation with Lexi in the toilets flashes through her mind and she cringes. At least her dad is letting her have the day off school tomorrow. She bet that Kate wasn't happy about that but she didn't care. At least her dad was taking her seriously and not treating her like a little kid. There was no way she was going to grass Lexi up again. She believed that she would come to the house and brick the windows and she had to protect her little sister. She wonders again why Kate couldn't just get another job, is it so hard? She says she'd do anything for this family, but she doesn't.

She looks at the address and decides to keep an ear out for when Kate is going out again. If it's for a reason which sounds suspicious, then perhaps she could catch the train into Reading and see if she can catch her out or something. She's certain that Callum will be up for that. She changes into her nightclothes and nestles under her duvet. She turns her phone on. After today, she decides to delete all social media except Facebook for now, but she wants to check that everything is totally private and delete some friends on her list that may be connected to Lexi. She doesn't need hundRed's of friends anyway; she doesn't need anyone.

She scrolls through her Facebook newsfeed for a bit and stops on her hometown's gossip page. A post catches her attention. At first, she rolls her eyes at yet another post moaning about the island in the town centre. Another car has been cut up and another crash spotted. The angry post says, *'When will the council make the road signs clearer?'* She reads the post again, it details the rough time that the crash was witnessed and the make and colour of the car involved. *Could that be Kate's car?* she wonders. It all sounds like the post is on about her stepmum's crash. But Kate was driving out of Mala's road, not going around the island in town. If she was coming home that way, then she could have come from the motorway. So she could have been coming back from Reading. Harper is now convinced that Kate is lying to her dad. She knew it. This is probably all that she needs to cause an argument between Kate and her dad. The truth will come out and her dad will throw her out. Harper jumps out of bed and takes her phone downstairs.

'Dad, can I show you something?' Harper says, holding her phone up to her dad.

He's sitting in the living room next to Kate, watching some drama.

'Sure, love,' he says, patting the seat on the other side of him for his daughter to sit down. 'What am I looking at?' he says, taking the phone.

'It's a post on the Bracknell gossip page. I think it's on about Kate's crash. People did see it.'

Kate sits bolt upright, suddenly paying attention and she reads the post over Jon's shoulder. 'What a funny coincidence,' she says. 'It's definitely not me. I was nowhere near that island.'

'The car mentioned here isn't the same make as your car, similar though,' Jon says thoughtfully.

'But it has to be,' Harper blurts out.

'I was at Mala's,' Kate says more forcefully. Then she relaxes her tone. 'It's good of you to check though Harps. If I had witnesses then I wouldn't be saddled with repairs I have to pay for myself.'

Harper's dad hands her phone back to her. 'Been a lively night on the roads,' he says. 'You get yourself off to bed, love. I'll call in sick for you tomorrow, so have a lie in.'

Harper tries to find the words to protest but realises that it's no use. Her dad isn't going to take her word for it. He's going to buy everything that Kate says. She says goodnight and heads back to her room. She texts Callum: *I know now for a fact that Kate is a big fat liar. I have an address and we have another mission. Call me tomorrow after school. I'm not going in. I'll tell you everything tomorrow. Hx.*

CHAPTER TWENTY-FIVE

'Did you not sleep well or something? You don't look so good, sister,' Mala says as I settle into my chair.

'No, not great, but no reason,' I say. I was hoping my eye bags weren't that obvious. Mala clearly knows me too well. I couldn't settle. Lying about the crash wasn't sitting well with me. When Harper showed us that post on Bracknell Gossip, I thought I was going to cry. So there I was, having to lie again to Jon and my stepdaughter. I wonder sometimes if she can see straight through me. She's insightful for a young lady, despite her angry outbursts. There was something about the way she looked at me, like all the trust was gone, like she just knew I was lying. I didn't want my lie to snowball but here it was, layer by layer, building. I decide not to tell Mala anything about my crash. It'd just be another story. The chances of Jon saying anything to her is slim. It's unlikely he'd take the opportunity to quiz Mala on anything. She can't know that I said I was at her house. I wouldn't know how to explain where I really was and what I was really doing.

'You have a teenage girl giving you grey hairs. No wonder you're not sleeping,' Mala says. 'I'm going to get us some strong coffees.'

I'm not going to argue with that and gratefully accept Mala's offer to do a coffee run. I make a start on the pile of mail in front of me. The first one that I open is filled with pink paper hearts. The accompanying letter tells of undying love and devotion and that she's counting down the days until they can finally meet. So they haven't even met yet, I tut. Another woman who thinks it's cool to form a relationship with a prisoner. These women seek out and write to inmates with the intention of romance and I just can't get my head around it. Romance or not, the paper hearts have to be binned. They can't be photocopied. I release the hand full of hearts over the wastepaper bin and watch them flutter down. I open and process the next few letters and then decide to leaf through the pile to see if Jason has anything. Yes, there is one. Jason Sawyer's name is scribbled on the front, in the familiar handwriting of Anna West. I eagerly open it and find another photo.

I find it annoying that, once more, Anna's face is not shown, just her breasts this time in a red lacy bra which reveals more flesh than is practical. There is a diamante heart dangling at the centre of her cleavage. I don't know why she never shows her face. I can only think that she doesn't like the thought of the other prisoners looking at it. Perhaps she's shy. None of her photos have ever suggested to me that she's shy. I read the letter and it's sweet. She says that she's thinking of getting a puppy so that she has something to cuddle now the loneliness is catching up with her. She says the house is cold and empty. She talks a bit about the family keeping well but not much else. It's signed, *I love you always Ax*

As the saying goes, no one really knows what goes on behind closed doors. From the outside of their house, it looks perfect. It looks like a well-cared-for and happy home. It wouldn't strike you as being cold and empty – that the owner was locked up for being a killer, and his girlfriend is desperately lonely. I feel frustrated that I've lost their address on the scrap piece of paper that I'd written it down on. It was an afterthought this morning to remember to take it out of my joggers' back pocket where I'd stuffed it. I'd left my joggers lying on the bedroom floor and when I rummaged for the address, it had gone. It must have fallen out somewhere. It doesn't matter, there's no name on the address. If it's picked up by Jon, he won't think anything of it. No one would automatically think that I was out stalking anyone. No, I was taking an interest, not stalking, I reassure myself.

I photocopy the letter and tuck it into the envelope along with the photo. This is genuine love and affection unlike the delusional ramblings from the first letter with the paper hearts. Anna has faith in her man; that he's innocent and she's standing by him. She wants to please him with her photos but she's too shy to show her face in case his cellmate or whoever looks at them. They are lucky to have each other. They love each other no matter what. I pick a paper heart out from the bin and pop it into the envelope. It's a little token from me. Not that he'll know and not that anyone will look inside now that I've already checked the contents. It won't be found. Jason can have a little heart from me. He'll just think it's from Anna.

Mala pushes back through the door, coffees in hand. A rush of excitement tingles up my spine. It's a small thing but I feel naughty, and I like it. I put the envelope on the completed pile.

'You're looking more awake already! All you had to do was smell the coffee,' Mala laughs handing me mine and inhaling the aroma.

'Don't think I've forgotten by the way,' I say to my bemused friend. 'Spill... who's your mystery date then?'

Mala throws her head back, grinning. 'Phil.'

'What?'

'Phil. He's taking me for dinner.'

'What? I'm sorry, you've lost me. Phil? Our Phil? Work Phil? Prison officer Phil?'

'Yes, yes Phil.'

'Hold up, I'm confused. What about the lack of hair issue? And not to mention the he's married issue.' My head is spinning with this bombshell.

'Okay. Firstly, I'm not that shallow and

secondly, his wife walked out on him months ago.'

'She did?'

'Yes.'

'He never said. So how did this come about?'

'When we left work last night, we got talking in the car park. You'd sped off home to look for Harper. Phil just blurted it out. He asked me out. I said yes. You can't deny he's got a good body on him. He's strong and—'

'Okay, I get it; I'm surprised that's all.' I think that at least he's tall enough for Mala; she tends to dwarf her dates. I let the news sink in as I sip my coffee. I'm not sure that dating a colleague is a good idea. If it doesn't work out then it could make things awkward at work. And if it does work out then Mala won't have as much time for me anymore. I'm feeling the same envy as when Mala introduced me to her new friend. I'm being ridiculous again and distract myself by taking a glug of coffee. I don't know where this insecurity is coming from. I can only pinpoint from when I first suspected Jon of having an affair.

Phil pops his head around the post room door, interrupting my thoughts. He's waving a packet of chocolate digestives at us.

'To go with your coffee, ladies.' He grins.

I wonder if this is how it's going to be now. Phil swinging by at every given opportunity. Mala takes the biscuits.

'Thank you,' she gushes. 'So what's the goss on

your wing?'

'It's been a quiet night. Don't trust 'em when they go quiet,' he smirks. 'I'm escorting Sawyer to a meeting with his solicitor shortly, so best make tracks.'

'How is he?' I blurt out. 'After being attacked, I mean.'

'He'll live. I'll catch you later,' he says to Mala, rather than to both of us.

'Mm-mmm, and I don't just mean the biscuits,' Mala laughs throwing her head back.

I shake my head.

I wonder what Jason's meeting with his solicitor is about. It's probably to do with his appeal. I haven't heard anything further about his niece being interviewed about her abduction. Not everything comes via post or e-mail. I miss out on information, not being the one to monitor phone calls. People assume that my job is boring but what is better than reading other people's post for a living? Doesn't everyone want to snoop? I get to do it and I get paid for it. Jon hasn't brought the subject up again of me finding a new job and I'm glad. He can't expect me to change career, and neither can Harper. I've already given up a lot for them, sacrificed a lot, but I draw a line at this. The very man responsible for Harper's mum's death is serving time for manslaughter. Surely they can see what an important job I have, the contribution that I'm making in keeping these criminals – these killers – locked away.

Mala looks amusing with her mouth full of biscuit and smiling to herself as she's reading through the e-mails. A blur of commotion catches the corner of my eye. I spin around and see two officers run past the door towards the garden. I jump up for a closer look through the window. I can only see a section of the garden but there are two prisoners engaged in a fistfight. The two officers are quickly upon them and the alarm rings out. I urge Mala over to come and see. She still has a mouth full of digestive and is crunching in my ear as we peer out together.

'Is Phil there, can you see?' Mala muffles with her mouth full.

There's a bigger crowd of officers now and they've moved over so are not in full view anymore.

'It's difficult to tell,' I say. I'm busy wondering if Jason is involved. I'm straining to see if I can see him.

'Phil can handle himself, he'll kick some prisoner's ass,' she says, sitting herself back down. She takes another biscuit.

Nigel walks past the door so I pop my head out. I just have to know.

'Hey Nige. Who's scrapping?'

'Just Harrison and Ben again.' The officer carries on and shortly later he is followed by two other officers marching Harrison towards the wing.

I sit back down and I cup my hand in time to catch a droplet of blood.

'Not again.'

Mala is quick to hand me a bunch of tissues. 'You okay, sister? You're getting these nose bleeds a lot. You stressed or something?'

I talk through my pinched nose, 'It's hay fever… or stress… or both.'

'Perhaps you should see a doctor or something? I worry about you. You take on an awful lot, with little respite.'

'I'm fine really.' The bleeding is already stopping. It's just a light one. I give my nose a last wipe. 'Fizzy spoke to Harper last night. Only a few words but she spoke. She then freaked out.'

'That's good, right? Well, not the freaking out.'

I nod a little. 'I don't know. I think Jon and Harper resent me. They resent how much Fizz needs me. I think that's why they're both being off with me so much lately. It's playing on my mind.'

'That little girl is lucky to have you. I'm sure they know that deep down. You can't help being an amazing woman.' Mala gets up and gives me a hug.

I still can't figure out what's amazing about me but it hurts to think that Jon can't seem to figure it out either.

'I'm always here for you if you need to sound off, you know that right? And take more you time. You need it.' Mala sits back down and takes another biscuit and offers me one.

'I'm surprised there's any left,' I mock her.

She looks wounded as I take two of the digestives. I remember my encounter with Jason in the toilets when I had my last nosebleed. It was potentially a dangerous situation but every time I think about it now my heart races. It flutters and I like it.

CHAPTER TWENTY-SIX
Gregg

Gregg was prepared for every eventuality. He knew that the scenario he'd mapped out in his head may not unfold in that way, but so far it was and he smiles smugly to himself. He insisted on only being able to make the meeting at four p.m. Enough time for Sophie Banks to get back from school and hopefully too early for her father to be home from work. He'd got that bit right so far. He had been hoping that the dad wasn't one of these 'finish work early on a Friday' types, and fortunately he wasn't. He just needs the next bit to go his way.

Sophie opens out her large portfolio of artwork. Gregg clocks that her hands are shaking a little. Her mum is standing beside her, beaming. It took all of twenty-four hours for Mr and Mrs Banks to contact him. It was too easy. Doting on their little blonde beauty clouded their common sense. *Idiots.* He thanks his lucky stars again, though, that Mr Banks isn't here. No one else is either, no siblings. Just one pandered little only child. The juicy fruit ready for collection.

'Let's get a closer look at these then,' Gregg says, taking the folder from the teen.

Sophie sits next to him on the sofa.

'Would you like a cup of tea or coffee?' Sophie's mum asks.

Bingo. Just what Gregg wants to hear; it's as predictable as he'd hoped.

'Yes please,' he says, 'Strong tea, no sugar.'

Mrs Banks leaves the living room.

Adrenaline surges through him. He can't waste time and seizes his moment; it's what he'd planned. It's how the scenario played out in his thoughts. He places the folder down and with a sudden movement, sweeps Sophie close to him, clamping his hand hard against the girl's mouth and whips out a large blade, holding it to her throat. He mouths a shush to her. The girl has completely stiffened, shock and terror taking over. He swipes a gag from his jacket pocket and has it strapped hard against the teen's mouth in a flash. She's not yet kicking and fighting back like the last little tramp, he notices.

'You're coming with me,' he says gruffly, forcing the girl up and manhandling her to the door.

The teen is muffling sobs, and resisting moving, so Gregg pushes her harder, flashing the knife close to the girl's pretty face. The blade gets her legs moving; it's as close to her soft skin as he can get it without damaging the goods. The struggle through the front door and the teen's loud whimpers alerts her mum. Mrs Banks is rushing at them, screaming for him to let her daughter go.

'Stay back or I'll take pieces off her face.' Gregg has Sophie around her throat and the knife in full view for her mum to see. He backs the teen out of the front door.

Mrs Banks raises her hands and cautiously follows them out. 'Please let her go. Please, I'll do anything, you can have anything, let her go…' Her voice is choked.

Gregg continues backing up to his car. He grapples to get the door open, keeping a strong grip on the girl. He forces her head down and shoves her into the car. He slams the door shut.

Sophie instantly hammers on the window, frantically trying the handle. With the knife away from her daughter now, Mrs Banks lunges herself towards the car. Gregg swiftly punches her square in the face, knocking her back, but she regains her composure fast and lunges again. Gregg blocks her and gets another punch in, throwing her to the ground with force. He boots her in the head, giving him the space to jump into the car and rev the engine. He reverses fast from the driveway, only catching a glimpse of Mrs Banks trying to raise her head from the concrete. His foot is down and he's away.

'Sit fucking still, or I'll go back and knife your mum. Do you understand?'

The teen is sobbing uncontrollably but is now frozen to her seat.

It all went to plan. He had hoped to avoid the mess of violence but knew the chances were high. A mother was never going to just hand their daughter over, even though she as good as did. *Stupid idiot,* Gregg smirks. He relied on gullibility, but he knew his plan was genius. He was no idiot and he had the balls to pull it off. He has new contacts and is putting his plan into action. He is on the up and he's looking forward to telling Riley to fuck off. Nothing will stop him from becoming his own boss now.

Half an hour later, and Gregg is pulling into a sweeping driveway in a remote out-of-town property. It's a large modern new build, owned and built by Charlie Coleman, who runs his own lucrative property development business. Talks with Charlie are finally becoming a reality. He has his trust. A regular customer already who could see Gregg's vision and has the means to make it happen. He wanted in. The man himself emerges from the front door.

'Good to see you, man.' Charlie firmly shakes Gregg's hand as he steps from the car. 'What do you have for us then?'

They both walk round to the passenger side. Charlie opens the door. 'Hello little love.' He winks at Sophie. She's shaking violently and desperately sucking in air through her nose.

Gregg gets her out of the car and they are greeted at the front of the house by a couple of heavies. Gregg doesn't recognise them but trusts Charlie to have discreet friends or staff. With the money the guy makes, he'd need security.

'Get her up to the guest suite, get her a drink, and lock the door,' Charlie orders the guys. 'We'll look after you pretty.' He turns to Sophie and winks at her again. 'Let me get you a drink, my man. Beer?' Charlie pats Gregg on the back and guides him through to the kitchen.

'What the fuck?' Gregg halts as he sees who's sat at the dining table.

'Hello Gregg,' Riley says.

Brian is sitting next to Riley and waves with a salute.

Realisation is quickly stabbing Gregg in the throat. 'You son of a bitch.' He turns to Charlie.

'Just business, my man,' Charlie shrugs.

Brian stands up and tells Gregg to take his seat. Gregg looks at him uneasily and declines.

'Sit the fuck down.' Brian grabs Gregg's collar and gut punches him, knocking the wind from him.

Gregg doubles over, coughing. Brian guides him down onto the chair but Gregg pushes against him in a rugby tackle. Coleman's two heavies burst into the room, overpowering him, and he's finally forced to sit down. He doesn't have a choice; the broader of the two men is now pointing a gun at him.

Riley stands. 'I'm sure you didn't mean to leave me out the loop like this, so I may still be able to forgive you. I want to thank you for the idea though. Credit where credit's due and all that. Thing is, I need you. We have a profitable business as things are. We have customers; we have obligations.'

The man with the gun steps forward, aiming the gun a little closer.

'We need a girl for next week, and you're still going to deliver. If you do then I might let you retire with your limbs and balls intact.' Riley takes a couple of beers and hands one to Charlie. They clink bottles. 'To expanding the business.'

Gregg glares at the man holding the gun. 'Get that thing off of me all right.'

The guy maintains the gun's position.

Gregg feels every muscle in his body tense. His jaw is set. He was close to being his own boss: he put all of the work in, he could feel the money. Now he's reduced back to being Riley's little lapdog. He imagines what he'd like to do to Charlie for screwing him over. He looks at him and can visualise gutting him open. It's almost like Charlie can read his thoughts and winks at him. Gregg curls his upper lip. *All in good time.*

Riley continues, 'Before I let you walk out of here, I need some reassurance. Jason Sawyer's niece, Chloe, has been taken in for further questioning over her suspected kidnapping by Michael before Jason murdered him. I'll ask you one last time: did you know about him taking Chloe? Were you there? Were you seen? Anything?'

'Do you think Michael would be dead if I was there? Sawyer wouldn't have made it out the door if I'd been there. No, and I knew nothing,' Gregg spits.

'Good, because we can't have this Chloe remembering anything that might make any connections to us. Michael was a fool for taking someone so closely connected. The only reason why we're here still operating is the fact Michael is dead. He can't talk.'

Gregg had to agree that Michael should have told him of his plans to take Chloe. It was a huge mistake; he could've made him see sense. His impulsiveness got him killed, but he was his mate and he's pissed at him for leaving him to deal with all of this without him.

'At the moment Sawyer is our loose end,' Riley says. 'If he wins his appeal, he's gonna come looking... revenge for his niece or some shit. He knows me, he knows you. You met him, right?'

'I sat in the car once when dropping the plants off to him with Michael. We never spoke. I don't know him and he doesn't know me. He doesn't know shit and he ain't getting out. He stabbed Michael to death, his prints were everywhere.'

Riley picks up a knife from the counter and points it in Gregg's face. 'You best be right. Now get the fuck out. We need a girl for next weekend. I'll be in touch.'

'Now c'mon, I want in. I've delivered tonight, haven't I? How about payment?'

Riley gestures to the man with the gun to help Gregg up. Gregg shakes him off. He's still hunched over from the punch to his middle. He never took Brian to have that kind of right hook, but to see his smug face now is far more painful. The two men march him out to the driveway with the gun still pointing. Gregg rips away the false plates, before getting into the car. He can't be driving around now getting himself caught. That gullible mother will have called the cops by now. He looks in his rear-view mirror and slides the dark toupee from his head revealing his shaven scalp. He's not being recognised; he's not going down for this. All of this for nothing. He slams his palms into the steering wheel, then starts the car. The two heavies are still standing there watching him. Riley's got him over a barrel and now he's going to have to source another girl. He drives away not knowing yet how to plot his next move.

CHAPTER TWENTY-SEVEN

I wake up with a start and freak out when I see the time. Jon lets out a loud snore and shuffles over onto his other side. It's Saturday. I inhale and breathe out a sigh of relief. I take a few minutes to try and piece together the jumbled dreams I was just having. I'm grasping at fragments of images, a baby is crying and I'm trying to run but my legs are heavy. I'm trying to call the police but my fingers keep missing the numbers. I think I stole a baby. I slide out of bed and allow the absurd fragments to fade away.

I trot downstairs to use the downstairs loo, deciding not to risk disturbing Jon by using the ensuite. I enjoy the peace before everyone awakes as it doesn't happen often. I flick the kettle on and rub my eyes. I slept well but it doesn't feel like it. I wonder what the world of Facebook has been up to overnight and scroll through my phone as the kettle bubbles away. All of the news pages are filled with reports of a teenage girl who was snatched from her family home yesterday early evening. A man claiming to be an agent for artists conned his way into the family home and took sixteen-year-old Sophie Banks by knifepoint. Her mother sustained injuries when she tried to fight off the kidnapper.

I put my hand to my mouth. How awful to have your child practically snatched out of your arms like that in your own home. Photos of Sophie are everywhere. She's a pretty blonde with big friendly eyes. There's an E-FIT of the man who took her. He looks respectable for an E-FIT image. I shudder. You don't know who you're letting into your home. The news reports go on to say that connections between the recent spate of kidnappings in the Reading area are not being ruled out. Naturally, there is growing fear in the town. I make my coffee contemplating the rising fear in Reading with kidnappings on the increase. Yet that's where I'm going today. I've not changed my mind. I'm keen to go and knock on Anna West's door one more time, just for a glimpse of her. I've considered that if she's not home again, then I'll leave it. I can only be so obsessed, and returning every other day to try and catch her seems borderline insane.

'Morning,' Jon says, breaking my thoughts. 'Sleep well? You went to bed so early last night.'

'Just a long week catching up with me,' I say, getting up to fix him a drink.

'As it's the start of half term, I'm thinking that the girls can't be sat around the house all week. Harper's done enough of that already.'

'What do you have in mind?'

'It's been a while since my mother has spent time with the girls, so thinking we could pay her a visit today, for starters.'

I struggle to swallow my mouthful of coffee. I had been trying to think up an excuse to go out on my own for a bit today, I hadn't expected this.

'I don't know. I'm not sure if I'm coming down with something. I've run to the loo this morning and feel icky.'

Jon just looks at me, weighing up what I've said. 'Okay, why don't you rest up then? I'll take the girls. You look… tired.'

I smooth my hair behind my ear and nod in agreement.

'I'll get the girls up,' he says and leaves me to think about how awful I look.

I push his comment aside and think about how this works in my favour. They can go off for a few hours and I can take a drive into Reading. It won't take me long and then perhaps I'll have time to put my feet up with a book before they get home and enjoy some peace. It'll be good for them to do something without me for once.

***

Two hours later and Jon and the girls are ready to leave the house. Harper hasn't stopped scowling; she doesn't see why she's been dragged out of bed so early on a Saturday. She refreshed her black hair colour last night and it's looking glossy against her pale complexion. She has her black ripped skin-tight jeans on, her black Slipknot T-shirt and her black leather jacket despite the sunny outlook for the day. Fizz is the polar opposite in pink shorts and a rainbow vest. She gives me a hug as they say goodbye.

I'm starting to doubt whether it's a good idea to leave Harper babysitting Fizz all week over half term. It'll be the first time, but neither I nor Jon could get the time off work and Jon is adamant that Harper needs to learn some responsibility. She's so angry at the world and I worry it will rub off on her sister. Jon let her stay off school for the remainder of the week and then with a week off for half term she can start fresh for the final term and the run-up to her exams. I'm not sure that burying his head in the sand is the right approach but there was no discussing it with him. It doesn't solve Harper's problems with Lexi but she doesn't want us going to the school again and Jon has agreed to play it however Harper wants.

I watch them pull off the drive and I dart upstairs to change. I slip on my linen trousers and a floral blouse. I run a brush through my hair and dab some concealer under my eyes. I stare at my reflection for a moment – no, I don't look tired. I grab my keys and my phone and dash out to the car. I can't be too long if I'm to get back before they do. I try not to let my skin prickle at the reminder of Jon going out again tonight. I'm finding excuses to go out on my own and he just does as he pleases.

Anna West's postcode is saved on my satnav from before. I still wonder what happened to the piece of paper with it on, but it doesn't matter. I pull away from the house and tell myself not to crash this time. Nerves are fluttering away in my stomach but there's nothing to worry about. I've planned what to say if Anna opens the door. I'll say that I have the wrong house and walk away. Nothing can go wrong and it's harmless really. Fortunately, the motorway is running smoothly for approaching a Saturday lunchtime, so I'm pulling up in the neighbourhood before I know it. I choose to park in the same parking lay-by as before and walk up. Perhaps an inner voice is telling me that I don't want Anna seeing my car.

I breathe. I compose myself. *Please be in.* I cross my fingers not wanting a wasted journey. I'm keen to know what kind of woman attracts Jason Sawyer and what kind of woman loves someone so dangerous. The best thing to do now is to not overthink it and just go up to the door and knock. So I do. I knock on the door three times in quick succession. I wait and then the door opens and I hold my breath. The woman who opens the door is beautiful. She has voluminous auburn hair, full make-up, and is wearing a sharp trouser suit. Stunning.

'Hi... I'm... I'm sorry I think I have the wrong house. I was... I was looking for an old friend of mine, Anna West, but I can see you're not her.' I just about get the words out through the nerves. I turn to leave sharply.

'Hold on, what makes you think she lives

here?' the woman says. Her tone is friendly.

'Oh, just looking up addresses for Anna West in the area. Just trying my luck.'

'There's no Anna here. I'm Carla.'

'Sorry to disturb you.' I go to leave again but a man appears at Carla's side.

'She's looking for Anna West; she's down as living here apparently,' the auburn woman says to the guy.

He goes to speak and then stops. His thick brows are furrowed and then he says, 'Nope, don't know her.'

'I'm sorry again,' I say, and this time I don't give them the opportunity to say anything else. I turn on my heels and walk off at pace.

When I reach the car, I suck in a deep breath. I suddenly feel ridiculous and plant my palm on my forehead. What was I thinking? Okay, nothing bad happened but they looked at me suspiciously and a bit amused. Was she lying about who she was? If they're unpopular in the neighbourhood, then perhaps she would be defensive and lie about who she was. It has to be her; the address is on all of her letters. But who was that guy? Is she having an affair? Is he a relative? A friend? No, I can't continue with this obsession. I did what I set out to do and the reality of it now is that I feel ridiculous. But she is beautiful. No wonder she's Jason Sawyer's girl. I picture them together and they do make a hot couple. A perfect fit. Perhaps now I can stop thinking about her but my next thought is wondering what she does for a living. Her outfit suggests a successful businesswoman. Why is she looking so immaculate for a Saturday lunchtime?

I start my engine, the unanswered questions racing through my brain. Setting eyes on her isn't going to allow me to move on. It's just made me even more interested. Yes, I feel ridiculous but what's wrong with taking an interest? I've reassured myself and I feel better and now I'm looking forward to having the house to myself for a bit. I'll make some lunch and read a book. Perfect. My phone rings and it's Jon. *Shit.* I kill the engine.

'Hiya, love,' he says. 'Just wondering where you went. We popped back because Harper forgot her phone.'

'Just in town getting something to settle my stomach.'

'We're back at my mother's anyway. Just checking you were okay.'

'Yes, I'm fine. Going to put my feet up now.'

'See you later. We won't be out long.'

'Bye, love.'

Damn it. Why can't Harper just be without her phone for just a couple of bloody hours? Why does Jon have to pander to her? I've had to lie again. But it's okay, I've done it now, no more sneaking around.

CHAPTER TWENTY-EIGHT
Harper

'Thanks Nan,' Harper says, taking her seat at the dining table.

Her nan has put on a good spread for lunch as usual. She's made enough sandwiches to feed the whole street and there's a huge Victoria sponge in the centre of the table.

'Shame Kate isn't here, would've been lovely to all be together like this,' her nan says. 'Is it something she ate, do you think?'

There's nothing wrong with her, Harper wanted to scream, picking at her sandwich.

'Not sure, but something's brewing; she looked pale this morning, It's best to keep the bugs away from you,' Jon says to his mum.

Harper had a gut feeling that her stepmum was lying, and when they popped back to the house and she wasn't there, she knew it for certain. She wonders if she's gone back to that address in Reading, the one on the piece of paper she swiped. If she didn't have to be here then it would have been the perfect opportunity to grab Callum and go to that house and try and catch her out.

'You not hungry sweetheart?' her nan asks her.

'Don't play with your food, just eat it,' her dad

says to her, and then he chuckles and says to his mother, 'She's already trying to look like the undead. I reckon turning to skin and bone will complete the look.'

Felicity laughs, almost choking on her mouthful of sandwich.

'I bet she won't turn down the cake,' her nan says. 'You've been having a hard time of it of late, haven't you? Is Lexi still being a bully? Do you want me to kick her ass for you?'

Harper half-smiles at her nan looking like she actually means it. Even though she's all but crippled with arthritis; she's sure she'd give it a go. Felicity giggles and makes karate chop actions with her arms.

'I don't think we should be encouraging any more violence,' her dad says.

'She's punched her one before. You can do it again can't you, sweetheart?' her nan winks at her. 'The school should be doing more.'

'Every time I grass Lexi up it makes things worse,' Harper says quietly.

'Oh love, you do know that karma will bite that girl on the ass. She'll have a bleak future ahead of her. She'll end up in prison like her dad, while you will be successful. You're beautiful and you've got your whole life ahead of you. You hold your head up, girl. Finish your exams and the world is your oyster. This sorry mess will be far behind you.' Her nan reaches over and lightly squeezes her granddaughter's hand.

Harper takes a bigger bite of her sandwich.

'Another thing, dear, is stop taking it out on poor Kate. She's doing an important job locking the bad guys away. She shouldn't be forced to change careers because of a bully. Don't let Lexi win. Isn't that right, Felicity?'

Everyone looks at the seven-year-old and she nods enthusiastically in agreement.

It dawns on Harper that her dad has arranged this especially for her Nan to try and talk some sense into her. She's always looked up to her Nan. She agrees that her Nan is right, bullies can't win. Perhaps she has been hard on Kate. She just wanted an easier life at school, but why should everyone change to keep Lexi happy? If Kate changed jobs then that bully would still find something to have a go at her about. It's not just her, she picks on everyone. Harper can perhaps stop taking it out on Kate, but it doesn't change the fact that she's convinced now that she's having an affair. She doesn't want to see her dad hurt, not after losing her mum. He deserves better and so does her little sister. Felicity is so dependent on her. It'll be the ultimate betrayal. She wonders if she could take a train ride with Callum on Monday into Reading and go to the house and just see who lives there. She'd have to take her sister too as she's babysitting. For her own sanity, she needs to rule out her stepmum having an affair.

CHAPTER TWENTY-NINE

Harper is making me a cup of tea. It's Monday morning and I told her that she could have a lie-in, but just to make sure she's up when Fizz is. But here she is making me a cup of tea. It's a small everyday thing that most people take for granted but nothing is making me feel more surprised. I didn't think anything could top yesterday. We had a wonderful picnic in the park, all of us. Harper was off her phone and kicked a ball around and we fed the ducks. There were smiles, and here she is now smiling and making me tea. I hadn't dreamt yesterday; it happened. The teenager is relaxed and smiling and making me tea. I can't stop saying it to myself.

'Does it ever get scary where you work?' she asks me.

She's never really taken an interest in my job role before, which I always put down to how much she hates it because of what her schoolmates think.

'No, I've never felt in danger. The prisoners are watched closely when they're walking in the areas near the post room.'

'Is it like on telly? Are there lots of fights?'

I nod. I'm not going to sugar-coat it to her. 'Yes, I think TV can glorify prison life sometimes but it can be violent.'

Harper's eyes widen. 'Any cool stories?'

'I did see a fight just the other day. I can see the garden from the post room and two guys were going for it but the officers were fast in breaking them up.'

'And you don't get scared?'

I shake my head. 'No, but I don't think I'd like to be a prison officer. They're the ones that are hands-on with the inmates.'

'It's cool you get to read their mail. Snooping for a living.'

I smile in acknowledgment, 'Yes, it's a lot like that.'

'Did you ever want to do anything different? When you left school?'

I'm aware of the time ticking by but I want this conversation to last forever. I don't know what's got into her; it could just be she's relaxed knowing she has a whole week ahead of no school.

'I wanted to be an air hostess, actually.'

Harper laughs. 'Really?'

'Yes, it's not that funny. I wanted to fly around the world.'

'So why didn't you?'

'I went on my first holiday abroad after leaving school and I was terrified of flying. It kinda put me off.'

My stepdaughter laughs again. 'So that would've been scarier than working in a prison.'

I nod, agreeing. 'And you're going to make a great nurse. And if you ever change your path, then don't be afraid to take that leap. Whatever you do always reach for—'

'Reach for the stars.' She finishes my sentence. 'Mum always used to say that to me and Felicity.'

For a second, I think that I've ruined the moment by mistake but Harper says, 'You do a great job and I'm sorry about all of the times I've shouted at you to leave your job.'

A lump catches in my throat. 'It's okay. I get how hard it's…'

'Right, I'm off to work.' Jon breezes in and kisses me on the top of the head. 'Call me if there are any problems all right Harps? I'm not in meetings today so I have my phone on.'

With that, he's out the door. He's in a good mood this morning too; he's been attentive and warm. I was surprised when he came home early Saturday night. He was only out a couple of hours and then we spent all day yesterday together. I'd almost forgotten that I suspect him of having an affair.

'I should get going to work too,' I say, picking up my keys.

Fizz walks in, rubbing her sleepy eyes. She comes straight to give me a hug. 'Now don't play your sister up, okay? She's the boss today. I'll look forward to hearing about your day when I get home this evening.' I blow her a kiss and wave bye to Harper.

I feel a little more comfortable leaving Harper with Fizzy now she's presenting as more relaxed. I still can't get my head around her sudden change of mood, but I'm going with it. It can all change again in a heartbeat.

***

I've beaten Mala to work for once then realise that she probably is already here but hanging out at the prison guard's office with Phil. I'm right. No sooner do I think it than she breezes in with a packet of ginger nut biscuits.

'What, no chocolate ones today?' I tut in disgust.

'I'll have you know that I'm partial to a ginger nut. I told Phil this and voila,' she says waving the packet.

'Aww, young love.' I mock being sick.

'You won't be wanting one then?' Mala says, already opening the biscuits.

'Really? Have you not just had breakfast?'

Mala screws her face up at me as if I'm talking complete nonsense and she pops a gingernut in her mouth.

'Are you on for yoga again tomorrow?' she says with her mouth full.

'Yes, I've not forgotten.' Mala had text me over the weekend to say what a great night out she had with Therese up Red's. She couldn't believe how drunk they had both got but Phil had picked them up and got them home safely. I felt a twinge of feeling left out but the weekend I've had with my little family has now pushed away those little green monsters, I'll look forward to getting to know Therese a bit better. If Mala likes her then I'm sure that I will too.

As I've started doing more lately, I sift straight through the pile of mail to see if there is something for Jason first. And there is. Seeing Anna West has only piqued my interest in their life more. It had to be her. I don't believe her name was really Carla. She must have thought that I was a reporter or something. You wouldn't give out your real name if a stranger knocked on your door and your other half is a killer in prison. You'd be wary and careful. I have so many unanswered questions about her now but there is no way I'm going back to the house for any reason or any excuse. I won't be pushing my luck.

I tear open the envelope and pull out the letter. It reads, *Hey Jase, do you know who this is? Who have you been giving our address out to? I'm not happy you've been giving out my personal details to any pervs you're locked up with. Was it one of their Mrs or something? She was actually asking for Anna West. Weird. Andrew is confused too. Get back to me or Andrew ASAP. Carla x*

It's like I'm reading the words in slow motion, and I realise there's another folded piece of paper inside the envelope. The colour is already draining from my face before I've finished unfolding it. Looking back at me is me, my photo.

An image captured by CCTV; a printout of my face. *Shit.* I feel like all of my internal organs have shut down. I shove the contents back inside the envelope and pray that I didn't just see that. Thoughts quickly whir around my head. I can shred it; no one will know. It landed on my lap; no one will know. There'll be no log, no trace. The shredder is next to Mala. Will she ask what I'm shredding? I don't know. Will she suspect that I've just shredded an inmate's letter?

'Any chance you can do a coffee run? I know you got them last time but I feel faint.' It's not even a lie. I could actually pass out.

Mala looks worried. 'Sure thing. Wow, you don't look good. Be right back.'

Thank goodness she doesn't hang about. As soon as she's out the door I shove the letter into the shredder and listen to the reassuring sound of its destruction. I rub my face and sit back down to steady my shaking legs. *So what the hell is going on?*

CHAPTER THIRTY
Harper

Harper steps from the train, holding her little sister's hand tightly. She feels relief at getting off at the right station. It's her first time planning a train journey on her own and she didn't want to get lost with her sister in tow. It's also the reason she decided on getting a taxi to number 15 Nelder Street, Whitley. This way is less stressful for Felicity. It's quicker and easier. She curses Callum for being on holiday; she had totally forgotten. She takes a moment to look around the bustling station and the signs. The majority of the passengers who have alighted all seem to be heading towards the same exit so Harper follows suit. So far, her sister has been no trouble and willing to just tag along. Harper didn't really know what reason she was going to give her as to where they were going. She just said that they were going to visit a friend of Kate's. She knew Felicity was never going to question her over it and she did feel a little guilty for using that to her advantage. Of course, it's likely that her sister will tell Kate where they've been but Harper decides that there's still time to think of a good explanation. She might even just tell the truth, that she suspected her of having an affair and wanted to find out for sure. Kate would hit the roof, and probably her dad would too, but she's willing to face the consequences.

Both girls find themselves outside the front of the station and Harper spots the taxi rank. She had emptied the cash out from her savings box so she's sure to have enough. It's not like she can have the tattoo she's saving for just yet anyway. She approaches the taxi driver and tells him the address. It's a short drive so even better. So far everything is going to plan. She'll have her sister back home by lunchtime at this rate and be back in time for when their dad calls to check on them.

Less than ten minutes later and the taxi is pulling up on Nelder Street.

'There you go ladies. Almost forgotten you were there you're both so quiet,' the driver says.

Harper hands him a ten-pound note. 'What's the taxi number so I can phone when we're finished?'

The driver hands her some change along with a business card. 'Enjoy your day and keep out of mischief, both.' He smiles warmly.

Harper thanks him and steps out of the car, taking hold of her sister's hand again. 'This won't take long. I just want to meet this friend of Kate's quickly and then we can go back home. I'm enjoying our little adventure so far.'

Felicity smiles at her but Harper notices that she looks a bit uncertain. There's no way she could've left her at home on her own and this is the perfect opportunity with both Kate and her dad at work, not questioning her every movement. She does still wish that Callum was here with them though. She faces number fifteen and admires the pretty front garden. It's much nicer than theirs, she thinks. It didn't really occur to her before, but she suddenly realises that it might not just be a man living here that her stepmum might be having an affair with. He might have a wife and children. The trouble she could cause starts to feel a little overwhelming and her heart quickens.

'Perhaps we should not bother them. Kate's friend might be busy.' Harper closes her hand around Felicity's a little more and gently tugs her to walk away.

Felicity stands firm and tugs her arm back and points to the door with the other.

'No, I've changed my mind. We shouldn't bother them when they don't know we're coming. C'mon.'

The sound of the front door opening sends a bolt of panic inside Harper's chest. A lady with deep auburn hair is in the doorway, arms folded. 'Can I help you both? You're staring at my house. You lost or something?'

'No it's okay,' Harper quickly says.

Her sister is rooted to the spot, refusing to be led away.

'Are you sure?' the woman asks.

The woman is beautiful and she's smiling. Perhaps she is just a friend of Kate's that she knows from work or something. There's no affair. Isn't that what she came here to find out? she reminds herself. She'd rather Kate wasn't having an affair now – she just wants what's best for her little sister and her dad. She realises that she can't keep blaming Kate for being bullied at school. Her Nan was right. If she can just rule out this problem then perhaps she can start to feel less angry about everything.

She takes a deep breath, 'Do you know our stepmum? I think she was here the other day.'

The woman raises an eyebrow.

'Kate Midwinter,' Harper clarifies.

The woman thinks a moment and then purses her lips. 'Yes I know her. Would you like to come in for some lemonade? She's an old school friend and it'd be nice to get to know you.'

Harper looks at her little sister who is nodding. Kate has just been catching up with an old school friend. Harper relaxes her shoulders a little.

'Yes please,' Harper agrees. Her throat is now so dry, lemonade sounds perfect.

'I'm Carla.' The woman smiles. 'Come on through.' She leads the way inside.

Carla opens the living room door and they are suddenly met with an excited West Highland puppy. Felicity's eyes widen and she immediately drops to the floor to fuss the puppy.

'This is Kylie. she's only ten weeks old,' Carla says.

'Kylie?' Harper sounds surprised. 'Funny name for a puppy.'

'I totally agree with you. I didn't name her.' Carla looks through some papers on the cabinet and hands Harper an image to look at. 'Just so we have the right Kate Midwinter, is this her?'

Harper looks at the image. 'Yes it's her but why ha—'

'It's okay. We have CCTV at the front of the house and I printed off her photo so I could compare it to old pics of her from school, that's all. It's been years since I've seen her. We didn't have long to chat; she just turned up out of the blue. I'll get those drinks and we can chat. Would you like ice?'

'Yes please.'

Carla turns to Felicity for an answer, and she nods.

'She doesn't really talk to anyone,' Harper says.

'Right. Well, I'll leave you for a few minutes to get to know Kylie and I'll be back with those drinks.'

Harper admires the décor in the lounge; the feature wall's paper was covered in striking red roses. The large plush grey sofa was covered in scatter cushions with various prints. It was mismatched but comfy and homely, unlike their own home which had a more sterile feel with white or magnolia walls and pine furniture. She couldn't wait to get her own house and decorate it in purples, blacks and dark Red's. It was her dream to own a gothic mansion but she'd settle for a flat, anything as long as it was her own place.

Carla returns carrying a tray with three glasses of lemonade, the ice cubes clinking away. 'Here we are. Please sit down; make yourselves at home. I must say this is such a lovely surprise.'

Felicity sinks into the sofa with Kylie snuggling next to her, demanding more fuss. Harper takes her drink and perches more cautiously on the end of the sofa.

'So does Kate know you're here? I have to ask: why are you here?'

Harper looks to her lap; she decides not to lie. Carla seems nice and she feels at ease. 'No, Kate and my dad are at work. They don't know we're here. I found this address in my stepmum's pocket and I just wanted to meet her friends, see where she's been going.' Harper gently shrugs and struggles to make eye contact.

'You mean you're snooping.' Carla raises her brows and grins.

'My dad hasn't been with Kate long, just wanted to know more about her, I guess.' It's all Harper could admit to. She realises how stupid she must sound.

'Well, I won't tell her you're here then. You have your reasons and I respect that.'

Harper takes a deep breath and relaxes her

shoulders a little. Finally, someone who just listens to what she says without nagging and questioning and going on.

'Were you good friends with Kate at school?' Harper asks.

Felicity sits up to listen more, as the puppy keeps nudging her arms for fuss.

'Erm, not really. Well, yes. Not the best of friends but we hung out. There was a group of us. To be honest, I don't remember much of school; I put it far behind me. I hated it.'

Harper nods in agreement. 'Yeah, I hate school too.'

'How about you?' Carla looks to Felicity who just shrugs.

'She has selective mutism,' Harper says. 'She can talk but she can't, but not to everyone. Sorry, I don't think that makes sense.'

Carla waves her hand. 'You don't have to explain to me, I get you just fine… both of you.'

Harper smiles at her and settles back into the sofa, sipping her lemonade.

'So, your stepmum is at work? Where is that? I was so busy when she turned up here that I didn't find out a thing about what she's up to now. I did say I'd be in touch for a proper catch-up very soon.'

'She works at Standington Prison, just outside of Bracknell.'

Carla coughs, swallowing a mouthful of the fizzy drink. 'Yes, I know it.' She coughs again. 'Is she a prison officer?'

'No, she's support grade. She mainly just opens the mail.'

'Does she now…?' Carla coughs and splutters some more. 'Excuse me a moment, I think I need some water.'

Harper looks to her little sister. 'You okay? We'll go home soon, okay?'

Felicity nods. She seems happy with Kylie giving her all of the attention. Harper pulls out her phone and sends Callum a quick text message,

I'm at the house now and it turns out the woman here is a school friend of Kate's. You were right all along, I was being paranoid. Love you mate x

The teen slides her phone back into her pocket as Carla enters back into the room.

'That's better. So how did you both get here? How are you getting home?'

'We got the train and then a taxi to here. We live in Bracknell so not that far.'

'Ah, taxis are expensive. Look, my other half will be here any minute. I'm sure he'd happily drive you back home.'

'Really?' Harper realises she should decline, not wanting to be a nuisance, but she didn't fancy tackling public transport again on her own and it would be faster.

'Absolutely. I'd like to see that you both get home safely. Look, I don't want you in trouble, so don't mention that you were here and I won't tell. I told Kate I'd catch up with her soon, so I'll swing by this weekend. It'd be so nice to catch up with her properly. I can already see by you two how well she's done for herself. I could bring Kylie too?'

Felicity nods enthusiastically, giggling at having her fingers licked by the puppy.

'That would be cool,' Harper agrees. She feels relief at not having to tell Kate anything. She can keep this to herself and say no more about it. She's not having an affair and hopefully she can now focus on building a relationship with her again. Today has gone far better than she ever expected.

The doorbell rang out and the puppy shot from Felicity's lap, barking as she ran to the door. 'Ah, that'll be my hubby. Bet he's forgotten his key again. You ready to go girls?'

Harper takes her sister's glass and places it on the coffee table. She takes her hand and they follow Carla to the front door.

'Hello, love,' Carla greets the man in the doorway and air kisses his cheeks. 'This is Harper and Felicity. Girls, this is Gregg. Honey, can you drive them home back to Bracknell?'

'Whatever you say, Carla. Ready, ladies?'

'Yes, thank you so much,' Harper says. 'Hope we aren't being a pain.'

'Not in the slightest,' Gregg grins. 'The only pain is my wife here. Ain't that right, Mrs Carla Riley?'

Harper clocks the stern look that Carla gives Gregg and she can't tell if she's joking or not but then she bursts into laughter so she relaxes again.

'I'll be back for me dinner in a bit then, woman,' Gregg teases again. 'Right let's get going girls. Who's riding shotgun?'

'I will,' Harper answers. 'I'll know the way once we get to Bracknell town centre, I can direct you.'

'Brains and beauty,' Gregg winks at the teen. 'Let's get this show on the road.'

CHAPTER THIRTY-ONE
Gregg

Gregg's phone flashes as he starts the engine; he quickly checks the message from Riley. *Not funny,* it read. He glances at her still standing in the doorway and he waves at her with a sarcastic smirk.

'You both buckled up?' He turns to the teenager sitting beside him and the younger girl sat in the back.

Both girls confirm that they are and he reverses from the driveway. He checks Harper out from the corner of his eye, her pale complexion and her dyed jet-black hair. He could say to himself that he stalks troubled teenagers for a living, so he knows one when he sees one. He grips the steering wheel a little tighter at the thought of being screwed over by Charlie Coleman again. Perhaps he should stick to the likes of Harper; it's what he knows best. He hasn't heard what's happened to the blonde piece he handed over on a plate. No news of her being found yet; the longer she's kept captive the messier it can get. Riley was a fool for excluding him from that one. But he knows that Carla needs him or else she wouldn't have called him for this urgent job. Pretending to be her husband was nothing short of disgusting though – the thought makes him wipe his cheeks from the air kiss.

'So, is it like half term or something? You not being at school?' Gregg breaks the silence.

'Yeah,' Harper answers. 'Thank goodness.'

'Not a fan of school?'

Harper doesn't answer. Gregg sees that she just shrugs.

'You're quiet back there.' He glances at Felicity in the rear-view mirror.

'She doesn't talk to anyone,' Harper says.

'That so?' Gregg winks at the little girl through the mirror then keeps his eyes on the road. 'Your mum is friends with Carla then, hey?'

'Stepmum… Yes, they are old schoolmates.'

'Sorry, your mum still around?'

Harper answers after a beat. 'No, she died.'

'Ah, sorry kid. Do you get on with your stepmum?'

Harper didn't answer.

'Sorry, I chat too much and ask too many questions. Tell me to shut the fuck up if you want?'

Harper smirks and her jaw drops a little.

'Excuse the French.' Gregg winks once more at Felicity in the mirror. He sees her smiling back.

Gregg turns on the radio and they continue in silence for a bit. He'll find out what the score is with these two soon enough. He didn't want to risk putting his foot in anything just yet, Riley hadn't given much away but she ordered him not to talk too much. Soon, they were taking the exit towards Bracknell town centre.

'It's right around the island,' Harper piped up. She continued to direct him for the last ten minutes of the journey.

'It's good you know your way around,' Gregg says, as he pulls up in front of the girls' home. 'Didn't have to use the old satnav.'

'I can't wait to drive,' Harper says, unbuckling her seatbelt.

'Nothing like having your first set of wheels, kid.'

'Do you want petrol money?' Harper blurts out as she opens the car door.

Gregg dismisses her with a brief wave of his hand, 'No, seeing you home safely is payment enough for me. Carla will be in touch. Nice to meet you both.'

'Thank you so much again.' Harper steps from the car and opens the rear door for her little sister to hop out.

Once both girls step away from the car, Gregg pulls away, waving to them as he does. He's made a mental note of the address. That's all that's required for now. That's all he was instructed – to get to Carla's immediately before Andrew got home, pretend to be her fella, drive two girls to Bracknell safely, don't say too much, and note their address. He hazards a guess as to what Riley has planned and he can't wait to find out if he's right.

CHAPTER THIRTY-TWO

Lunch break is over in a flash. It was good to speak to Harper and Fizz on the phone; it grounded me and took my mind away from the giddiness. This is the most unsteady that I have felt at work, ever. What if Mala had opened that letter and seen my face? How would I have explained that one? Why was it even posted by Carla anyway? Who the hell is Anna West? I feel so stupid. I shouldn't have let my curiosities get the better of me; I should never have gone to that house. It was meant to be harmless, but I have a sick feeling that it was anything but that. I try and shake it off; it's done and no one will be any the wiser. I'm going to stay well away from Jason, his house, and push all thoughts away. I won't be found out for stalking an inmate's home and my job will be safe. The trouble with pushing thoughts away, though, is that they slam back in your face with force. There will be a phone conversation between Carla and Jason; she'll ask him if he's checked the photo. He'll say 'What photo?' because he hasn't seen it. She'll send it again. What if I don't open it again?

'Food not helped?' Mala says, breezing into the post room. 'You still look pale. Are Harper and Felicity okay?'

'They're fine. They sound like they're coping well, being home alone. I'm fine, honestly.' The pen I'm holding slips from my fingers. As I bend to pick it up, I knock a pile of paperwork to the floor.

Mala pulls out my chair and sits me down, picks up the papers for me then hands me a ginger nut.

'Seriously, what's going on? You're not yourself. I know when something's not right.'

I nibble away at the biscuit. I can't stomach it and I don't know how I'm going to swallow it, but it delays answering my best friend.

'I'm just tired; I'm fine. Perhaps I'm coming down with a bug.' I'm rapidly trying to weigh up whether I should just come clean and tell Mala what an idiot I've been. No, I can't risk her judging me and being disappointed in me. I can't have her thinking I'm one of those nutters who are obsessed with inmates. I'm not, I don't think I am. I shuffle the papers out of the way and start scrolling through the computer screen, hoping Mala will just leave me be but I hear crunching in my ear. She's chomping on a gingernut and staring me out.

'Honestly, I'm fine.' I smile at her.

She looks at me, unsure, but raises her hands in defeat, backing away to her own desk. I'm grateful that she has decided to back off for now. We've been friends since childhood; she can almost read me like a book but even some books don't reveal everything. I need to focus on my work. There's nothing more I can do about my photo getting into Jason's hands except pray that it doesn't. I'll have to take it on the chin whatever unfolds – if it does. I should start thinking of some rational explanation just in case. *It'll be fine.*

There's a batch of mail to be distributed, so I tell Mala I'll take it over. I want to stretch my legs and keep busy. Mala's been doing it more and more lately just to catch up with Phil for those extra few minutes, but I insist this time that I'd like to do it.

'It's starting to rain,' I say, as I load the trolley.

The inmates are starting to congregate in the garden. Mala joins me by the door to inspect the level of rainfall.

'What are they doing?' Mala asks.

I'm suddenly aware that the rain isn't why the prisoners are huddled together.

'Shit,' Mala gasps.

We see a glint of steel; a guy slashed to his face with a knife. Five inmates jump on him raining down a frenzy of kicks and punches, as the alarms reverberate around the grounds. I ensure our door is locked in time as the fight escalates fast. Another group of prisoners set on the attackers, erupting into chaos. The brawl is dangerously close to spilling through the doors. None of the men are backing down, despite the prison officer's threats. Jeering shouts erupt around the wing above the alarms. We both back away from the door. Prisoners spill out onto the walkways, running in our direction. *How did they all get through?* Mala grabs the stapler.

'What's that going to do?'

She shrugs at me, her eyes wide. I link her arm. Two prisoners overpower an officer, slamming his head face-first into our door. Blood streaks the glass. He slumps to the floor, the men stamping on his defenceless body.

'What do we do?' I mouth to my friend.

'We have to leave it to the guys.' Mala looks desperate. 'Can you see Phil?'

I lunge forwards and slam my hands on the glass pane, 'Leave him alone.'

A guy with a mop of curly hair raises his head, his top lip curled up tight. He faces me through the door. I leap back as he punches the glass. He punches again and again. More officers are deployed, armoured up. The man is dragged away, screaming obscenities. The prisoners from outside have now broken through inside, and the guards are desperately standing their ground, containing them as best they can. A tall skinhead lifts the wheelie bin and rams it at the guards. Another bin comes crashing through the doors, rubbish becoming missiles.

'Where is he? Where's Phil?' Mala is shaking.

I doubted her feelings for Phil. I really did. It's like she just decided on the spur of the moment that she had the hots for him when there was nothing there before. We've both worked here long enough and she's never looked twice at him. But I see genuine fear in her eyes. I see something I haven't seen in her before.

Officers have managed to pin an inmate up against the door. I couldn't be more grateful for the reinforced glass. Riots this big have never been so close to our office. The reminder is like a punch to the guts, just who we are working with – the dangerous and the unpredictable. I should never have got so interested in the life of Jason Sawyer, of a criminal. At the thought of him, I wonder where he is. The numbers are dissipating now the prisoners are retreating to their cells or being restrained, but there are still a few unwilling to give up. Mala puts her head on my shoulders.

'It's going to be okay,' I say.

She's still holding the stapler. 'Yeah we had 'em,' she says, waving it towards the door.

'Phil will be fine. You know he can hold his own.' I try to reassure her.

Her eyes shine and then mine do. Before we both know it we are both in tears.

'That was fucking scary,' Mala sobs.

'I think I forgot to breathe,' I gasp.

Slowly but surely, the remaining prisoners are under control, and everywhere is locked down. Some of the officers start to clear away the aftermath, the rubbish strewn across the walkway. Simon, the young officer, knocks on the door and I let him in.

'You okay ladies?' he asks. He's holding a bucket of bleach. 'I'll get this cleaned up.' He points to the blood smeared on the door. 'Bastards.'

'Is he okay?' I ask.

'His nose is smashed up. Medics are looking after him.'

'Anyone else hurt?' Mala asks.

'Nah,' Simon says, putting on his gloves ready to clean the door. 'I think Phil took a hit but— ah there he is.'

We see Phil approaching over the officer's shoulder and Mala is straight out of the door to greet him. She throws her arms around his neck and I see him wince. I step out of the post room to check he's okay too. Simon continues to sponge down the door. I see that Phil has a cut lip and a slight gash above his eyebrow and Mala is fussing over him. He's trying to reassure her he's fine.

'It's nothing,' Phil says.

'Could've been though,' Simon chips in. 'Having a knife held to your throat is hardly nothing.'

'What?' Mala yelps.

'If it weren't for Jason, jumping that prick like he did—' Simon continues.

'Sawyer?' I ask.

'Yeah, saved his skin. At least we have one of these convicts on our side.'

Phil half nods in agreement.

'What the hell happened?' I ask.

'Investigations are beginning straight away, but I think this has been brewing for the past few weeks. Thankfully it wasn't any worse.' Phil rubs his head. 'Put you off the job yet mate?' he says to the younger recruit.

'Talk about throwing me in the deep end. Christ, is it too early to ask for a pay rise?' Simon finishes drying off the window.

Phil puffs out some air. 'I've got to get on. The paperwork now is going to be ridiculous. Thankfully no one was killed. I'm glad you're both okay.' He turns to Mala, 'Don't worry, I'll see you tonight after work?'

'Yes, I need a stiff drink. One I'll be raising to Jason Sawyer by all accounts.' Mala says.

Phil nods again and strides away, the younger officer following on.

Why would Jason protect Phil? The fight flashes through my mind – the faces of the prisoners. Given more of a chance, they would have seriously harmed or killed each and every officer. Even us. *If that one had gotten through our door...* I shudder. So why would Jason not join in the riot? If he defended an officer, he's not going to be a popular guy on the wing by any means. Here I go again, overthinking Jason's every movement. I smile at my best friend.

'Are you okay?'

'I'm rethinking my career choices,' she says.

'You do really care for Phil, don't you?'

'It could be the real thing this time. I could actually hug Jason. Never thought I'd say that about one of these convicts.'

I throw my arms around my best friend. 'I'm happy for you.'

I am and I really mean it, so why do I feel like I'm losing her? My stomach knots and I pull away. She doesn't need me to comfort her; she'll run to Phil this evening. He's going to be the one there for her now. Where does that leave me? This environment feels volatile in multiple ways now and I'm keen to get back to the warmth of my home and my little family. If I'm ready for any day to end, it's this one.

CHAPTER THIRTY-THREE

I must have been on autopilot during the journey home. I'm pulling up onto my driveway next to Jon's car and I'm not sure how I got here. I'm alert now though and looking over to the Black Mazda parked opposite. The driver, who I can't make out clearly, is staring at me through the partly open car window. He's holding a cigarette and puffing out smoke. Because he's staring directly at me, I think I must know him, so I stare back longer than I should. He flicks the cigarette with force to the ground and then revs the engine, still not taking his eyes from me. He revs again before wheel-spinning away. As if I wasn't feeling unnerved enough today.

'Hey, I'm home,' I shout, slipping off my shoes and dropping my bag to the floor. Silence.

I poke my head into the living room and Jon looks up briefly from watching the TV.

'Hiya, love,' he says, but his eyes are back on the screen.

'I'll start dinner then?' I say.

He stretches but it feels exaggerated to me. 'If you could, love. Hard day of meetings today and I'm whacked.'

He's still not looking at me. I had fifty-odd men rioting outside my office today and one tried to batter down the door. I could have been raped and beaten. I saw an inmate get stabbed and an officer's face was pummelled into my door. That's what I want to say. But my day is never going to be as exhausting as his. The wonderful day we spent together yesterday is all of a sudden a distant memory and we're back to reality, where my husband is as pleased to see me at the end of the working day as an irritating fly buzzing around.

I head to the kitchen and Jon shouts after me, 'Make me one too, love.' I pick the kettle up and I burst into tears. It takes me by surprise but I just let the fat teardrops fall; it feels like the release that I need. I don't see Jon approach me; his arm around me makes me jump.

'What's happened?' he soothes.

'I think it's just the shock of the day kicking in,' I say through my sobs. I wipe my tears and take a deep breath so that I can get my words out. I fill him in on the details of the fight.

He hugs me briefly. 'At least you were safe. You will insist on working there. Oh, can we use the mince for a shepherd's pie tonight instead of bolognese for a change?' With that, he leaves the room.

I think about Mala and Phil now, ordering food in, snuggled together on the sofa sharing the pains of the day between them; feeling secure and loved. It looks like I won't be getting that, I rarely do. The moment I feel like my husband worries about me, he changes. I feel loved and then I don't. Perhaps that's how he thinks about me? That I don't care about his day and his boring meetings. I do and often ask him about his day, but over time, when you get nothing in return, you stop bothering. I think that's what's happened. The truth is, I don't know who stopped bothering first, or how or when these changes occurred. Is it me, is it him?

Fizz breaks my thoughts; she skips in and throws her arms around me like she always does. I can depend on Fizz being pleased to see me, always.

She looks up at me. 'Have you been crying?'

'What's up?' Harper says, joining us.

'Oh, it's okay. I'm being silly. Tough day at work that's all. There was a nasty fight which was a bit scary. But I'm okay.'

'Whoa, you literally have to tell us everything.' Harper sits at the table, props her chin up in her hands, her eyes wide in anticipation.

At least Harper's good mood has remained, and it brings a smile to my face. I start taking the ingredients out to prep dinner and fill the girls in on the action. I sugar-coat it a little so as not to scare Fizz.

'Are the bad men still locked away? They didn't escape?' Fizz asks quietly.

'Yes, they are securely locked up,' I quickly reassure her.

'You're a total badass,' Harper says.

I don't know how I've gone from being uncool to a badass in Harper's opinion but I'm not going to knock it at all. 'I'm not really. I was safe behind locked doors. It's the prison officers that were in the thick of it. They're the brave ones. I honestly don't think I could do it.'

'You help keep the world safe,' Fizz says as a matter of fact and wraps her arms around my waist again. It's a relief to see Harper nodding in agreement and not glaring at me. I know how uncomfortable she feels at times when Fizz talks to me and shows me affection. For once, she isn't storming out of the room. Instead, she offers to help peel the potatoes and I gladly accept.

'Anyway girls, tell me all about your day?'

Fizz immediately puts her hand to her mouth and giggles and Harper puts her finger to her lips to shush her little sister. I raise my eyebrows, 'Sounds like you've been up to no good?'

'We're just messing.' Harper winks at her sister. 'We've done nothing much.'

I dismiss any doubts that I have. They are both relaxed and in a good mood and they're safe and I'm safe and that's all that matters. I'm filled with love again as both my stepdaughters help me prep dinner. Perhaps it's too much of me to expect any kind of sympathy or support from Jon. It is the nature of the job I'm in; it's to be expected, right?

Smash! The three of us look alarmed at each other as the sound of shattered glass rings out from the living room.

'What the...?!' we hear Jon shout.

I drop my oven glove and run to see what's happened. The girls follow. Jon is standing over a rock sitting amongst the carnage of broken glass. A large, jagged hole now in the centre of the window.

'What on earth?' I blurt out, looking at my husband's stunned expression.

'I don't know,' he says. 'I jumped up and saw the back end of a black car speed away. 'Jesus.' He throws his arms up.

'Is it the bad men?' Fizz cries, burying her head into my stomach.

'No sweetie, it'll be stupid kids messing around. You go upstairs so we can clean the glass up.' I stroke her hair before she runs from the room. 'Was it a Mazda?' I ask Jon.

'Could've been, why?'

'Saw one parked outside when I got home. The driver was looking at the house. Just thought it odd.'

'I know who did it,' Harper pipes up. She's hugging herself, her lower lip trembling.

'Who?' Jon asks.

'Lexi said she'd come and brick our windows. I keep telling you she has it in for me. She said she would if I grassed on her for being nasty to me. She said she'd do this. I'm so sorry.'

'It's not your fault.' Jon embraces his daughter. 'That girl needs locking up. I'll have to report it to the police.'

Harper starts to cry, 'But it'll make things worse. I know I told Nan that I'd be braver and ignore Lexi and focus on my schoolwork, but it's going to be too hard.'

'We need to stand up to her. She can't go around pulling stunts like this.' Jon sounds like he won't back down on this one. Not this time.

I go to fetch the dustpan and brush and vacuum. So Harper's nan managed to talk her around then. Her change in behaviour is down to her? Why does her nan's opinion hold more influence than mine? Haven't I been giving Harper the exact same advice for months now? I know her nan has been there throughout her whole life and I'm just this strange newcomer and I will always be made to feel like that. Harper is making an effort with me now, though, and that's all that matters, isn't it? I start to sweep up the bigger chunks of glass. It's still broad daylight outside. I can't believe the nerve of some people. I shudder at the thought of the black car and I hope that it was just Lexi, like Harper thinks.

I wait for Jon to get off the phone to the local police before hoovering up the smaller shards.

'An officer will pay Lexi a visit, hopefully later on,' Jon sighs. 'I'm going to finish off dinner before it's spoiled and then get the window covered with something. At least it's not a cold night.'

I look at the fractured windowpane and think

that it just about sums the day up perfectly. I head upstairs to check on Fizz. I shouldn't have said anything about work in front of her. I should have known better. 'Fizzy?' I knock her door before poking my head into her room. She's sitting on her bedroom floor with her favourite blanket wrapped tightly around her.

'Don't be scared, okay? I promise you there are no bad men. They are locked away. It really will be some stupid kids. Do you still trust me?' I sit down next to her and hold out my little finger. She links her little finger around mine and we shake on it.

The severe anxiety that she experiences stems from witnessing her mother's attack. Any talk about violent men is going to have an adverse effect on her. I slipped up and I shouldn't have. I have her trust and I nearly blew it. If she loses faith in me then she has no one else to confide in.

'I can take the day off work tomorrow if you want me to. I can call in sick?'

Fizz shakes her head. 'I'm okay with Harper. We had a fun day today. I'll be fine.' Her voice is barely a whisper, so I know she's not quite herself. Perhaps I should call in sick anyway, especially after what's just happened. What if another window is bricked and Jon and I aren't around?

'Kate?' Fizzy whispers.

'Yes?'

'Can we get a puppy?'

We've talked about getting a dog before. I've looked into dogs and how therapeutic they can be. Dogs can be trained as therapy dogs to assist in easing anxiety attacks. One would be perfect for Fizz but Jon has held back on the idea. He doesn't think it would be fair on the dog to be left alone all day as we both work full time.

'I'll talk to your dad again, but you know that having a puppy is a huge commitment,' I remind her.

She nods. 'If we can have one, can I call it Kylie?' She put her hand to her mouth and giggles.

I look at her bemused. 'Funny name for a dog. Where did you get that idea?'

Fizzy just giggles even more and shrugs her shoulders.

'Like I said, we can talk about it some more. I'm going to help finish dinner and fix the window. You sure you're okay and not worried about anything?'

'I'm fine,' she whispers.

I kiss her forehead and head back downstairs to Jon. I find him emptying the boiled potatoes into a colander. He curses as hot water splashes back at him.

'Can you start mashing these?' he says. 'Bloody day is just getting worse.'

'You're having a bad day?' I even shock myself with the venom in my voice. 'Am I supposed to sympathise with you when you don't bat an eyelid at everything I've been through today? Do you even care that my life may have been in danger today? It's like I don't exist to you sometimes and you expect me to care about your sodding day?' I'm shaking now.

'You were safe the whole time though, weren't you? Sometimes you tell me you don't want the fuss or anyone to overreact. I was giving you your fucking space.'

'Don't swear at me Jon. It's obvious that I was upset—'

'I don't need this.' Jon throws the potato masher down. 'I can't do right by you, say the right thing, act the right way. I can't win. Finish dinner, I need to sort the window. I'm not doing this now.'

Angry, hot tears slip down my cheeks.

'Why are you shouting at dad?' Harper appears in the doorway.

'I'm not; we're just having a bad day.' My voice is more raised than intended and Harper glares at me before stomping away.

'Well I can't flaming well win either,' I curse out loud. I walk out into the garden in desperate need of fresh air. I freeze. There's a man looking over the hedge at me. He's wearing a black hoodie. He grins before walking away. I hurry back inside and lock the door behind me. Something doesn't feel right. I feel like we're being watched. This isn't just Lexi. A dangerous prisoner's family have my photo and tried to get it to him. What if they've found me? I don't know why; I haven't done any harm. They couldn't want anything from me. I'm trying not to sound ridiculous, and my imagination is whirring. It's Lexi; it has to be. She has an older brother or something. It'll blow over. I'd rather that than the alternative.

CHAPTER THIRTY-FOUR

It's just gone three-fifteen a.m. I've been clock-watching all night. I'm envious of Jon's gentle snores. I'm tired enough to sleep but I just can't. I know that I clench my teeth at night because my dentist has told me there are tell-tale signs. My inner cheeks are pinched and my tongue has scalloped edges from where it pushes against my teeth. I was never aware of it happening, but I am now as I lie here. Every muscle in me is tense and my teeth are clenched. I can't seem to unclench them. I don't know how I'm going to function at work. Jon is insisting that he will stay home with the girls so I'm not needed. I can go to work. I argued that Fizz will want me here if she's anxious, but he still insisted that I'm not needed. He'll be here for the girls, just in case, and that was that. It's the first time that I feel like he's pushing me away from his daughters. Paranoid thoughts will always be magnified in the middle of the night.

Harper looked relieved when the police officer said that they'd paid Lexi Keggans a visit and there was no one home. A neighbour said that Lexi had gone away for the week, for half term. She couldn't have bricked the window then. So if it wasn't her then who was it? I'm not feeling so relieved and every one of my fibres is screaming that at me. I hate going to bed angry after an argument and Jon's gentle snores are telling me he's not so bothered. Sounds are also magnified in the middle of the night and I'm sure that I can hear rustling, shuffling and footsteps at the front of the house. I sit bolt upright.

I slip out of bed and gently pull the curtain back to see two men on the driveway. My heart hammers against my ribs; I drop the curtain.

'Jon,' I say, rushing to shake him.

He splutters then shoots awake. There's hammering on the door. My heart stops. Jon jumps out of bed and pulls the curtain back. We watch the two men jump into a black car; they rev the engine before speeding away.

'Is anyone still out there?' I whisper.

Jon pulls on his joggers and a jumper.

'Don't go out there. Let's just call the police.' I take his arm.

'I don't know what the hell is going on. I'm just gonna look through the spy hole.' Jon says as he rubs his face and now looks wide awake.

He heads downstairs and I follow him, grabbing my phone first.

'What the hell?' Jon says looking through the spyglass on the front door.

'What?'

He unlatches the door.

'Don't,' I beg.

'It looks like a ...' Jon opens the door wide and

steps out.

I immediately see her lying on the drive and rush past my husband. I brush the blonde hair away from the face of the girl who's lying on our driveway, unresponsive. The lamppost illuminates the ground enough for me to see that she looks to be about sixteen years of age and she has cuts and bruises on her face.

'Is she breathing?' Jon asks, crouching down next to me.

I shake her gently. 'Can you hear me?'

There's a soft whimper.

'Yes.' I hold my phone up and punch in 999 with shaking hands.

Jon jumps up as I make the call; he looks up and down the street to see if he can see anyone. He rushes back past me into the house and returns with a throw, placing it over the girl to keep her warm.

'I'm staying on the phone until the ambulance arrives,' I tell him. I'm back talking to the operator. 'No, I have no idea who she is or how she got here.'

Jon interrupts me. 'She looks like that missing girl who's been on the news.'

'No, I can't find any ID on her,' I continue on the phone. The girl is wearing leggings and a T-shirt and a quick inspection shows no signs of pockets or a bag or anything. 'My husband thinks she looks like the missing girl...' I can't recall her name fast enough.

'Sophie Banks,' Jon says.

'Sophie Banks, I don't know though,' I blurt down the phone.

The operator is telling me that the ambulance is nearly with us and we're doing really well and to keep calm. I suddenly remember Harper and Fizz. They must still be fast asleep. Fizz can't see all of this. I pray she stays asleep. I can hear the sirens now and I tell the operator. The lady on the phone says she'll hang up now and I thank her. *It can't be the missing girl.* I think Jon and I are just lost for words. We're just looking at each other confused. Jon stands at the end of the driveway and flags down the ambulance and the police car that approach.

The paramedics are quick to take over and assess the young girl. They carry out their observations and work together to get her lifted onto a stretcher. Another police car pulls up and I start to see lights coming on and curtains twitching from the neighbours.

'I hope she'll be okay,' I say to the paramedics as they secure her into the ambulance.

'We'll do our best for her,' the female paramedic says.

The ambulance departs, followed by one of the police cars. The other officers remain, and the two policemen ask if they can come inside to ask us some questions. We can't refuse them but I'm panicking about waking up the girls but then I realise that it's too late. They are both standing in the doorway. Harper has a protective arm around her little sister who is trembling in the cold.

'What's happening?' Harper says alarmed.

'Go back inside,' Jon soothes. 'There's been an accident, but everything is okay. Kate and I just need to tell the policemen what we saw. I promise everything is okay.'

I bend down to Fizz's level and tell her not to worry. She's trembling all over. 'I'll come up and tuck you in with some hot chocolate in a bit.'

'I'll sit with her,' Harper says.

The girls head upstairs and I invite the two policemen inside. We show them through to the kitchen and Jon puts the kettle on.

'I'm PC Johnson and this is PC Patel.' Both officers take a seat at the table. 'You say that you don't know the girl, so you've never met her at all? She's not someone your daughter might know from school? I noticed they look a similar age?'

Jon answers, 'No, we have no idea who she is at all other than she looks like the missing girl. Do you think it's her? Harper didn't see her but if it is her she doesn't know her. If it's not then I still don't think it's anyone she knows. She has no real friends at school other than Callum.'

I do a quick search online and pull up a picture of Sophie Banks. I hold it up to PC Johnson. 'It does look like her.'

'We'll have to wait until we find out for sure,' Johnson says.

'So run us through everything you heard and saw leading up to finding her on your driveway?' Patel asks, taking out a note pad.

I answer first. 'I couldn't sleep and just heard shuffling and footsteps outside the front of the house. I went to take a look and saw two men. But they were both dressed in black and I couldn't make out what they looked like or anything. They banged on the door. That's when Jon woke up, they then sped off in a black car. I didn't see the girl at first, not until we opened the door.'

'Did you get the make of the car at all or the registration?' Patel asks.

'No—'

'We had a brick through our window yesterday evening and I saw a black car speed off then,' Jon interrupts.

'And before that, when I got home from work, I saw a black car outside of the house. The driver was staring at me before driving away. It was definitely a Mazda.'

'Same car, do you think?' Patel asks, still scribbling everything down.

'Possibly. It looked similar, but it was so dark and they drove off so fast.'

'Anything unusual happen before all of this happened? Can you think of anything at all, any issues, arguments, run-ins with anyone?' Johnson asks.

'Not at all,' Jon says defensively.

'It's just that the girl looked like she has been

assaulted and we need to find out why she was left here specifically,' Johnson says.

'Mistaken address? I don't know,' Jon is sounding more irritated. 'We thought our window being bricked was something to do with a girl who's been bullying my daughter; she threatened to do it. But one of you guys went to her house and she's away for the week. But I don't know what this has to do with that. I don't know what's going on.'

Johnson asks if he can see the broken window, so Jon leads the officers through to the living room.

'Clutching at straws here,' Jon says suddenly, 'but Kate works at Standington Prison. It wouldn't be the first time she's received abuse for working in a prison by friends or family of convicts.'

'Oh hardly,' I snap. Of course Jon would bring up my job; anything to get another dig in at me for where I work and make it my fault. I look at the policemen who are looking seriously at me. 'I'm support grade. I work in the post room and vet the mail. It's all I do. I've had the odd remark but hardly abuse.' I glare at Jon.

I shouldn't snap but the truth is my visit to Anna West is eating away at me. I'm not going to mention it, I can't. None of this can be connected, surely? It was harmless. I knocked on the door, pretended I was looking for an old school friend, Anna or Carla whoever she is, said it wasn't her and that was that. Okay, she then sent my image to Jason Sawyer to find out who I was but he didn't get it. It was nothing. She doesn't know where I live; there's no reason for her to have issues with me – none at all. There is no way that any of that has anything to do with a teenage girl being dumped on my driveway.

PC Patel's phone rings and he answers it. A few moments later he hangs up. 'The girl has been identified as Sophie Banks. She has injuries consistent with serious sexual assault.'

I gasp, my hand flying to my mouth.

He continues: 'There will be detectives and forensics on their way. Your driveway will need to be cordoned off for a while. We'll do a door to door, see if anyone saw anything.'

'Whatever you need,' Jon says. 'I just can't get my head around this.'

My tears make an appearance and Jon actually puts his arms around me. I'm rigid though and unable to return the hug. Kidnapped Sophie Banks was dumped on our doorstep. *Why*? It can't be anything to do with Anna West. And then I remember and it's like a punch to my stomach. Jason Sawyer's niece, Chloe, was being interviewed for her suspected kidnapping. That's why Jason stabbed that guy. Detectives were exploring all options, trying to crack down on teenage girls going missing. There is a link. There is a connection of sorts. What did I get us into? The words don't come. I can't say anything.

I can't explain it. I can't admit to Jon that I was obsessed with an inmate and went snooping. I can't risk my job and it still might not be relevant. I'll keep quiet for now and hope that this all blows over without me having to admit to anything. I think of what must have happened to poor Sophie Banks. By not saying anything, I could be holding back their investigation. Bile rises into my throat, so I rush from the room. I need to be sick.

In the privacy of the downstairs toilet, I let my tears flow freely and splash water on my face. The last twenty-four hours have been overwhelming, and I can't make sense of it. I just know that I'm the cause of it somehow. Jon was right. It is me and it is my job but little does he know how right he is. I can't admit it. I can't, not now. I can't lose us, my little family, everything. I can't. I have to hope that the police find who did this without my help and just pray it all goes away. It has to be okay, it just has to be.

CHAPTER THIRTY-FIVE

It's approaching midday and the forensics team are finishing packing away. From what I can gather, they haven't found anything. No footprints, tyre tracks, items left behind. Goodness knows what the neighbours are saying. If the police have discovered any useful information, then they aren't giving anything away yet.

'Are you going into work?' Jon asks me.

There was no way I was going to make it in this morning, so I called in sick. I can't remember the last time I did that. Mala text me on her break to find out if I was okay and I haven't replied – I don't know what to say. The lies just keep snowballing.

'No point in me going in now.' I lower my head. 'I'm shattered. I wouldn't be able to concentrate.'

'This whole thing is nuts. Feels like we're in a real CSI drama on the TV.' Jon half smirks.

'Why don't I take the girls to the park? An hour or so away from the house will do us good. I'll grab us some sandwiches whilst we're there.'

Jon looks hesitant to start with but then agrees it's a good idea. He says he'll stay behind just in case the police come back for anything. He also admits he could do with a nap. I could do with a nap too, but I don't think I could. Getting away from this house is all that I can think about.

'Girls,' I shout up the stairs, 'We're going to the park, get your shoes on.'

I hear stomping down the stairs and Harper appears with a thunderous expression.

'What?' she snaps.

'I know we're all tired and stressed but Fizz needs the distraction. C'mon, do it for her.'

Felicity walks in carrying her shoes, sits herself down in the middle of the floor and starts to put them on.

'Fine,' Harper agrees.

Moments later, we are buckling up in the car.

'I know you don't want to hear it, but I am proud of you, Harps. You handled being questioned by that detective really well.'

She gives me a little appreciative smile. There wasn't much that she could tell the detective; she just confirmed that she didn't know Sophie Banks and she spoke about Lexi Keggans bullying her, but other than that she had nothing else to suggest.

'I wonder what happened to Sophie,' Harper says.

'The main thing is she's going to be okay.' I smile at Fizz in the rear-view mirror. 'None of this makes sense, but the police will get to the bottom of it and we don't need to worry.'

'It's on the local news,' Harper says, scrolling through her phone. 'Missing, Sophie Banks found, is currently in hospital being treated for some injuries.'

I can't swallow. 'What else does it say?'

'Nothing, that's it. No other details yet.'

The last thing we want is for our address to be splashed all over the news about where she was found. The sudden thought about the public thinking that we are connected to it fills me with dread. What if they think we were in on it? What will the girl's parents think? And it won't be long before the neighbours are spreading their gossip. A few minutes later, we are pulling into the car park. The park looks quiet for now which is a relief, and we find a parking space with ease.

Fizz is the first out of the car and she is already skipping over to the swings.

'She is remarkable,' I say to Harper. 'She has severe anxiety yet look at her. Her ability to cope, all things considering, is remarkable.'

Harper looks thoughtful for a moment. 'It's all down to you.'

I'm taken aback as my older stepdaughter starts to cry.

'Mum would be grateful to you for everything you've done for Felicity. Wish I was brave. I'm not; I'm scared. Why did someone leave that kidnapped girl at our house?'

'Oh Harps.' She lets me give her a big hug. I know that was difficult for her to say. 'Good people can get caught up in terrible situations. It's how we cope together that matters. Look at how far you've come. Don't forget how much you've been through. You're so much braver than you think.'

Harper pulls away, wiping her eyes. I rummage in my bag and hand her a tissue from a pack so she can blow her nose.

'Can you go and watch Fizzy while I nip over the road to get us some sandwiches and snacks? I don't know about you but I really need food.'

Harper admits she's starving and heads over to her sister. I watch them for a few moments to ensure they're okay before walking away. I lightly jog across the road, not bothering with using the lights. I want to get back as quickly as I can. As I walk through the automatic doors to the store a man pushes past me, nudging me out of the way. He doesn't look back and he doesn't apologise. After the last twenty-four hours, I can do without it and feel myself wanting to scream at him. I hope not to set eyes on him inside, in fear of what I might actually do to him. But it's too late. There he is by the sandwiches as if waiting for me. He's just standing there, watching me approach. He's rough-looking, ugly, like he's been in numerous fights over his lifetime, like his nose has been rearranged, and he has deep creases in his face. He's not the type you'd want to meet in a dark alleyway or in the aisle of a supermarket. I avoid eye contact and forget the need to scream at him. My nerves are on edge and I have to have faith that he's just checking out what to have for lunch and nothing more sinister.

I throw a few packs of sandwiches into my basket without overthinking what fillings to choose and quickly head to the crisps. Again, I grab three packs of anything and head to the next aisle to look for a packet of biscuits. He follows me. I see him at the end of the aisle watching me. He's not looking at the products; he's watching me. I grab the chocolate digestives and hurry to the till. I choose the woman at the till over the self-serve as if she could offer me some protection. I tap my card and glance up and yes, he's there. My heart is racing, and I need to get back to the girls. harper

I run back across the road this time, taking a risk with the fast-approaching cars. I make it, look back and he's close behind. I run across the car park to the entrance of the park, with people in view as well as my stepdaughters. I rummage for my phone. It's in my hand ready, but the man has caught up and he grabs my arm. His grip hurts.

'Don't scream,' he growls.

'Who are you?' I yelp. I can't look at him; I'm frantically trying to keep my eyes on the girls.

'They'll be safe if you listen carefully.'

'Get off me! I'll call the police.'

He takes the phone from my hand. 'I said "Listen carefully." You work at Standington. We need you to do a little something for us and if you don't, the next girl to disappear will be yours.' He nods towards Harper and Fizz.

I can't believe this is happening, what he's saying. 'Did you leave Sophie Banks at my house?'

'To show we mean business. It will be Harper next.'

'How do you know—'?

'Shh, listen up. Jason Sawyer. His appeal is due soon. You need to stop that going through. Plant something on him. Do something to harm his appeal. We don't want him getting out.'

'I can't. I don't know how. It's not that—'

Harper looks over at me and waves.

'Think of something and just do it. We'll be in touch.' He points over at Harper who is back to pushing Fizz on the swing. 'She's a pretty one.' He strides away. I watch him get into a silver car and he drives away. *He actually followed me here.*

My knees buckle and I just about make it to the bench before bursting into tears. I'm now certain that this is all down to me. It was my visit to Jason and Anna's house. It's too much of a coincidence that I go there, a picture of me is captured and it's Jason Sawyer that I'm being blackmailed to sort out. *But why*? Why would Anna West want to keep Jason inside? I've read her letters to him. She loves him, unless Carla is really Carla and not Anna. Who is Jason to Carla? Carla wrote to him with my photo. The letter was friendly enough, just asking who I was. There was another guy there that day – Andrew, I think his name was. Who was he? I'm desperately trying to piece everything together. I want to kick myself. I gasp for breath as the enormity of what's just happened sinks in. *How did they find me?*

I frantically wave the girls over.

'Are you okay?' Harper asks me, slightly out of breath from running.

She can see I've been crying. 'Perhaps I'm not so brave either. C'mon, let's eat.' I hand out the sandwiches and both girls sit either side of me.

They feel like my walls, my protectors, and I'm in the middle, vulnerable, helpless. It shouldn't feel like this. We're sat on mine and Fizz's bench. The bench we met on like we always do. Our favourite bench; the bench where it all started. I gained a family, love and security. Even with the downs, I wouldn't be without them and now here I am sat on this sacred-to-me bench feeling like I've put my little family in danger and I'm ripping us apart. The day Jon met me, he couldn't have foreseen this day coming. He was in awe of me. Fizz connected with me and then so did he. He put me up on a pedestal and even though that pedestal hasn't felt secure for a long time now, he will never ever forgive me for putting his daughters in harm's way like this. He's going to hate me.

I have to think but I don't know where to start. My head is spinning. If I go to the police, the chances are that man will get to us before the police get him. We're being watched. The thought makes me look around the park. I'm suspecting everyone. If I call the police then there's no going back. The truth comes out and I'll lose my family. I could try and handle this on my own, but what do I smuggle into Jason's mail – drugs? It's not possible; I wouldn't know how to get drugs. We're searched regularly. I'll lose my job. I'll lose my family. Isn't it worth the risk to keep Harper and Fizz safe? Isn't that what parents do for their children? I imagine Harper as the girl battered and terrified, lying dumped on the ground and my blood runs cold.

'Shall we go home?' I try to control my voice shaking. 'I think I'm too tired after all.'

'Who was that man you were talking to?' Harper asks.

'Don't know, he was just chatting about the weather. Ready Fizzy?'

She scrunches her empty sandwich packaging up and nods. The urge to get them home to safety is overriding my thoughts. I need to step up and come up with a plan. Now is not the time to feel like the vulnerable one. I have to sort this mess out. I'll do anything it takes to keep my girls safe.

CHAPTER THIRTY-SIX
Gregg

Gregg toys with the butter knife at the table. He's sitting across from Charlie Coleman, thinking how he'd like to damage that disgusting grin of his. Carla is pacing around, waiting for Brian to return. Gregg didn't think that Brian was the best choice to go and threaten the woman; he's conspicuous with his big ugly face. Picking him out in a line up would be a piece of piss. But Gregg knew that he wasn't the best choice either. The two girls, Harper and Felicity, had seen him before. They know his face. Little did Gregg know that when he dropped the two girls at home, Carla had plans this big.

Gregg did help dump the blonde girl at the Midwinter's property. He tutted when he saw the mess of the girl's face. So much for a more classy, upmarket operation. Charlie Coleman is a disgusting man. It's like Charlie can read his thoughts; he winks at him across the table. *Cocky bastard.* Gregg knows they have him over a barrel and he's been dragged into this mess, but he wants Sawyer to stay locked up more than anyone. He killed Michael. Carla was also waving a lot of cash at him and that always talks the loudest. Always. He just hopes that Brian, the ugly muppet, has done enough to get the message across to the Midwinter woman. He's about to find out because Brian is at the front door.

Charlie lets him in and Carla wastes no time.

'Well?' she asks.

'Oh, she'll cooperate,' Brian sneers. 'No question about that.'

'I want their house watched constantly. Gregg, you don't go near the house. Is that clear? The girls know you. But if it comes to it, you need to be ready to do what you do best.'

Gregg mock salutes Carla. He knows that if the Midwinter woman doesn't deliver or she tries to pull a fast one, he'll be ready to act fast in taking Harper. Should that not be needed, he may just take her anyway. The money he's making from this job should be enough to get a deposit down on a flat up north. Start again. Take the girl with him and make sure that Carla and none of her minions can find him.

Carla opens a bottle of whisky and pours herself a measure before passing the bottle to Charlie. She takes a large swig.

'When it comes to it, I want you to take the younger Midwinter too. Take both of them,' she says, draining the remaining whisky.

'Whoa, I ain't takin' no little kid. C'mon Carla, she's too young. The kid don't speak. She's disabled or something. The older sister is enough.'

'You're taking both of them.' Carla pours another measure.

'Thought you welcomed new business opportunities,' Charlie says. 'Whole new market right there. And what's more perfect than a kid that doesn't shout back.'

Carla laughs and clinks glasses with Charlie, 'Bet she's still a screamer though.'

'You're disgusting,' Gregg spits.

'Oh, wind your goddamn morals in,' Carla snaps. 'We need both girls hostage that's all. We'll be giving Kate zero options but to do what we ask. Besides, it might not come to it at all if she hurries up and gets results.'

'Calm your nerves and have a dram,' Charlie says, passing Gregg the whisky.

Gregg stands, pushing his chair back with force. All he wants to do with that bottle is smash it into Charlie's face. He sees Brian smirking and imagines smashing the glass into his face too, not that it would have an impact on his looks. *Ugly prick.*

'Just call me when you need me,' Gregg says to Carla. 'I'll see myself out.'

CHAPTER THIRTY-SEVEN
Harper

Harper shuts herself in her room and puts her earphones in, turning the sound up loud. She needs to drown the outside world out. Her dad said that he's arranged to be at home for the rest of the week, telling work there was a family emergency. This disappointed Harper to begin with; she was looking forward to a week of independence, for quality time with her little sister. She enjoyed their trip out together yesterday, feeling like the responsible one, the big sister. She couldn't help but get her hopes up that Felicity would start talking to her the more time they spent alone together. She knew she couldn't push it but she felt like the chance was there. Despite all of this, she did have to admit that perhaps she was glad to have her dad around now. The world feels that bit scarier.

Thinking about yesterday's trip out, Harper wonders if Carla will still pop round this weekend like she said. With everything that's going on, perhaps she should tell Kate about Carla visiting. It might not be great timing. At least Kate can get in touch with her and cancel her coming until another time. It would be a shame to ruin the surprise but with everything that's happened, Kate might not like it. But then again, her stepmum could probably do with a friend. She has Mala, but you need all the friends you can get when times are difficult. It might be just what she needs as a distraction – a fun surprise visit from her old school friend. There is also how angry Kate might be with her for sneaking out with Felicity to see Carla in the first place. With how stressed Kate is at the moment, Harper doesn't want to add to that right now. She decides to keep quiet and just wait and see if Carla turns up.

Harper rips her earphones out. The thought of needing your friends makes her desperately miss Callum. She picks up her phone. She doesn't want to interrupt his holiday but she needs to hear his voice. She hits his name and calls. *Please answer.*

'Hey Cal.' Harper grabs a cushion and settles back on her bed when her friend answers.

'Hey Harps, you missing me?'

More than you know. 'I'm missing your ego and how awesome you think you are.'

'Look, you know it and I know it. How's Bracknell?'

'How's Devon, that's more exciting?'

'The arcade here is massive. It's pretty cool. And I've met someone. We're hooking up to hangout again later.'

'What? You've only been there a few days. Fast mover, aren't you? What's she like then?' Harper felt her chest tighten. This is not what she wanted to hear.

'Being here has given me some head space. I'm just going to say it. I'm gay, Harps. It's a guy.'

Silence.

'Harps, you there?'

'Sorry, you've thrown me. Why didn't you say before?'

'Did I have to?'

'No, but I'm your bestie. You can tell me anything.'

'Just needed time to tell myself first, I guess.'

'Does this guy know what a loser you are?'

'I do love you, you know, Harps.'

Harper catches the lump in her throat. It was painful enough that Callum didn't have feelings for her but this revelation made it more impossible. She knew for certain that Callum would never be hers.

'Harps, talk to me, stop going quiet. Don't fall out with me.'

'I'm not.' Harper sucks in a big breath. 'Something happened, I'm scared. You know that missing girl on the news – Sophie Banks? The kidnapped girl? Well, she was found in the middle of last night, on our driveway. She was dumped there. She was unconscious and beaten up. Forensics have been here and everything.'

'Holy shit, now I'm lost for words. Tell me everything.'

Harper fills her friend in on all the details and how she was questioned by a detective. She told him about the rock being thrown through the living room window and how she didn't know if it was all connected.

'Please don't put this on social media or anything,' she adds.

'What do you take me for? I'm home Friday, alright? I'm all yours. Just call me if you get scared or anything. I'm always here for you.'

'Thank you.'

'It's what best friends are for. I know, I'll take you shopping. I'm gay so apparently I have to like that now.'

Harper manages a chuckle. 'Loser.'

'Love you.'

'Love you.'

'I'll call you later.' Callum hangs up.

Harper places her earphones back in, curls up into the foetal position and bursts into tears.

CHAPTER THIRTY-EIGHT

'I'm not going to yoga,' I tell Jon for the tenth time. I shouldn't have told him that Mala had text me asking if I was still up for going.

'Isn't it meant to be relaxing though?' Jon says. 'Just go; it'll do you good.'

'I've not slept, I'm knackered, and I'm not leaving Fizz this evening.'

'It's only an hour, isn't it? Go. I'm here for her.'

He's pushing me away again. Last week, he was making me feel irresponsible for going out and about and now he's practically pushing me out of the door. I know he believes deep down that I am somehow responsible for all of this, that it's something to do with my work. He's right; he just doesn't know for sure. Yet.

'We need CCTV,' I say.

'I've already been looking online,' Jon says.

'The sooner, the better.'

The thought of someone watching the house gives me shivers. I walk over to the window and peek out. I can't see anything unusual.

'Is there something you're not telling me?' Jon asks.

'No, of course not,' I snap.

I would have thought getting CCTV would be obvious and he shouldn't have to read into me suggesting it. If we had caught the two men on camera leaving the girl on our driveway then they would be behind bars already and I wouldn't be in this terrifying mess. I rub my arms and take a deep breath.

'I'll go to yoga.'

Jon nods to me and I go upstairs to get ready. Whoever we're dealing with are clearly dangerous and mean business. The girls need protecting but if I tell Jon everything he'll want to go straight to the police. Of course he would. I'm not putting the girls in more danger. I have to play it my way and hope I can come up with something quickly. I need to do what that man told me to. I need to hinder Jason's appeal, but how? I need a plan and I need some space to think. I reassure myself that nothing will happen tonight because whoever these people are at least need to give me a chance to get to work tomorrow to put something into action. And Jon is right; he is here at least. I'll go to yoga. I need my best friend.

'You okay, Fizzy?' I say, seeing my youngest stepdaughter enter the bedroom.

'I think I heard Harper crying,' she whispers.

'I'll go check on her. Are you okay though? Do you want to talk about anything?'

Fizzy shakes her head. 'The police were scary. Are you and Daddy in trouble?'

'Oh my goodness, no. Never. We're just helping them.'

'I remember Daddy speaking to the police when mummy died.'

'You remember that?'

Fizz nods.

'You were so small,' I say. 'It's amazing. Do you remember much?'

My stepdaughter shrugs. 'Just him crying.'

'Come here,' I say, giving her a big hug. 'You are so brave. But I promise you there is nothing bad happening and everything is fine.'

'It's okay. I'm not scared when you're here.'

I'm overwhelmed with love for this little girl and have to catch the lump in my throat. She looks up to me and look at what I've done. I can't bear the thought of anything happening to her. I'll do whatever it takes to keep her safe.

'Right, I'm going to take a cup of tea into Harper. Check she's okay before I head off to yoga.'

'I bet it's boy trouble,' Fizzy chuckles.

Moments later I'm heading into Harper's room with a hot tea and a couple of chocolate digestives. She's stretched out on her bed with her earphones in and her eyes do look puffy.

'Your dad's buying CCTV if that helps you feel better?' I say.

'It's not that,' Harper sits up and takes the mug of tea. 'Callum's gay. I thought we might be more than friends one day, but no chance now.'

'Told you it was boy trouble,' Fizz pipes up, listening in from the doorway.

'Scram, you!' Harper shout's but playfully.

I smile gently. It's not like Harper to disclose what's wrong. I'm not being shouted at to mind my own business. I knew she was close to Callum and did wonder if there would ever be romance. Jon was convinced there would be.

'Oh love, I can't think of anything much worse than loving someone you can't have. But he's still Callum and still your best friend and he always will be. Better he's in your life than not at all.'

'I guess... but it just sucks.'

'There'll be the right person out there for you. I know you hate me saying it but you're so young and yet to meet so many people.'

Harper rolls her eyes and sips her tea. 'You can go now,' she says.

I grin at her and leave her to it. Both girls are everything to me. I have until tomorrow to think of a plan to get us out of this mess. It's time to head out to yoga so I grab my stuff and don't even bother saying goodbye to Jon. It doesn't feel like he'll even notice that I'm gone anyway.

The moment I reverse out onto the road, I notice headlights come on from a parked car at the side of the road behind me. My stomach lurches. I tell myself it's okay and drive away, but the car pulls away too. It's following me, driving up my rear and now it's beeping its horn. Shit. I don't know what to do. It's still light and it's a residential road. People are walking past, watching. There are witnesses. The car is still beeping its horn, I pull over hoping that it will just overtake. If it's them, they can't do anything to me in broad daylight surely.

The car overtakes slowly and pulls up in front of me. A tall man steps out and I recognise his ugly face straightaway. It's him. The same man who threatened me earlier. I'm paralysed and just about manage to press the button to open the window, but not too much.

'Hello again.' He grins through the gap in the window.

I quickly check that the light on the dashboard is on indicating that all of the car doors are locked. It is.

He looks over his shoulder then passes me a small package. I can't speak.

'A little gift for our Jason. Be a good girl and pop it in his mail. Make sure someone finds it in his cell.' He winks then strides casually back to his car. He drives away.

I suck in a huge breath. That man was actually waiting outside my house. Is he going back there now? My head is spinning. I drop the package on the passenger seat like it's burning my fingers. I need to get away from here.

The short drive into town is a blur. I'm still shaking as I park up. I pick up the package and I have a sick feeling that I know what it is. And I'm right. Drugs. Goodness knows what kind. Peeling back the brown paper reveals a bundle of white powder. I slump back in my seat and throw the package back down. There's no way that I can do this. I could be searched on the way in through the doors. I can't just put it in his mail and let it make its way into Jason's cell. I'm the one that's supposed to be checking for this stuff. How would I explain why I didn't report it? It's impossible. It wouldn't work. I don't think that the ugly man will want to hear that it's not that simple.

Mala is approaching from across the car park. She's spotted me and his waving. I thrust the package into the glove compartment. I step out to greet her.

'You sure you're feeling better?' my best friend says, greeting me with a hug. 'I said that you've not been looking right.'

I hate keeping secrets from Mala, if she found out the trouble I'm in and I didn't tell her she'd probably never forgive me. She'd be hurt; I know I would be. My eyes well up. I decide to tell her about the missing girl being found on my driveway and nothing more.

'And that's the real reason I couldn't come into work today,' I finish.

Mala links my arm. 'Well sister, this is gonna need more than a yoga session. We're walking over to Red's. There is an element of stretching involved when lifting a fruit cider.'

'But—'

'No, we're going.' She marches me away from the direction of the gym and towards the bar. I look back at my car, knowing what's in there.

'I really can only be an hour though. I have to get back to Fizz.'

A few minutes later, we are nestled into a booth inside Red's. It's quiet; it would be on a Tuesday evening. I think back to the last time we were here. It suddenly feels like a lifetime ago. Feeling carefree, drinking, laughing, and flirting with those men. I find myself flushing at the memory.

'So what's Jon's reaction to all of this?' Mala asks me.

'He's as baffled as me.' I don't want to mention that he suggested it may be something to do with where I work. I don't want Mala to start wondering that too. I know she'd advise me to report it.

'You should've just told me straight away. You know you can call me any time of night if you're in trouble or scared.'

I squeeze my friend's hand. 'I know but the police asked us to keep it quiet. just for now.'

'I can't get my head around why she was left at your house. How random is that?'

'You and me, both.' I take a gulp of my cider. It's washing down the guilt of lying. 'How's Phil after yesterday?' I feel a strong urge to change the subject.

'He's been in the job so long, I don't think it phases him anymore. He's made of tough stuff.'

'What, you haven't broken into his vulnerable

side yet?'

'Oh, he has a soft side all right... right between —'

'Whoa! Stop right there.' I laugh covering my ears.

Mala throws her head back, laughing. She downs the remainder of her drink. 'Right, next week, no excuses. Kidnap victims or not, we are toning our bums and tums at yoga. Deal?'

'Yes.' I reluctantly nod and finish my drink off too.

I thank my best friend for everything and for just being there for me like always and I wave her off from the car park. It was a temporary distraction from the package sitting in my glove box. I don't know how I'm going to get out of this mess yet but it won't be by planting drugs. I can't see a way of doing it without getting caught and losing everything including Mala. I start the engine and drive off slowly, ensuring that it doesn't look like I'm being followed. I drive up to the park and pull over. Again, I look all around me. I take the package and walk across the park and along the path to the river.

It's still light and it's a mild evening, but there's no one in sight. One final look around and I throw the package to the centre of the river. It disappears under the ripples. My stomach sinks along with it. I don't know what I'm doing. I'll tell the ugly man I've done it. Hopefully it will bide me more time. I'll do what they want. I have to. But not like this. Not this way.

CHAPTER THIRTY-NINE

Getting into work that bit earlier has paid off. I'm in before Mala. I set to rummaging through the stack of mail. Nothing. No post for Jason. I wanted the time to process it unseen if there was another photo of me, or any clue as to who or what I was dealing with. It's got me thinking again. Who is Anna West? Who is Carla to Jason? Who was the guy at Nelder Street with Carla? There is a kind of link connecting Jason to the kidnappings of local teenagers but could it really be anything to do with Anna or Carla or whoever the hell she is? This woman sends my image to Jason and, before I know it, my family is being threatened. But why would she want to keep Jason inside? I've read the letters from her; the heartfelt letters full of love and support for him.

I'm going around in circles, nauseating unrelenting circles. I might be completely off the mark with whoever these people are. I've always told Harper to stand up to her bullies and to tell someone. It's the only way to take action. This is different though, isn't it? I can't tell anyone without exposing that I went to Jason's house in the first place. There he is. I spot Jason heading towards the exit to the gardens; he's taking out the bins. I'm still on my own so take the opportunity without really thinking. I burst out from the post room and head him off before the exit to the gardens. He looks at me bemused for a moment as I can't catch my words. There's a prison guard further up the walkway watching and one visible just inside the garden. I have to be quick.

'Who is Anna West?' I blurt out.

His face drops. He goes to brush past me.

'I think she's threatening my family. She wants me to sabotage your appeal. Tell me who she is. She wants to keep you locked up and we can help each other. Who is she?'

'Do you have a screw loose or something, lady?' He starts to walk off again.

'I'm being deadly fucking serious.' I'm shocked by my own assertiveness. I glance at the guards nearby. Any moment, they could come over to check that everything's okay.

'Look, I don't know what you're on about, but you're mistaken,' Jason says, his voice calm.

'I work in the post room. Someone wants me to plant something on you to harm your appeal. They dumped a kidnapped girl on my driveway as a threat, for God's sake. I can't say yet how I know, but it's someone from your address. I'm almost sure of it.'

Jason rubs his head and is now checking to see where the guards are. He leans in a bit closer and my heart is thumping against my rib cage.

'Anna West isn't a real person,' he says, in a

hushed tone. 'I'm gay. I live with my boyfriend, Andrew, and our friend Carla lodges with us. Carla sends raunchy photos of herself along with Andrew's letters to me. He uses the pen name Anna West. I use the photos to hand out to the other guys in here. It keeps them onside. I need my time in here to go smoothly so I can get out of this shithole and back to Andrew. I shouldn't be here.'

I don't have the time to let that bombshell sink in. 'Does Carla have a grudge against you? I need to know what to do, how to stop them. Who wants to screw you over? Help me.'

'Look lady, it's not them. And I don't know who —'

'Don't tell anyone. We'll talk again.' I have to walk away. The guard standing nearest to us is now walking in our direction. I depart quickly.

I walk back into the post room and Mala is close behind. I turn and jump at her presence behind me.

'Jumpy,' she laughs, 'Boo.'

I feign a smile.

'Everything all right at home?' Mala asks.

'Yes, no more bodies on my driveway.' I try to joke, but I feel weak. I wriggle the pins and needles in my fingers. *What have I done*? I've no idea if I've done the best thing – going to Jason. I collapse into my chair with a slump. It all dawns on me now. When I went to Nelder Street asking for Anna West, it's no wonder Carla tried to send my picture to Jason. It's a made up name that only they know about – of course that set alarm bells ringing for her. *How was I to know that*? As I've tried to justify to myself over and over, I was just taking an interest in the life of the partner of a murderer. I couldn't have anticipated any of this. That's if Carla and Andrew are behind all of this. So Andrew wrote those letters. They love each other. None of this makes sense.

I realise that I should go to the police. I know their address; I could tell them everything. I did say that I'd do anything for my family to keep them safe, even if that did mean losing them when the truth comes out: losing them and my job and probably my best friend too. I don't know how I can be sure though. I don't know who the ugly man is. I could go to the police and say I've got it all wrong and then my family are still in danger and even more so. I rest my forehead on the desk.

'You okay?' Mala asks.

'I'm just so tired.' I sigh.

'The post won't read itself. Buck up, sister. And don't think I'm doing the coffee run for you again.'

I lift my head and smile at Mala. She mocks cracking a whip at me. All I know right now is that I have to try and get to Jason again and beg him not to say anything to anyone. I had hoped he'd just know who would have it in for him and that he'd know people on the outside who would sort them out for him. Isn't that the sort of thing that happens in movies and stuff? I don't know what I was hoping for, but nothing feels like the right plan. Mala is concentrating on her computer screen, working through the incoming e-mails and an idea occurs to me.

'Do you mind if I stay on the mail all day? I think less time staring at the screen today might help this headache I've got.' I ask her. We usually swap roles, so my idea won't work if I'm not the one opening the mail all day.

'Sure. You know I prefer e-mails anyway.'

I thank my friend and snatch up a piece of paper and start to write, occasionally glancing at Mala to make sure she's not taking an interest in what I'm doing.

Jason,

It's Kate from the post room. I spoke to you earlier. I'm begging you not to tell anyone what we spoke about. My family is in very real danger if I don't do what they ask. They have already given me drugs to plant in your mail. I won't do it. Please, please, please can you think of anyone who would want to harm your appeal and keep you inside? If we know who is behind this, then you can help me stop them and protect my family. I'm risking everything telling you all of this. I assumed Anna was your girlfriend because of the letters, and the reason I suspected her is because my image was sent from Carla to you from your address. I intercepted it because I was scared. She had my photo. She tracked me down and then I'm getting threatened. Are you sure it's not her? Please don't confront her yet just in case. I need to hear your thoughts. Write me a letter and address it to Felicity Harper. That way I'll know it's for me. It will land in my hands. Put this letter in the envelope too so it can never be found. I'll destroy both of them. I'm begging for your help.

Kate.

I stuff the letter inside an envelope, seal it, then open it again so it looks like I've checked it. I scribble Jason's name and the prison's address on the front. I take a stamp and stick it on. The letter looks unremarkable and hopefully it will get passed on to him without any suspicion. Mala is still typing away, oblivious. My clammy fingers set to processing the bulk of mail in front of me. I can't work fast enough; the sooner this mail gets distributed the sooner I can hear back from Jason. I just pray that he replies today.

'The wing is rowdy this morning, isn't it,' Mala pipes up.

She's right. Even though we are set a fair way back from the cells, raised voices and commotion can be heard.

'We don't need a repeat performance of Monday, do we?' I say.

'Hell no to that,' Mala stands up and stretches her legs and arms. She peers out of the door. 'There's the man of the moment, Mr Sawyer.'

My heart skips a beat. I look up in time to see him stroll past. He looks at me and carries on walking.

'That man can do no wrong in my eyes now. He ain't no killer to me. He's too good. What he did for Phil... Well, it doesn't add up does it? Phil could be dead if he'd been stabbed—'

'You can't keep up the what-ifs. It didn't happen.'

'No, and all thanks to Jason. If I could hug him, I would, and you know I'd never go near any of these dirty criminals. So that's saying something.' Mala sits back down.

I actually have no idea how I'm going to keep all of this up, all of this lying and hiding everything. Mala has no idea and I want to reach out to her now and break down and tell her everything. She'll be disappointed in me and I don't want to drag my best friend into my sorry mess. I've landed enough people that I love in danger. I burst into tears.

Mala is quick to wrap her arm around me. She rubs my back.

'Should you be here? Is it what happened the other night?' She hands me a tissue.

I nod and take a breath. 'It scared me. I'm overtired that's all.'

'This isn't like you. C'mon, get it together. The police will catch whoever kidnapped that girl and with a bit of luck, they'll end up in here and we can make sure they have a miserable existence.'

She has no idea how much I do want them to suffer.

'Dry your eyes. I'll go grab us a coffee. How about we take your girls somewhere this weekend? Have a fun girls' day out? It's been a while since we've done that. Start thinking and it will give us something to look forward to.' Mala heads out of the postroom.

I take the letter that I've just written to Jason and think about destroying it. It's no good; I've already spoken to him now; it's done. I have to follow through with it whether I've done the right thing or not. He has to see this letter. I shove it back in the processed pile of mail. I carry on opening and reading through the rest of the post, none of it holding the same interest anymore.

**

The day is going painfully slowly. It's just after three-fifteen p.m, so just under a couple of hours left. Jason's reply wasn't in the last batch of outgoing mail handed to me, but I didn't expect it to be; it was too soon. I've watched him go in and out of the gardens a number of times throughout the day already. I can go days without spotting him at all, but today, there he is: everywhere, working hard, keeping busy, doing everything except being in his cell, reading his bloody mail. If I don't get his reply before the end of the day, I run the risk of the letter landing in different hands, and then everything is screwed. The day is going painfully, nauseatingly slowly. We do usually get another batch of outgoing mail around this time of day – so any time now. I discreetly cross my fingers and silently beg.

If this mess disappears, I vow to never be this much of an idiot again. I'll be a better wife, I'll leave this job, find something else like Jon has always wanted me to. I'll never risk putting my family in danger again. Mala will always be my best friend; I'll see her all of the time, it won't matter that we won't be working together anymore. I think back to lunchtime and getting choked up hearing Harper and Fizz's voices over the phone. They both said a quick hello and just knowing that they are safe and happy filled me with enormous relief that I found hard to contain.

'Five o'clock, hurry up already.' Mala yawns, stretching her toned arms out. She wheels her chair over to me. 'You thought of a plan for the weekend yet?'

I don't know how to answer. I'd love nothing more than to go out and have fun with Mala and the girls, but I need to keep Fizz and Harper safe inside the house.

'Hold that thought,' she says. before I can speak. 'Incoming hot man alert.'

I swivel round to see Phil's face at the door

window. He lets himself in and hands me a batch of outgoing mail. My heart stops. I'm no longer aware of the chit-chat between Mala and Phil. I'm now completely frozen in time. My heartbeat quickens and I'm back on full alert. I need Phil to leave so I can sift through this pile of mail.

'Put her down, Phil, she's got work to do.' I try to sound like I'm joking.

Phil holds his hands up in protest to show he's not even touching her.

'Lock her up,' Mala says to Phil, pointing at me.

Phil jangles his bunch of keys and laughs. 'I best get back anyway. Call you after work,' he says to Mala.

Mala mouths, 'Okay, love you.'

'Whoa, this is all escalating quickly,' I say to my friend. 'You love him now?'

'Hush, sister, you've work to do.' Mala shoots me a wicked grin and slides her chair back to her desk.

I waste no time. I flick through the mail. There it is: *To Felicity Harper.* I tear it open and remove the contents with shaking hands. I'm instantly relieved to see the letter I had written to him. I know I can now destroy it. I put a lot of faith in a criminal I don't know at all to follow my instructions. I unfold the other piece of notepaper and start to read:

Dear Kate,
I'll tell you straight out. I've spoken to Andrew

and my friend Carla over the phone already and asked them outright about what you said. No reason for me not to. I trust them completely. They both sounded shocked and confused at the thought and have no idea who could be threatening you and me. But it's definitely not them. It might be the family of the man I stabbed? I'm no killer, you know. We're good people that got caught up in some crap which turned nasty. I need out of here and I'm scared now that someone's trying to put a stop to it. I've worked hard, kept my head down and done everything to make life in here as easy as I can. Giving inmates money, giving them photos of women. Andrew and Carla have helped me with all of this. We're close knit. You have to tell the police. Do something. If you don't, I'll have to talk. I'm not risking my release for nothing.

Jason.

Shit. I shove the letter back inside the envelope as if it were burning my fingers. I need it destroyed and I don't have the time to worry if Mala will question what I'm shredding. I just do it. The mechanisms whir away as the letter goes through and Mala doesn't bat an eyelid at me.

I absently start looking at the rest of the post so it looks like I'm working and that the colour isn't fast draining from my face. Jason has already spoken to his boyfriend and Carla. He had better be right about them or else they'll now know that I haven't followed through on their instructions. Harper and Fizz's lives will now be in danger. The office is closing in on me – suffocating. I can't let this happen.

CHAPTER FORTY

I see a grey car parked opposite my house as I pull into the street. Even though I've not seen that particular car before, I know it's one of them. I suspect every car that's following me now, but I'm certain that whoever is sitting in the car is waiting for me. I slow down to a crawl and pull up kerbside, just out of view of the house. I wait a moment. I'm right. I see a tall guy step from the grey car and he heads towards me. It's the ugly guy. He's going to want to know if I planted the drugs and what the outcome was. I can't tell him that the stash is at the bottom of the river.

I wind the window down. The ugly man gives me a toothless grin.

'I have something for you,' he says, handing me a black hoodie.

I unfold it and hold it up. I know it straight away. It's Harper's. It has Slipknot's logo on the front – her favourite band.

'How did you get this?' I say, with my lower lip trembling and a shaky voice.

'That careless girl of yours left it at the park earlier. Lucky I was there to pick it up.'

'Just leave us alone.' My eyes start to burn.

'I can't do that, love. You see, you didn't plant them drugs did you?'

'I did, I… I—'

'Save it. Give me your phone number.' The ugly man discreetly flashes a knife blade at me.

My dry mouth barely gets the numbers out as he punches them into his phone. A moment later, my phone beeps and he tells me to take a look. I unlock the screen and open the messages to see a video clip. It's a fairly close-up clip of Harper and Fizz kicking a ball to each other at the park. The phone alerts me to another message and I open the second video clip. I immediately gasp, throwing my hand to my mouth. I throw my phone down. The horrifying scene has me retching.

'Is that real?' I sob. I can't hold back the tears.

'It's going to be that careless girl of yours next. I won't just have her jumper. I'll have her too. She'll be inside it and then lots of men will be inside her.' He sneers and then spits on the floor. 'Don't go snitching to Sawyer again, and if you don't fuck him over then it'll be that girl of yours getting fucked over. Give me your phone.' He flashes the blade again.

I hand my phone back to him, unable to look him in the eye. He shows me that he's deleted the video clips. He smirks and walks away. I reach for a carrier bag that's stuffed inside the glove compartment and vomit into it. What I've just seen will not be Harper. I'm not sure if that clip was the girl found on my driveway, but the young girl had blonde hair. Her face was hidden by some monster on top of her. *What he was doing to her...* I retch again, bringing up the last of the contents of my stomach. That's not going to be Harper. I'll do absolutely anything. I wish I'd just planted the drugs. But then I have to rationalise that it was highly likely that I'd get caught and then I'd be the one in trouble and Jason would be no worse off. The girls would be in danger and I'd be locked up unable to help keep them safe. *Keep them safe.* I dig my own nails into my palms. I've done nothing to keep them safe. I hate myself for everything that's happening. I pull up onto my driveway and the grey car hasn't moved. He's still there.

'You took the girls to the park?' I snap at Jon, who has his feet up in the lounge.

'Yes, and?'

I've just walked through the door and I suddenly hope that he doesn't question how I know that.

'I don't know. It just doesn't feel safe,' I change my tone, now aware that I might give something away.

'You're being ridiculous,' Jon jumps up from the sofa. 'I'm not keeping the girls locked up.'

'When are the security cameras arriving?' I ask.

'A couple of days.'

I bite my tongue. I don't know why he just couldn't go to a store and buy them there and then, so they'd be installed quicker. I want to scream that at him but I can't let on the danger that we are in.

'Is there something you're not telling me?' Jon looks at me, searching my face.

'I'm just on edge, that's all, and I'm tired.'

'There's no reason to suspect that there's anything to worry about, okay?' Jon squeezes my shoulders. 'I'll start dinner, although I won't be eating. I'm heading out with Alan for food.'

'What?'

'It's a work thing. Can't I even leave the house now?'

I throw my bag down and storm away. He follows.

'Are you having an affair?' The words just tumble from my mouth. The words I've wanted to get out for a long time now. I can't see why else he would go out when his daughters have been frightened by the recent events.

Jon looks at me blankly. 'What? Where did that come from? Are you serious? You're really asking me—'

'You keep going out for dinner. Who is she? The girls have had a scare and you're sodding off out. Who is she?'

'It's Alan and we're preparing for a big meeting next week. I've not been at work, have I? And I'm not going in this week to be with the girls because they've had a scare. How dare you accuse me of not putting them first? What the hell has gotten into you?'

My temples are pulsating. I have a list of reasons why I suspect him of having an affair. He lied about the hotel he was staying at; he lied about the last time he went out for dinner. He hasn't come near me in months. I'm about to reel off this list to him, but Harper appears.

'Oh my God, are you two arguing again? Wait is that my...?' She takes the hoodie that I'm still clutching. 'It is. Where did you find it?'

'Just outside on the ground,' I say hesitantly.

'Could've sworn I left it at the park. Weird.' Harper barges past us to get into the kitchen.

'We'll talk about this later.' Jon glares at me. 'Go take a shower and sort your head out.'

Once more, I find myself locked away in the bathroom in tears. I perch on the toilet, head in hands. I heard Fizzy singing to herself as I passed her room and couldn't bring myself to say hello to her, not in this state. I've let her and Harper down in the worst way possible. If Jon had been more affectionate and I didn't suspect him of having an affair, none of this would have happened. I wouldn't have got so curious about the lives of someone else, leading to all of this. I need to think. I blow my nose and take some slow deep breaths. The ugly man knew that I'd snitched to Jason. Those were his words. So it has to be coming from Carla and Andrew. Jason had phoned them and told them and now this. But Jason was adamant that they were tight-knit. Those were his words. It doesn't make sense. Do

Carla and Jason's own boyfriend secretly hate him and are glad he's out of the picture? But then why would Andrew go through the bother of writing all of those lovely letters? Why would they both still help him out by sending money and photos to help keep him onside with his inmates? They could easily cut him off, being locked away for murder.

If it's not Carla and Andrew, then who? Unless Jason confided about what I said to him to another prisoner, who happens to know what's going on, and it got out that way. I feel like I'm sending myself crazy. I turn the shower on. I need to wash away being so close to that disgusting ugly man. If the grey car is still outside, I could just call the police, but then I don't know what evidence there is. If the police drag him from the car and take him in for questioning, I don't know how many other people I'm dealing with. I also know where Carla and Andrew live so I could send the police there, but how can I when I'm not certain it's them? Again, there's no evidence to arrest them for anything. It would be my word against theirs, wouldn't it? No, I can't call the police. That video clip proved beyond doubt how dangerous these people are. The image is haunting me. That won't be Harper. I turn the heat up in the shower. I need to feel the hot water sting my skin. I'll find a way to do what they want.

When I step out of the shower I hear a gentle

knock on the door.

'I'll be out in a sec, Fizzy.' I know it'll be her. She'll have noticed that I haven't said hello to her yet since coming in from work.

I quickly towel dry and wrap a bathrobe around myself. I open the door to see Fizz sitting crossed-legged on the carpet, waiting patiently for me. I grasp her hands and help her up and she wraps her arms around my middle. Her touch feels extra reassuring.

'How was your day?'

'We went to the park and me and Harper played football.'

I catch my breath. I think about that disgusting man watching them, filming them.

'Has your dad got any more plans for you to go out anywhere for the rest of the week? Has he said?'

Fizz shrugs. 'We might go and see Nanny.'

I exhale. That sounds safer than being out in the open right now. 'Whenever you're outside, you stay close to your dad, okay?'

My stepdaughter nods and she takes my hand, leading me downstairs.

'I smell dinner,' She giggles.

I leave her to walk ahead to the kitchen. I divert into the living room and take a look outside. I can no longer see the grey car, or any car parked opposite. Relief washes over me for the time being. I join the others in the kitchen.

Jon is removing some breaded chicken

steaks and chips from the oven. He doesn't acknowledge me standing there as he plates up the food and places it on the dining table. Harper and Fizz sit down to tuck in.

Jon picks his keys up. 'I'll be back later.' He still can't look me in the eye.

'Have a good time,' I mutter. I hug myself close. I hate this.

I join the girls and push the food around my plate. The image from the video clip is nauseating.

Harper puts her fork down, 'You should cut Dad some slack, you know,' she says. 'He works really hard and he's looking after us.'

I can't argue against her opinion because she doesn't know the full story; she doesn't know everything. She's always going to take her dad's side, no matter what I do for her or have done for her in the past. I wonder how Harper would feel if Jon was having an affair and she knew. Would she care about my feelings at all?

I think back to when Mala and I went to try and catch Jon out at the pub and it turned out he wasn't even there. I'd be doing it again now if I didn't have more important things to worry about. Suddenly, Jon having an affair seems nothing in comparison to being blackmailed by some gangsters.

'I know,' I say gently to Harper.

I notice Fizz is now pushing her food around. 'I haven't forgotten about asking your dad again about getting a dog. I reckon the three of us can persuade him.' I try and lighten the mood.

Fizzy's eyes instantly light up and she takes a mouthful of chicken again.

'Can we get a Doberman?' Harper asks.

'Erm, I was thinking something a bit smaller and cuter,' I laugh, almost choking on a chip.

'I'm going to call it Kylie,' Fizz says with her mouth full.

Harper kicks her sister under the table and Fizz's hand flies to her mouth.

'I think it's a brilliant name for a dog.' I wink at Fizz.

I pause for a moment in thought. 'I want you both to know that I'm going to start looking for a new job. The stress is affecting everything, and I want us to be happier as a family.'

Harper gasps. 'Please don't do it because of things I've said. You love your job, I see that now.'

'No, it's not that, love, I'm tired of it. I'll find something less stressful.'

Harper is looking at me unsure, so I reassure her again that it's fine. I look at her pretty, pale face with her huge eyes and suddenly she's in that video clip and I can no longer swallow my food. It does spark an idea and I let the seed grow into a plan that I can put into action first thing tomorrow. I have to do it; there's no time and there's no choice.

CHAPTER FORTY-ONE

'Like I said, give me until the end of the day and I'll get it done, then leave my family alone.' I hang up on the ugly man, not giving him the chance to get one more threat in. I get the message. I'm giving in to him, to them, to whomever. I look around the prison car park and ahead to the building. Security is everywhere and even though I'm sitting in my car, I'm paranoid that someone heard every word of my conversation. Eyes, ears, cameras are everywhere in a place like this. My heart is in my throat, but I remind myself that Jason Sawyer is a criminal. Even if he isn't guilty of murder, he's guilty of violence, of dealing in drugs. He's connected to criminals; it's the lifestyle he leads. This is what happens. His life was never more exciting than mine. Anna West's life was never more exciting and it turns out she's not even real. My mundane existence is more real and so much better than theirs and all of this. I see that now.

I step from the car, still convinced that I'm being watched and that someone knows. I'm through security, I've signed out my keys and I make my way through the gauntlet of locked doors. I don't turn to the post room though; I briefly wave at Mala who's letting herself in, then

I head straight to the office to see Phil, who is today's custodial manager. He's there chatting to another officer and a couple of inmates.

'Can I talk to you?' I butt into the conversation. Phil looks concerned into my pleading eyes.

'Excuse us a moment.' Phil gestures for the small group to step away from the office.

The glass walls of the office aren't as private as I'd like but I know we can talk now without being overheard. I look at the hustle of the prisoners getting ready to head for breakfast and I spot him. Jason. I turn, shield my face and collapse into a chair. My eyes are full of tears and Phil is quick to pass me a tissue.

'What's going on, Kate?'

His voice is warm and he pulls his chair closer to me. I see his caring side now and I understand Mala's attraction to him. My tears are for many different reasons, but it helps for what I'm about to do. I suck in some air and dab my eyes with the tissue.

'Do you remember, a little over a week ago, I came in here with a nosebleed?'

Phil nods, listening carefully.

My voice breaks again. 'I'm finding this hard as I should've said something straight away.'

'It's okay; take your time.' Phil passes me more tissues.

'It's just... I felt so stupid and I knew I put myself in that situation.'

'What happened?'

'I unlocked the staff toilets for Jason so he could go in to clean. I wouldn't have gone inside with him—'

Phil raises his eyebrows and sits up to attention.

'But my nose just started bleeding and he beckoned me in and handed me some tissues. At first I thought he was just being nice and as I went to walk away...' I suck in more air to steady my shaking voice. 'He grabbed my arms, he grabbed me between my legs and then my—' I put a protective arm across my chest.

Phil drags his hands down his face and looks thoughtful for a moment, thinking back to that day. 'I do recall you looked a bit shaken up, but I assumed you would with a heavy nosebleed. I really wish you'd said something—'

'He threatened me; he said he was handy with a knife and when he wins his appeal he'll come looking for me and my family.'

'Have you told anyone else this... Mala?'

I shake my head, 'I shouldn't have put myself in a situation where I was alone with a prisoner. I didn't want to get in trouble.'

'You should know that wouldn't happen. This is not your fault. I have to ask: is there a reason you're speaking up now? Has he done anything else?'

'No. Mala keeps singing his praises after he helped protect you during the riot. Yes, he did a good thing, but he's dangerous. I couldn't keep listening to it. After what he said, I knew there was a strong chance that he is guilty of killing that guy. He could walk free and kill again.'

'Look,' Phil says gently, 'we'll have to investigate this and file a report. I'll arrange for you to check in with the welfare team. For now, do you want to go home?'

'No, I need to work. I just need that piece of shit away from me.'

Phil half-smiles at me. 'We'll pull him in. Don't worry.'

I stand and thank him. He tells me that I've done the right thing and that I can go to him anytime. Sadness washes over me at his kind words. I picture going to my own husband for support, knowing that I'll only get the cold shoulder. I know I may have to tell Jon all of this but I'll try to avoid it; all of this lying is eating me up inside as it is. I'll have to confide in Mala though. Even though Phil may take confidentiality seriously, I can't completely trust that he won't spill everything to his girlfriend.

I greet my best friend with a coffee which I picked up on the way back.

'Finally decided to rock up then, sister?' Mala takes the cup with a look of mock disapproval. She sees that I'm not smiling and her expression quickly changes to that of concern. 'You okay?'

I sit down, my shaking legs unable to hold me up any longer. I'm all too aware that my lies are appalling and now having to repeat them to Mala makes me feel sick. But I'm desperate and my hand is forced. There's no going back now. I relay the events of Jason groping me to Mala and she sits and listens with her mouth aghast.

'Bastard,' she says. As Phil did, she takes some time to think back to that day. 'I do remember you having blood on your collar from your nosebleed and you were flustered, and thinking about it, you haven't been yourself since. This explains everything.' She then looks cross. 'Why have you kept this to yourself all this time? You know you can tell me anything. We've been friends for decades. I don't call you "sister" for nothing. All this time?'

'I felt embarrassed and stupid. I thought I'd brought it on myself being alone with a prisoner in a space where there aren't cameras.'

Mala is right. We've been friends for decades; she's been there for me through some of the most painful moments of my life. I'm scared that she will see straight through me but as I'm sitting here talking, I feel like I'm starting to believe my own story.

'You are stupid for not speaking up.' Mala gives me a brief tight hug and lets go, 'You can't let these filthy criminals get away with shit like this. Goes to show you can't trust any of them. I thought I had Sawyer pegged as a decent person after what he did for Phil. In fact, Phil has always said that he's never bought into his good guy act.'

'It got harder for me to tell you after you were

singing his praises.'

'Yes, I'm grateful for what he did, but there's no excuse for this. He's still a criminal and he deserves to rot.'

'Well, it's out in the open now. I'll be seeing the welfare team and Jason will be in the shit.'

'You've certainly been through a lot in the last couple of weeks. Has any more been said about the girl found at your house?'

I shake my head. 'No, nothing. Until they catch her kidnappers, I don't suppose I'll ever find out why she was left there.' I take a gulp of my cooling coffee. My mouth is drying out from the lies. 'We need to get some work done. The post won't sort itself. I need to take my mind off it all for a while.'

Mala hugs me again and slides her chair back to her desk.

I routinely flick through a batch of mail and stop at one addressed to Jason. The excitement and the intrigue of reading his post has now been replaced with nausea. I feel like I can't take any more as I tear it open.

Hey Gorgeous,

I'm writing this straight after our phone call. I know you wouldn't let me get my hopes up over the phone and that's the last time I let you shush me. You will win your appeal and when you're out, we have so much to look forward to. I'm planning a Christmas getaway for us. You will be out by then.

How does some winter sunshine sound? Or we could be carefree in snowy Lapland. Fancy getting pulled along by some huskies? We will do this and more. You need to believe it's going to happen and start looking forward to the future. Nothing and nobody can stop us. Good will win. Every piece of me believes in you. Oh, and I forgot to mention that I'm taking your mother shopping for a new dress for Aunt Trish's wedding. God help me. I'll send you the pics. Oh, and Kylie sends her love.

Love always A x

Along with the letter from Andrew is another photo of a pair of breasts cupped by a lacy red bra. I now know the photo is of Carla and not Anna West. I have to read the words a few times over. I don't get it. These aren't the words of someone who hates their other half and wishes for them to be incarcerated forever. Carla is still showing her support too by sending more pictures. It can't be them behind all of this. *Good will win.* I mull this over. Jason could still be innocent of murder and was simply protecting his niece from kidnapping and gang rape. Anyone would do the same. Haven't I just proved what I'd do for my girls? I won't let the guilt of what I've just done eat into me. Just like him, I have to protect the ones that I love.

I take a copy of the letter and finish logging it on the system. I quickly move on to the rest of the mail, keen to push away any doubts. Mala is using the shredder and the internal phone starts to ring. The noises are setting every one of my nerve endings on fire. The walls are closing in again and I know today is going to drag.

'It's Phil, for you,' Mala says, offering me the phone.

I feel the colour drain from my face as I take the handset. I say hello and listen to him for a few moments before hanging up.

'I'm so sorry,' I say to Mala. 'I've been called for a quick meeting about everything. I don't know what Jason has said, but I have to answer a few questions.'

'I wouldn't worry. Phil will have your back no matter what that prick says. Stay strong. I'll sort us some cakes for lunchtime, okay?'

Mala blows me a kiss and I feel like I'm going to need more than cake to get me through the day this time.

CHAPTER FORTY-TWO
Gregg

'Do we have to keep meeting at this shithole now?' Gregg says to Riley, who greets him at the door to Charlie Coleman's house.

'What can I say? The place is growing on me. I have you to thank for sourcing this location.'

'What's so urgent, Carla?'

The redhead folds her arms and Gregg feels the sting of her glare.

'Okay. Riley, what's so urgent?' He rephrases his question, knowing the woman's hatred for her Christian name. He decides that he shouldn't deliberately try and wind her up yet until he finds out what the deal is. Besides, he can think of other choice names he could call her which she'd like much less.

Riley beckons him to follow her inside. Once in the kitchen, she gets straight to the point.

'We're taking the Midwinter girls.'

'Black, two sugars please,' Gregg sits down.

Riley looks irritated and fills the kettle.

'So where is Coleman? You're well at home here. You fucking him now?'

'You can think whatever the hell you like.'

Gregg relaxes further back into his chair. 'So what's developed?'

'Andrew had a phone call from Jason. Kate Midwinter has accused him of sexual assault and said that he's threatened to knife her and her family.' Riley pours the coffee and hands one to Gregg.

'Nice,' Gregg says. 'If anything will shit on his appeal, then that's it, right? So what's the problem?'

'The hare-brained woman had already given Jason the heads up that she was being blackmailed into ruining him. He spilled all when he was questioned so now it's his word against hers. Jase has also been advised that even with this charge against him, it wouldn't necessarily stop the re-investigation into Michael's murder. He can still be cleared of that regardless.'

Gregg mulls this over, 'So what was the point in all this again? Why get this woman to try balls up his appeal if nothing would make a difference?'

Riley all but slams her mug down, 'Sawyer killed Michael. Is that not enough for you? We look after our own, don't we?'

Gregg wonders what Riley's definition of *looking after our own* actually is. It's not like she hasn't screwed him over enough times already.

'Least we caused old Sawyer a bit of shit. What say we leave it? All of this is messy, right? I ain't risking my ass to stare at Sawyer over porridge.'

'No, we're taking the girls.'

'I'm telling you, it's too risky.'

Riley leans into him and cocks her head to the side. 'Where did your balls go, huh? They'll fetch a good price, and that Midwinter bitch deserves it.'

Gregg rubs his forehead. 'I'm gonna need a bigger cut of the profits.'

'Done,' Riley says, holding out her hand.

Gregg doesn't take it. He takes a glug of coffee instead. Riley withdraws her hand and runs it through her hair.

'Let's plan. We need to act fast,' she says.

Their thoughts are interrupted as Charlie walks in. 'Well this looks cosy,' he sneers, making a beeline straight for the fridge. He swipes out a bottle of beer and rips the cap off with his teeth. 'Want to tell me what's going on here?'

Riley gets up to help herself to a beer too, 'It's time to step things up; we're planning on snatching the Midwinter girls.'

'And you're still including this buffoon?' Charlie gestures to Gregg.

'He's good at what he does, okay?' Riley answers.

Charlie starts to pace the kitchen, 'Who is he to you anyway? You, making your cosy little plans the two of you.'

Riley stands next to Gregg, bending her knees so that her face is level with his, 'What's the matter? Can't you see the family resemblance?'

'You're kiddin' me,' Charlie scoffs.

'That's right, you're fucking my sister.' Gregg winks at him.

Charlie howls, spitting out his beer as he does. 'Some family business you two started up, Christ.' He turns to Riley. 'Don't forget whose house and security guys you're using. Keep me in the loop. No decisions are made without me, got it? I need a leak.' Charlie walks off laughing, 'Brother and freakin' sister.'

'What's the matter, Carla, your crown slipping?'

Riley takes a large carving knife from the stand and points it at her brother. 'Men don't control me.'

Gregg raises his hands in submission and Riley places the knife back down. He wouldn't put it past her to stab him one of these days. She was dealt a cruel blow of a start in life thanks to their crack whore of a mother. This is the way of life she's always known and she fought all her life to take control and dominate. Gregg is all too aware of the times his sister has bailed him out each time he found himself on his knees. But his gratitude is wearing thin. Dangerously thin.

'Tell you what, Carla. You get back to me when you and Charlie decide what you're doing. I've got places to be.'

Gregg leaves the room and hears what sounds like a cupboard door being kicked and he smirks to himself. He'll wait for her phone call and he'll be ready to take the Midwinter girls. He also promises himself it'll be the very last job he ever does for his sister. He drives away feeling content in the late afternoon sunshine.

CHAPTER FORTY-THREE

I can't take any more. The text message says to meet the ugly man at 17.30, at the lay-by along Mile Lane. It's a remote lane and not on the route I'd normally take home. My stomach and heart sink. Mala waves from her car as she drives past me; a few others are also leaving the car park. I can't bring myself to start the engine. Today has sucked the life from me. I've done what I can; I can't do anymore. It's now Jason's word against mine and so far I feel like the management is on my side. Jason can't prove that I spoke with him or that we wrote back and forth to each other. It was all destroyed. I sat there and looked Phil in the eyes and denied all knowledge of being blackmailed to hinder Jason's appeal. *He's a disgusting liar,* I said again and again. Perhaps ugly man just wants to find out what I've done today. It has to be enough. I don't have the strength for anymore. I'm not a calculated criminal mastermind. I don't know what I'm doing.

I start the car, press the accelerator, then stall the engine, forgetting to put it into gear. I don't know why I have to meet him down some remote lane. Being seen in public during broad daylight hasn't stopped him from approaching me yet.

There's nothing inside the car that I can use as a weapon; it's just another thing I've overlooked. I have gangsters after me and I have no protection in the car. This is a far cry from the movies where people in this situation seem to just have their shit together. I start the car again.

The clock reads 17.26 as I slowly drive along Mile Lane, keeping an eye out for the lay-by. I round a bend and there it is. I can't miss the black Mazda that's parked there. It's him. I pull up behind and the ugly man steps from his car and my skin instantly crawls and itches.

'Get out the car,' he says.

I think about the girls back home and think that I don't care what happens to me now. I got into this whole mess; he can do what he wants to me as long as he leaves the girls alone. My trembling legs barely hold me up as I step from the car.

'Well, haven't you been a good girl?' He grins, his smile making him look more sinister if that was possible. 'You played a good card, accusing old Sawyer of sexual assault.'

'How do you know all this?'

The man steps into me. His face is now against my cheek. I can feel his tobacco breath through his rubbery cracked lips. He places his hand between my legs.

'Did it make you all hot, imagining Sawyer's hands all over you?'

'I'll scream.'

Ugly man backs away laughing, then spits. 'That was payment for the drugs you threw away.' He heads back to his car and opens the door.

'Is that it now? Will you leave my family alone?' I shout, the fear evident in my plea.

'You upheld your end of the bargain. I'm going to miss our chats.' He blows me a kiss, smacking his lips together as he does, then gets in the car.

I will him to drive away and he does. I fall back against my car and let out a guttural sob, catching it with my hands. I fumble with the door handle and then the keys in the ignition, trying to breathe through the pressure in my throat. I have to get home. I have to hug my stepdaughters tight and I have to wash away the stench and touch of that vulgar man. He's leaving us alone; they are leaving us alone. The rest of the drive home takes me longer; I take two wrong turnings unable to concentrate. How did he know about today already? Jason had the opportunity to phone home; he'd fill his boyfriend in, wouldn't he? Who else would know? I talked through everything with Phil. Who would Phil know? Who would he tell? It's not possible is it – that Phil is in on it and has been feeding info back to the gangsters? But if these people knew Phil, why wouldn't they just get him to set Jason up? They needed someone on the inside, didn't they? I want to slap myself hard around the face, to knock the paranoia out of me.

I arrive home and relief fills me to find there are no cars outside spying on our house. I burst through the door to my startled husband.

'You're late back,' he says. He looks at me for a moment. 'Have you been crying?'

'Hayfever, that's all. Just stood chatting to Mala for a while after we finished.'

'You see enough of her during the day, don't you?'

I muster a smile and head upstairs.

'Hey Fizzy,' I greet my youngest stepdaughter with a big hug.

'You smell funny,' she says, pressed in my embrace.

I let her go. 'I'm hot and sweaty. I'll take a shower. Have you had a good day?'

'Bit bored, but alright. Harper is on the phone to Callum again. You can't go in there yet.'

I pull a mock worried expression, 'Does she sound happy or mad?'

Fizz giggles, 'Callum is coming home from holiday tomorrow, so she's happy.'

I exaggerate a big sigh of relief. 'I'll see her after my shower. Apparently I smell really bad.'

Fizzy holds her nose and laughs. 'Do you want my special perfume?' she says, still holding her nose so she sounds funny.

I bend down to her level. 'I'd love that.'

Fizz slides out her box from underneath her bed and fishes out her bottle of *Reach for the Stars* perfume. I hold my wrist out and she gently pumps some of the scent onto my skin.

'Perfect,' I say, holding my wrists up to my nose.

Fizz looks satisfied and places the perfume bottle carefully back in the box and slides it back under the bed.

'Why don't you go and see if your dad needs help with dinner? I'll be down very soon.'

'Okay,' she says, and skips out of the room.

I lock myself in the bathroom. The reality is the perfume doesn't hide the stench of that bastard and I rip away my uniform. I pray he meant what he said and they would stay away. I can't think about what will happen if my accusations against Jason don't come to anything. What if they come back for me, for my family? I'll hand my notice in at work tomorrow. It doesn't matter that I don't yet have another job to go to. I can't face it anymore. If I don't work there, they can't blackmail me. I have to take myself out of the situation. I'll tell Jon it's stress. It's making me ill. He knows that I haven't been myself lately. He never liked me working there anyway. I have to get out and the sooner the better.

CHAPTER FORTY-FOUR
Harper

Harper stirs, stretches, and slowly opens her eyes. As her thoughts come into focus, she sits bolt upright wide awake. *Callum is coming home today.* She pads over to the bathroom, passing her dad on the way.

'Ah, the undead is awake,' her dad mocks.

Harper runs a hand through her messy black hair. 'Has Kate already gone to work?'

'She left about twenty minutes ago.'

'Are we doing anything today?'

'No plans, why? Oh, I know, lover boy is back today, isn't he?'

'You're gross.' Harper pushes past her dad and shuts herself in the bathroom.

Moments later, a piercing scream comes from Felicity's room. Harper bolts from the bathroom; her dad close behind. Hurrying into Felicity's room, they find her sitting up in bed plastered in sweat and shaking all over. Her dad places a hand on her forehead.

'Bad dream, sweetheart? You're okay.' He takes her into a hug but Felicity lashes out thumping at his arms.

'It's okay, little sis,' Harper soothes, helping to gently prise her away from her dad, but the seven-year-old continues to lash out.

'Felicity, stop it.'

'Don't yell at her,' Harper continues to try and stroke her sister's hair, 'Shh, it's okay.'

Jon pulls back, allowing Felicity to relax into her big sister's arms.

'Stupid dream, you're safe now.' Harper soothes.

'I'll make you both a cuppa,' Jon says, leaving them to it.

'Want to tell me about your dream?' Harper asks her sister as she feels her trembling body relaxing.

Harper is not surprised that Felicity doesn't answer. Her sister does, however, lean across to her bedside drawers and pull out a sketch pad and pencil. She does a rough sketch of a large person filling the whole page. She draws an angry face on him. Harper studies it for a second.

'He looks like a bad, scary, old man, but you know what?' Harper takes the pencil and adds to the picture. 'There.' She shows her sister what she's drawn. A picture of herself kicking the man between the legs. 'That's sorted him out.'

Felicity manages a chuckle, then she screws up the page and throws it across the room.

'Good girl,' Harper says. 'Right, I'm going to bring that cuppa up to you.'

Harper joins her dad in the kitchen. She notices that he looks fed up.

'Did she say anything?' he asks her.

Harper shakes her head. 'Are you okay?'

'I just want my daughter to talk to me.' Jon drags his hands down his face.

There's a knock at the front door. Harper continues to make the tea whilst her dad goes to see who it is. She stops stirring the hot drinks and her heart stops, something's not right. She hears a thud, a commotion, something. She wearily steps to the kitchen door. Another thud, a groan. Her hands start to tremble. 'Dad?' She spots the front door wide open. 'Dad?' She's suddenly met with two men in balaclavas. They storm at her. Before she has a chance to scream, they are both on her, clamping her mouth, forcing her hands behind her back and tying them together. She sees another man head up the stairs. Harper's eyes bulge as she desperately tries to scream through the gag. The men are too strong. They march her past the living room but they halt for a brief second to allow her to see her dad collapsed on the floor, tied up and gagged with blood oozing from his temple. She hears her sister screaming, and moments later, Felicity is being bundled down the stairs by the third man. She's gagged and restrained, sobbing hysterically. They are both forced towards a black car with blacked-out windows, which is parked on the driveway. One of the men opens the boot and Felicity is thrown inside. The door is shut. Harper wriggles and squirms but the men are too strong, their grip crushing against her skin. Her head is forced down and she's shoved into the back of the car. One of the men climbs in next to her, whilst the other two jump in the front. The car wheel spins and speeds away.

The masked man leans closer into Harper, 'Don't worry your pretty little head. We'll look after you.'

The three men start to jeer to each other.

'Smoothly done, lads.'

'Piece of cake.'

'Told you it would be.'

They're driving through the town centre and Harper is silently pleading for someone to see her. The commute traffic is heavy, there are a number of people passing by on foot, but no one can see in through the blacked-out windows. Harper's nostrils flare as she rapidly intakes the air. She has to get to her sister; she's going to be terrified in the boot. Why have these men taken them? She's too terrified to think about where they're going and why. There's no time. She thinks about Felicity's drawing of her bad dream. Harper promised her that she was okay. She kicked the bad man in the picture and protected her sister, but this was real and she was powerless and failing her.

The driver accelerates as they take the slip road to the motorway: cars, buildings, trees now whooshing past. She has to get out. Harper twists herself slightly so that her bound-up hands can feel for the door handle. She hooks her finger over the handle and pulls. The door flings open, letting in a blast of air.

'You little…' the man next to her shouts.

'Child locks, damn it.' The man in the passenger seat clouts the driver's arm.

Harper is grabbed by the man sitting next to her. A horn blasts out from behind, then another. The driver looks behind for a second and hits the brake. A car in front has slowed down. Harper throws her head back and thrusts it forwards, headbutting the man hard on the nose. He loosens his grip on her, and as the driver swerves sharply to overtake the vehicle in front avoiding a near collision, he is thrown, unbalanced and loses his grip altogether. The door is still wide open; Harper shuffles into a better position and thrusts herself out of the car. She hits the tarmac hard, feeling her skin burn. The sounds of horns blasting and skidding tyres ring in her ears right before everything turns black.

CHAPTER FORTY-FIVE
Gregg

The black car skids to a halt on the vast driveway of Charlie Coleman's property. Gregg jumps out from the driver's seat and confronts Brian who has jumped from the passenger side.

'What kind of shit show was that?' Gregg grabs Brian by his throat.

'Get off of me, you dumb prick. You didn't set the child locks!' he spits in Gregg's face.

'You sourced the car,' Gregg growled back, spittle forming at his mouth.

The man from the rear of the car jumps out and attempts to separate the two men.

'What the hell?' Carla is striding towards them, followed by Charlie.

The three men straighten themselves up.

'The older Midwinter girl got away. She jumped from the car.' Gregg says, raising his hands.

'Where?' Carla says her tone remaining calm.

'The motorway.'

'She jumped out of the car onto the goddamn motorway?' Carla's voice was now rising. 'So that was seen by how many people?'

'Look, we didn't stop. I floored it and we got away, all right? No one could follow us.'

The other man opens up the boot, reminding everyone that there was a young girl in there.

'You got her sister? For Christ's sake get her inside. She can't see me; she knows me. You do realise cops are going to be all over this by now?'

Charlie addresses all three of the men. 'If you've put my ass and business in jeopardy...' His voice trails off and he follows Carla back inside.

Gregg glares at Brian and spits on the floor. He moves around to the boot of the car and looks down at the fragile-looking young girl, her eyes wide and body rigid.

'Let's get you up.' He lifts her slight frame out of the car and carries her inside. He takes her straight up the sweeping staircase to the bedroom which has been allocated to her at the far end of the landing. He places her on the double bed and gestures for her to be quiet, then he gently removes her gag. He's still wearing his balaclava so that she doesn't recognise him. Felicity curls herself up into a tight ball and cries into her hair.

'It'll do you no good to scream, kid. If you look out of the window, there's nothing but fields. There's a bathroom just for you through that door there.' Gregg points to the ensuite, not that the girl is looking. He then opens a drawer and takes out a nightdress. He places it next to the trembling young girl. He had felt the dampness of the pyjamas she was wearing whilst he was carrying her. 'Put this on, kid. Might be a bit big but you'll feel fresher.'

Felicity still doesn't look. She has her knees tucked tightly up to her chest; her eyes leaking through her scrunched-up eyes.

'Your sister got away, kid. But don't worry, we'll get her back. That make ya happy? You won't be here alone for long. Want anything to eat? I'll get you some milk or somethin'.'

Gregg doesn't get a response. He moves over to the window and looks out. Apart from cows grazing in the distance, there's nothing but fields. He wonders how a prick like Charlie Coleman managed to get all of this. Some people get everything just handed to them. Charlie looks like he's never had to graft in his life, yet he's a successful piece of shit. He has all of this, yet it's not enough. He wants in on dealing with this nasty business.

'Get changed, alright kid.' He takes a last look at the fragile-looking creature and leaves the room, sliding bolts across as he does.

'Christ's sake,' he mutters under his breath, then heads back to the kitchen.

Gregg rips off his balaclava and wipes away the sweat from his forehead. He surveys everyone in the kitchen, noting the atmosphere is far from relaxed.

'Where's Brian?'

'Sortin' the car's plates,' Coleman answers.

Carla is pacing the kitchen, swiping at her mobile phone, then looks up to glare at Gregg.

'I'm refreshing all newsfeeds to see if there are any reports of a teenager found on the motorway after jumping from a moving vehicle. For Christ's sake, Gregg.'

'Hey, I told you we should've done it my way. Snatchin' and grabbin' is messy. Broad daylight too. It was too rushed. I told ya, grooming and luring 'em is the cleanest way.'

'No time for that shit,' Coleman butted in. 'The element of surprise is best, strike fast. It's you three stooges hashing it all.'

'I usually work alone and I ain't been caught yet, That tell ya somethin'?'

Brian walks back in, interrupting to announce that the plates have been changed. He walks over to Gregg. 'You can scrub inside the boot of the car. It stinks of DNA evidence. Then how about you get rid of it?'

Gregg squares up to the larger man in front of him.

'Now is not the time to get all macho,' Carla butts in. She rummages under the sink and pulls out some rubber gloves. She hands them to her brother. 'He's right, someone has to do it and fast. Then we've got to plan our next move. What are we going to do about Harper Midwinter? You better all hope she never saw any of your sorry asses.'

'Shouldn't we just leave her?' Brian says.

'No we shouldn't,' Carla snaps. 'We have an order to fill and I want her. Kate Midwinter has to pay.'

'She might be dead for all we know. She hit the ground hard,' Gregg says.

Carla starts scrolling through her phone again, irritated.

Gregg puts on the rubber gloves and sets to filling a washing-up bowl of water and roots around for other cleaning stuff. 'Take the girl a drink and make sure she's changed. Find a maternal fibre in you,' he directs at his sister.

'Fuck you. I've got to get to work,' she replies, snatching up her bag and marching away.

Gregg grins at her and takes what he needs outside. He'll do the dirty work if it gets him away from the rest of the morons for a bit. He soaks a sponge in the bleachy water and starts to scrub the floor of the boot. He's not convinced that Harper will be in any fit shape but what Carla wants, she gets. All they can do for now is play the waiting game.

CHAPTER FORTY-SIX

Phil pulls out a chair for me to sit down. I knew there was a strong chance I'd be questioned more today over my allegations towards Jason. I'm holding my breath. I couldn't face breakfast before leaving the house, which I'm glad about because I'm sure I'd be bringing it back up right now.

'You look tired, Kate. How are you?' Phil asks me.

'I'm not sleeping.'

'Are you getting support at home?'

'I haven't… Jon doesn't know. Things are difficult at home. I'm ashamed and I can't add to the stress.'

'Look, Kate, I urge you to—'

'Can you just tell me what's going on?'

Phil's expression remains neutral as he logs into a laptop. 'We have to take any allegations seriously, and we have to look into Jason's side of things. I'm sure you understand.'

I just about manage to nod my head. He asks me to move around to get a better view of the screen.

Phil continues, 'Jason claims that you approached him regarding being blackmailed by someone on the outside to harm his appeal. That your family are in danger, so you asked for his help in finding out who it was blackmailing you. I've checked CCTV footage at the day and time he said this happened and, as you can see, you are clearly seen talking to Jason by the exit to the gardens, backing up what he said.'

I feel my cheeks burning and my hands go clammy. 'No, it's him. It's the other way round. He called me over and was checking that I never said anything and was reminding me what he'd do to my family if I told.'

'Why did you go over to talk to him?'

'I don't know… I was scared, not thinking… I don't know.'

Phil is looking at me, unsure. I have to stick to my story, going back on everything will put my family at risk and, not to mention, land me with a criminal record.

'Jason also claims that you wrote him a letter, asking him to reply addressing it to Felicity Harper to ensure that you knew it was for you when it landed on your lap to process. Those are the names of your stepdaughters, aren't they? How would he know that?'

My eyes are now full of hot tears. 'That didn't happen. He's lying. He's got friends on the outside. They must already be stalking me. Oh God.' My voice breaks.

Phil hands me a box of tissues. 'Look, Kate,' he says gently, 'this is a serious allegation if you believe he's threatening you on top of sexual assault. Have you noticed anyone suspicious hanging around where you live? Anything unusual at all?'

'No,' I sniff.

'Jason is adamant that he's telling the truth; he's not backing down. The police will be involved, and they'll want to interview you. If he's threatening your family, we need to ensure you're kept safe. This isn't going to be a clean-cut case. The police will investigate his side of the story. So, I am going to ask you: are you being blackmailed by someone to fit Jason Sawyer up?'

I can't find the words straight away. The enormity of the situation is bearing down heavy on my shoulders. I stare at the custodial manager through watery vision, 'That prick put his hands on me. That is what happened and he's full of shit.'

Phil gives me a slight nod and sits back in his chair. 'You should take a few days off, some compassionate leave, whilst this gets resolved. Your safety and welfare are paramount.'

I haven't got the strength to argue with him. I need out of this place, this mess and this nightmare. 'I'll be handing my notice in.'

'You don't have to be hasty.'

'Jon and the girls never liked me working here... It's for the best.'

'Get yourself home and give yourself time.'

I stand, thank him, and head for the door.

'And Kate,' he calls after me. 'Talk to Mala, she's

worried sick about you. You need a friend.'

I feign a smile and close the door behind me. I'm sure Phil doesn't believe me. I imagine him and Mala curled up on the sofa together last night discussing what a liar I am. I've made such a hash of everything. I wish that I could go back and handle it differently, or better still, go back even further and not take that trip to Nelder Street. Calling myself a foolish idiot is an understatement. At least I can go home now and spend some time with the girls. I need to pop in and see Mala in the postroom first. I need some affirmation that she's on my side.

When I reach the post room, I can hear the buzz of chatter and laughing. I let myself in to find Heather from reception sitting at my desk. Mala jumps up to greet me.

'Hey, Heather is filling in for a bit whilst you take some time off. The office staff have shuffled around a bit.'

I can't catch my breath. Phil has only just asked me to go home. This has already been arranged. *They must know I'm guilty.*

Mala continues, 'I'm just showing her the ropes and how unexciting it all is. But she did bring coffee with her, so I know she'll be just great.'

They both laugh and clink coffee cups. Mala guides me further up the post room, although it's not a huge office and won't offer any more privacy away from Heather.

'Are you okay?' she asks, 'You didn't reply to my message last night.'

'I'm just worn out. Sorry... yes, I'm okay. I didn't want to just drop this on you but I want you to hear it from me first. I'm handing my notice in today. I'm leaving.'

'What, no way, sister. Don't let that piece of scum—'

'It's not just that... it's not for me anymore.' I'm aware of Heather glancing over at us, pretending not to be nosey.

Mala throws her arms around me. 'Eight years in this office together, sister. No way can you leave me.'

I feel an ache in my heart. Mala wouldn't be saying this if she knew the truth. She must still be on my side.

She lets me go. 'But it's probably for the best. I get that.'

The ache in my heart now turns to a sting. She does think it's for the best. My best friend has been discussing me with Phil and probably Heather too. The urge to bolt from the room is strong.

'I've got to get going.'

'Call me tonight, okay?' Mala looks at me with concern.

I don't answer; I just leave. And I'm sure I hear Heather laugh as I do. I feel like everyone I pass on the way out is staring at me, like they know something. I want to scream. They would do the same if it was to protect their family. Light rain hits me as I step into the fresh air. I jog over to the car and collapse into it. I need to compose myself before getting home. I don't know how to explain all of this to Jon yet. I check my phone, no missed calls or messages. It's close to midday and the rain is starting to come down a little heavier. If it wasn't for the rain, I'd take myself off for a walk to try and clear my head but I figure that's not even close to being possible. I just need to tell Jon what's been happening, stick to my story and ride it out.

Nearing home and the rain is now hammering down on my windscreen; the wipers working hard against the onslaught. Visibility isn't great from the surface spray and I welcome the need to concentrate on the road, momentarily distracting my thoughts. I pull up onto the driveway next to Jon's car. I'm not surprised that they haven't gone out in this weather. It's only a few steps to my front door but I brace myself before stepping out into the rain and making a dash for it. I don't even have to fumble with my key in the lock because the door is already open; just a little ajar, but it's open.

'Hi,' I call out. 'That rain—'

Groaning interrupts me and turns my blood cold. I burst into the living room to be met with my husband lying on the carpet, his mouth gagged, desperately groaning. I drop to the floor next to him. His wrists are cuffed to the radiator.

'Oh my God. What…?' My hands are shaking, I rip away the tape from his mouth. Blood is smeared down his face from a gash at his temple, his one eye swollen and bruised.

He sucks in some air as his lips are freed. 'The girls.'

I run from the room and bolt upstairs, all air leaving my lungs, my head light and fuzzy. 'Girls, girls.' I cry out swinging open each door. Silence. Nothing. I run back down to Jon. 'Where are they? What the hell?' I get a closer look at Jon's cuffs but I can't unclasp them.

'Just call the police,' Jon pants. 'I don't know. There were three men, they burst in…' He starts to sob. 'They've taken my girls.'

I grab my handbag and fish out my phone.

'Hello, police.' I blurt everything out to the operator, who is reassuring me to stay calm.

I kneel down next to my husband to get a closer look at his head wound, then put my arms around him.

'Who would do this?' His tone angry through his sobs. 'Is it connected to that girl who was dumped here?'

I can't talk. Shock is setting in. The realisation that someone has kidnapped the girls is burning through my entire core. *They actually took them.*

'Kate, what's going on? Do you know something? What are you doing home?'

'I… I think… it could…' The lump in my throat is painful. I can't process what to say fast enough.

'Kate?'

'I was recently assaulted at work by a prisoner. He threatened to harm my family if I told anyone and I did. I don't know; it could be him—'

'And you didn't tell me? Jesus Christ.'

'I couldn't… I couldn't face you sniping at me, telling me that you told me so. You've always hated me working there.'

'But someone was threatening the girls, my daughters. If anything happens to them… Oh, Jesus.' Jon breaks down further.

I can hear sirens so jump up to wave them down outside the front. Two officers step from the car and greet me in a relaxed way.

'My husband's chained to the radiator inside. My two stepdaughters have been kidnapped.'

The one officer opens the boot and takes out a small bag of tools.

'Hurry,' I snap, frantically waving them on to follow me.

Inside, one of the officers tells Jon that an ambulance will be here shortly to look at his head. He introduces himself as PC Stokes and his colleague as PC Clarke.

'My daughters have been taken,' Jon cries.

PC Stokes shows him the bolt cutters and sets to breaking through the cuffs. 'Let's get you free and check you over. We'll take a full statement in just a sec.'

'Do you know your attackers or did you get a look at them?' Clarke asks.

'No,' Jon says, sounding frustrated. 'My wife might have an idea.'

More sirens sound outside. 'That'll be the ambulance.' PC Clarke goes to greet them.

Jon is now free from his handcuffs and rubbing his sore wrists.

Clarke reappears followed by two paramedics, one of whom goes straight to Jon to assess the gash on his temple. The paramedic gets him to sit down.

The spacious living room now feels small and crowded, the walls closing in.

'Can we go somewhere else to talk?' Stokes asks me.

I nod and he follows me through to the kitchen, where we take a seat.

'Obviously, we have a lot to get through here,' he says. 'We'll need full statements from both of you and the forensics team will be here soon. Detective Matthews is on his way and will take over the questioning. Firstly, do you have any idea where your stepdaughters have been taken?'

'No.'

'We'll need recent photographs of them as soon as you can. Your husband said that you might have an idea?'

'I was sexually assaulted by a prisoner at work recently. I work at Standington. His name is Jason Sawyer. He threatened my family if I told.' I just let the words tumble out. 'He has a boyfriend, Andrew, and someone called Carla who lives with them. Those are the only contacts that I know of on the outside. You could start with them.' I have no proof that they have ever been involved, but it has to be them, there are too many coincidences. I can use this fabrication to get the police around there. I have to stick to this story; it's all I have now. The worst has happened, and I will lose Jon forever if he finds out that this was all me from the beginning.

My nails dig into my palms as PC Stokes makes some notes. My mobile vibrates on the table making me jump. I swipe it up not knowing the number. It could be ugly man.

'Hello,' I say clearing my throat.

I listen to the woman's voice on the other end and I burst into tears. 'We'll be right there.'

I hang up and throw my hand to my mouth. 'That was the hospital. Harper's been found.' I rush from the kitchen. 'Jon, Jon, Harper is at the hospital.'

My husband jumps up, knocking the paramedic out of the way. 'Is she okay? Where's Felicity?'

'I don't know. I don't know all the details. Harper is okay, that's all I know. A head injury or something.'

'We're going.'

The paramedics warn Jon to slow down. One of them says, 'We're taking you there anyway. You need some stitches at least and checking over for concussion. The dizziness you're experiencing is cause for concern.'

'I'll follow in the car,' I reassure him. 'God, I hope she can tell us where Fizz is. It'll be okay, love, we're going to get them back.'

PC Clarke says he'll hang behind for forensics. Stokes phones Detective Matthews to update him. I don't even hang around to listen to Jon protesting that he's fine to come in the car with me. I just run.

CHAPTER FORTY-SEVEN

As soon as Harper sees me, she bursts into uncontrollable sobs. There is a large dressing covering the right side of her beautiful face. I perch on the side of her bed and wrap her up in the biggest hug. She winces and I loosen my hold. I allow her time to cry despite being desperate for some answers. I look to the nurse who showed me to her room.

'She has a nasty graze spanning the right side of her face,' the nurse confirms. 'She sustained a head injury and was unconscious for a while. She's being treated for concussion and she has a fractured rib, but other than that, she's done well considering she jumped from a moving car.' The nurse smiles warmly.

'Is that what happened?' I gasp.

Harper pulls away from me and sits more upright, clutching her side as she does. She takes her time, taking a few deep breaths through her pain to slow her tears.

The nurse says, 'There was a police officer here earlier, but she wasn't up to talking much.'

'There is one on their way now,' I say, and it hits me that I need Harper to talk to me and fast.

'I'll leave you both alone for a while.' The nurse heads out.

'Where's Dad?' Harper sniffles.

'He's okay. He has a wound on his head. He's being checked over here; he'll find you very soon. You have to tell me everything, love. Where's Fizz, what happened?' I don't think I can breathe.

Harper closes her eyes, reliving the moment that the masked men knocked on the door and attacked her dad, then bundled her and her sister into the car.

'They put her in the boot,' she cries, looking at me in total anguish. 'I was sat in the back with one of the men, my hands were tied up. I just wanted to escape; I had to get out. I had to save my sister; it's all I could think about and I got the door open and jumped.'

'Did the men say anything? Where they were taking you, anything?'

Harper shakes her head, breaking down further. She hangs her head low avoiding eye contact. 'I saw the number plate before getting in the car. I was sure I'd remember it. I can't now. I thought I could tell the police; they'd track the car and find Felicity. I just thought I'd save her... but I just left her. I shouldn't have left her, she's all alone, she'll be so scared. I just left her...'

I want to reach out to my stepdaughter, but she looks so fragile and small. 'Don't you blame yourself. You're safe and that means everything to me and your dad. We'll find Fizzy. We will.' I scrunch my eyes shut briefly at the thought of how scared she will be and pray she's not been hurt. 'She'll be back home with us before we know it, skipping around the house, you'll see. We'll dig that vegetable patch that she wants and get her a puppy and she can even call it Kylie.' I try to manage a brave smile.

'It's your old friend, Carla, who has a puppy called Kylie. That's where Felicity got the name from.' Harper sniffs, looking ashamed.

'What?'

Her words startle me. She takes a tissue and blows her nose.

'I'm sorry. This is going to sound bad, but we went to see her, me and Felicity.'

'What do you mean, who?' *Surely they didn't? It's not possible.* I feel a rapid rise in a sense of panic.

'I found Carla's address, so we went to visit her on Monday. I couldn't leave Felicity alone so she came with me—'

'Hang on, what address?'

'It had fallen from your back pocket when we were outside looking at your dented car after you crashed. I took it, I'm sorry.'

Her words are like a solid punch to my guts. 'Nelder Street?' My voice breaks saying it.

Harper nods, hanging her head low again.

'Monday? When? Why? Just why...' I stop and think, 'The address didn't have a name on it. Why would you go there? You didn't know who you were going to see. Why would you do that? Why?' I can't help raising my voice.

Harper looks directly at me. 'I said this would sound bad. I thought you were having an affair.'

My eyes widen, 'What on earth?'

'I can't explain it. I thought you were acting strange at times. You went out late one night and other stuff.'

'And that made you think I was having an affair? So let me get this straight... You took your sister to some random address to find out if that's where I was going to cheat on your dad?'

'I'm so sorry,' Harper crumbles again. 'I'm such a bitch. I wanted evidence. I wanted Dad to throw you out. I hated being bullied at school because of you. I hate that my sister only talks to you and not me. I wanted you gone.'

Now I know how my stepdaughter is feeling from being thrown from a moving vehicle. I feel the impact, the tarmac burning along my skin. It hurts. I can't speak.

'I'm sorry,' she cries again. 'I don't think that now. I was a stupid bitch. You have been everything to me and my sister. I see that now. You're a mum to me, to us. I'll never doubt you again.'

I wipe my eyes to hold back the tears, 'Tell me everything. You saw Carla?'

'We took the train and then got a taxi. It wasn't far. Carla answered the door and I asked her if she knew you. She said she was an old school friend of yours and you'd gone to visit her to catch up. She said she didn't have time to talk to you much though because she had to get to work. She showed me a picture of you. She was really lovely and has the cutest puppy called Kylie.'

'Did you stay long? What else did you talk about? Did you say anything about me?'

'Just where you work and stuff. Her husband drove us home.'

'Home? To our front door? What's his name?'

She nods, 'Gregg. He was lovely too. Carla said that she'd come to surprise you this weekend for a catch-up so not to say anything. I didn't mean to keep it from you.'

So that's how they found me. The realisation sinks in and everything starts to make sense.

'What does Gregg look like? Not very tall with an ugly face full of scars and missing teeth?'

Harper looks bemused. 'No, I wouldn't say he's that tall, but big built and no scars. He had no hair. Why?'

'Doesn't matter.'

'I didn't do anything too wrong, did I? It'd be great for you to meet her properly again. She's so nice... Actually, she might be back again in a bit.'

I jump up. 'What do you mean, back again in a bit?'

'She was here not too long ago. She popped in and said that she thought it was me. She couldn't stop, but said she'd be back with some treats for me.'

I stride over to peer out of the room. A number of staff are hurrying back and forth. I hold onto the doorframe to steady myself. I turn back to see Harper sobbing loudly into her hands.

'I need my sister back,' she howls.

I stroke her hair, whilst looking around me. The man that Harper describes as Carla's husband didn't sound like ugly man or Andrew. But if I wasn't sure before that Carla has been behind all of this, then I am now. A doctor walks in and apologises for interrupting.

'I have your scan results. You have a slight fracture to the skull but nothing that looks too serious. We'd like to keep you in overnight to monitor you.'

'That's a relief, isn't it, Harps?' I say squeezing her hand.

The doctor continues. 'You were a very lucky young lady. I'd say you've used a life up though.'

'I don't care about anything. I just need my sister back.' Harper says weakly.

The doctor looks sympathetic. 'I understand the police will be here any moment to help you.'

'Where's my dad?'

'I'll get a nurse to chase things up, find out what's happening. You just rest up, be strong for your sister.'

I thank him and he briefly nods before leaving us alone.

We're not alone for long though. PC Stokes walks in.

'How's the patient?' he says to Harper.

She clams up, looking away.

'Can I talk to you outside for a minute?' I say to the officer.

We step into the corridor. 'I told you before I may know who's behind this. Her name is Carla. I'm not sure about other names except an Andrew who lives at the same address. Carla was here. She was here seeing Harper. She's in danger here. That woman has found her.'

'Okay. It might be best if you come down to the station and tell us everything from the beginning.'

'There's no time for that. You need to get round to Nelder Street and talk to them. Jason Sawyer assaulted me in prison and they are his contacts on the outside. He threatened my family, then this happens, and that woman has been here. You have to get there now.'

PC Stokes takes out his notepad and scribbles the address down that I give him.

'We have to question your stepdaughter but I'll get on the radio to Detective Matthews now.'

I listen in as Stokes talks to Matthews. I rub my arms and look back into the room to see Harper still sitting there hugging herself.

Stokes ends the call. 'A car is being sent to Nelder Street now. But we do need you to get to the station to make a full statement. Detective Matthews will meet you there.'

'I'm not leaving Harper. She needs me whilst you question her.'

'We'll wait until her dad is with her. He's

already here being checked over. He won't be long. We'll need a full statement from him too, but it's important we speak to you if we're to find Felicity as quickly as we can.'

I reluctantly agree but I have to leave now for Fizz's sake. I go and kiss Harper on the forehead and tell her not to worry.

'Keep it together, okay? We'll find Fizzy. Your dad will be up with you any minute, and I'll be back as quick as I can.'

I go to leave but turn back, 'If Carla comes back, you tell someone straight away, you hear me?'

'Why?' the teenager looks confused.

'I'm not sure I trust her. I'll tell you everything later.'

I walk away, leaving her with PC Stokes. My mind is whirring with Harper's revelations. I think back to when I realised the Nelder Street address was missing from my pocket. Harper taking it and then travelling there was the furthest scenario from my mind. It's the last thing I would have expected. As if I couldn't blame myself and hate myself enough already. My heart is being ripped apart thinking how terrified Fizz must be. She needs me. She's my little rock and I'm hers. She won't cope without me. I'm going to get her back and then I'm going to kill Carla.

CHAPTER FORTY-EIGHT
Gregg

'You don't talk much, do you kid?' Gregg says to the seven-year-old who is sitting up on the bed, wearing a slightly oversized pink nightdress and squeezing a brown teddy bear. The little girl is still unable to look at him even though he's wearing a friendlier mask – a fancy dress Bugs Bunny one. 'Here, take the milk. You need to keep your strength up.' The girl still won't look at him. Perhaps she doesn't like bunnies, he thinks.

His phone rings. 'I'll be back in a minute, kid,' he says, placing the glass of milk down. He takes the call out on the landing.

'Riley.'

'The police are calling me in for questioning.'

'What they got?'

'They've been to my house and have spoken to Andrew. That Midwinter woman has been shooting her mouth off, suspecting I'm involved. She's been putting the pieces together.'

'Told you you shouldn't have tried to find that teen in the hospital, I told ya—'

'I was there anyway. Now we know she's okay, we can plan to snatch her back.'

'You're outta your mind. The police are sniffin' and you wanna carry on? What's drippy Andrew said?'

'Nothing. They'll have nothing on him because he knows nothing. I'm heading to the station now for voluntary questioning. They'll have nothing on me either.'

'Told you this'd get messy.'

'That bitch is a mere thorn, that's all. She's still sticking to her story that Sawyer assaulted her. We've caused him some shit and Midwinter has no proof against us. What's messy about that? Get planning with the guys. I'll call you later.' She hangs up.

'*What's messy about that?*' Gregg mimics in a sarcastic, childish tone.

He goes back into the bedroom. 'Hey kid, drink your milk. We're getting your sister back.'

The girl slightly glances up at him.

'You too old for milk, that it? Want a beer or something?'

She looks away again.

'Ah, talking is overrated anyway... especially from a woman. Is your sister a pain in the ass too? I tell ya, mine is up there with the worst.'

The girl wipes away a stray tear.

'You know what she did to my teddy bear when I was a kid? She set fire to it. Yeah, she had her problems and she'd take it out on me. Still doing it now. Sisters, eh?'

The girl hugs the bear tighter.

'Her problems made her a fighter though. It'll make you one too. You've a rich and powerful life ahead of ya.'

The girl sniffs and rubs her watery eyes.

'C'mon tell me something. What do you like? What's your favourite food? Want some chicken nuggets or something? You don't talk at all? Not to your sister either? Why?'

The girl slides from the bed and goes to the far corner of the room. She slumps down to the floor, clutching her knees tight to her chest and burying her head down. Gregg takes the milk over to her.

'Look, just drink the milk. You haven't had anything all day.'

Gregg steps closer and offers her the glass. As he does, the girl swiftly kicks him in the shin. The milk sloshes. 'You little—' He takes a moment and backs off, placing the glass down. The girl now has her hands over her ears and is pressing herself against the wall.

'I guess I deserved that,' he smirks. 'You know, I didn't want you here. This ain't my idea, alright kid? Just tryin' to make it all a bit more comfortable for you.'

He meant it. Whoring out minors is a whole different game; it's disgusting in his eyes. There has to be some standards. This whole set up is branching deeper into depravity. But the girl shaking in front of him now is his ticket out. The money that Carla's contacts are willing to pay extra for a seven-year-old is enough to see him merrily on his way out of this shit show and away from his toxic sister for good. It's a sacrifice he's willing to make for want of a better life. He smirks, kidding himself that he's capable of a better life. He'll settle for just vanishing off Carla's radar and that already smells sweet to him.

'Well, kid, I'll check in on you later. I need to prepare to get your sister. Thanks for the conversation.' He laughs before locking the door behind him.

CHAPTER FORTY-NINE

I don't understand why it's taking them so long. I'm now pacing around the interview room, adrenaline keeping me from sitting still any longer. They kept me in the waiting area for ages, moved me to this room, and still no one has spoken with me. My little girl is missing and there's no urgency in this place. Is a missing child not important to them? The door suddenly opens.

'Sorry to keep you. I'm Detective Matthews.'

The silver-haired man holds his hand out to me. I briefly shake it.

I don't give the detective chance to continue. 'What's happening? Felicity is vulnerable; she has selective mutism. She's going to be terrified. What are you doing to find her?'

'Mrs Midwinter—'

'We need to get her home. I need to get back to the hospital. I've been here for hours.'

'Please, just take a seat.'

I do as he says and he pulls up a seat opposite.

'I know this is a distressing time for you.' His face mellows. 'I want to reassure you that we have been acting fast and doing everything that we can. Forensics have been going over your property—'

'Have they found anything?'

'No, I'm afraid. Nothing that can help us identify the gang. We have taken a copy of a photo of Felicity which was on your fireplace and the image is being circulated as we speak. We have already been in touch with members of the public who witnessed Harper jump from the car. We have descriptions of the vehicle, but the number plate appears to be fake and the occupants were wearing balaclavas. We've put a call out to anyone else who may have been a witness but hasn't yet come forward.'

'So you have nothing? Did you speak to Carla and Andrew? Have you been to their house?'

'We have spoken with Andrew West at his home and Carla Riley is here in another interview room. She has come in voluntarily for questioning.'

I push my chair back and jump up.

'Please sit back down. Can I get you a drink?'

'No.' My head is spinning at the thought of being under the same roof as that woman. 'She has Felicity; she needs to give her back to me. Get her to tell me where she is.'

'Please just take a seat, Mrs Midwinter, so that we can get to the bottom of this without further delay.'

I sit back down opposite him, every one of my nerves on fire.

'Both Andrew and Carla have a different story to tell, in that you turned up out of the blue one day at their home looking for someone who you thought was Jason Sawyer's girlfriend, Anna West. They explained the situation that Andrew is in a relationship with Jason and used the name of Anna in order to help hide Jason's sexuality whilst inside, and to help keep other inmates onside by sharing semi-naked pictures of his so-called girlfriend around. These pictures were modelled by their good friend Carla Riley. They realised that you must work at the prison as no one else could've known the name Anna West. We've been shown a CCTV image by Andrew, placing you at their home before your allegation of assault against Jason Sawyer.'

My eyes fill with tears and I can't hold them back. I inhale deeply. 'Okay, you have to listen to me. No, Jason didn't assault me. After I went to Nelder Street, they found me and blackmailed me to harm Jason's appeal to stop him getting out. They threatened to kidnap my girls if I didn't.'

'So, let me get this clear. Andrew and Carla directly blackmailed you. It was them?'

'Yes. No. Well, yes. Not themselves but they got someone to do it for them. There was this guy. I can describe him. He was watching my every move. He was following their orders.'

'Both Carla and Andrew have been interviewed separately and their stories corroborate, and they are claiming that you have some unhealthy infatuation with Jason Sawyer.'

'What? So I'm that much of a crazy lunatic, that I'm making all of this up and I kidnapped my own stepdaughters because of an infatuation.'

'Why did you visit them at their home?'

Shame washes through me, but there is nothing left to lose, 'Yes, I was curious about the life of a woman who loves a murderer, and I was being nosey. I crossed a professional line. but I'm telling you that after that they found me, they blackmailed me and then kidnapped the girls.'

'They found you because Harper and Felicity went to visit their address too. Harper has been very cooperative and has told us everything. She said that she suspected you of having an affair because you were acting secretive and strange.'

'Yes okay, but you see it has to be them. And Carla turned up at the hospital to see Harper. She's dangerous and Harper isn't safe there. You have to listen.'

Detective Matthews relaxes his shoulders, leaning in. 'Carla Riley is the Director of Clinical Governance, covering hospital trusts in the whole of Berkshire. She is in a position of great influence and respect and had business to be at the hospital this morning. It was a chance encounter with Harper.'

I try and let that sink in and wipe away my angry tears. 'Well, that doesn't mean anything. People in authority can still—'

'Tell me more about this man that you say has been watching you and, as you say, carrying out orders.'

I tell Detective Matthews as much as I can remember about him: his ugly appearance, the drugs he handed me, the video clip he showed me, the threats he made, the time he groped me. Everything.

'We'll be continuing our door-to-door enquiries around your neighbourhood, see if anyone saw this man and the car at the times you've stated. See if we can gain any vital information in tracking him down. We can't rule out that someone else is responsible for the kidnapping of your girls. Both Andrew and Carla have solid alibis for this morning and we are yet to find any connection. We need to focus on finding this man. We'll get an E-FIT drawn up.'

'Are you letting Carla go?'

'She wasn't under arrest and we've no cause to hold her. Please be reassured that we're doing everything that we can.'

My voice breaks and I buckle into uncontrollable sobs. 'She'll be so scared. I need my baby girl back.'

He looks at me like he's a machine programmed to see me as just another distraught victim. 'Get yourself home, there's word that the forensics team is close to packing away and your assigned family liaison officer will be with you. If there are any other details, remember you can contact me anytime. We'll keep in touch.'

The urge to get out of this building is strong and I don't hang about. I know I'm not crazy. I know Carla is behind this; I can feel it. Yet I'm made out to be the lunatic. I don't care what that hard-faced detective thinks of me. It's all out there now and all that matters is getting Fizz home unharmed. I hurry from the station and a refreshing splatter of rain hits my face as I step outside. I grapple for my phone from my bag and call Jon.

He answers, 'Kate, I'm just on my way home. Meet me there. We need to talk.'

'You've left Harper?'

'She needs some stuff. It's okay. There's a police officer and family liaison officer with her for now.'

'I should—'

'No, Kate. Home now and you can explain to me what the hell has been going on.'

CHAPTER FIFTY

I brace myself as I near home. I'm prepared. Nothing matters now. Jon can hate me, he can be angry at me. The important thing is finding Fizz. He's going to know everything; he'll know about how Harper went to Nelder Street. I don't know what other information the police have fed back to him – that I've known we were in danger all along, that I kept quiet about being blackmailed, that it was my stupid behaviour that started it. Hindsight is that evil dark presence that torments you when the shit hits the fan. It's not a wonderful thing. It's hell.

I pull up kerbside behind Jon's car as the forensics van is blocking the driveway. My husband is talking with PC Clarke; he spots me and calls me over.

'Forensics are just leaving,' he says.

I feel uneasy, watching the team removing their white suits and ripping away the police tape surrounding the drive.

'You'll be able to go inside now,' PC Clarke confirms. 'Beware though, that there may be some mess from the searches carried out. I'll be remaining here for the rest of the evening at least to keep an eye on the house. We'll be arranging regular drive-bys also.'

'Thank you,' I say, thinking that nothing is going to make them feel safe now.

A dog walker slows his pace and stares as he walks by. I'm certain there'll be more eyes on our house, peeking around curtains. The forensics van pulls away. Detective Matthews didn't think that they found anything useful, I'm praying that he's wrong.

'I'll grab some clothes and toiletries and stuff that Harper needs,' Jon says, flustered as we enter the house, leaving PC Clarke on the doorstep. He bolts upstairs. I head straight to pour myself a glass of water, downing the contents. Things have been moved around in the kitchen. The feeling of violation is unsettling; the thought of people combing through our home. The violation from the men that broke in and attacked my family though is much worse. Jon returns, placing the bag for Harper on top of the kitchen counter. He looks at me, darkness clouding his eyes. He clutches his hair and kicks out at the unit in front of him, 'Where the hell is my little girl?' Jon glares at me, his eyes wild.

'I don't know who has her,' I say, my voice nearly a whisper.

'Start explaining because the police are full of facts that I know nothing about.'

My legs feel like they could give way and I collapse into a chair at the table. I can't look at him. I just start talking and I don't stop until I've told him everything, every detail. Exhausted and spent but nothing spared, Jon listens in silence, not interrupting even though I can see the disbelief and rage in his features. I finish and he stands. He lets out a roar and punches the kitchen cupboard. He slumps against the unit, his shoulders shaking as he sobs. My heart breaks.

He wipes his snot away with his sleeve, 'The girls' mum would be turning in her grave. You knew that some scum was threatening my daughters and you said nothing?'

'Please, I thought I could handle it. I was so scared. I just wanted to do what they said to protect the girls. I... I thought I was doing the right thing.'

'The right thing? The right thing would've been to tell me, to tell the police. We could've got out of the area somewhere safe. We could've caught the evil scum who was sat outside our house in broad sodding daylight, watching our every move.' He roars and punches the cupboard again.

I flinch and step back.

Jon grabs the bag for the hospital, 'I need to get back to my daughter, and if anything ever happens to Felicity...' He goes to walk away but turns back. 'Why? Why would you go round to the house of a murderer in the first place? It just doesn't make sense.'

'It's hard for me to explain,' I plead.

'It's hard for me to know that some monster

has his hands on my little girl.' His voice breaks again. 'Tell me.'

'It sounds ridiculous now, but I was curious that's all. I was seeing provocative photos from this woman to a murderer, and I just wondered what kind of person she was. What life she had. I don't know; it added some excitement for me.'

'Excitement? This is exciting for you?'

'I never imagined any of this, did I? If I could've foreseen this, of course I wouldn't have gone.'

'So you were bored, is that what you're saying?'

'Jon, I thought you were having an affair. You've been distant, I've felt lonely. I guess I was looking for something.'

'Not this again.'

'Yes, this again.' I start to get angry myself. Remembering what led to all of this. It was how Jon was making me feel, his lies, his coldness. I tell him how I found out he was lying about the hotel he was staying at, that he wasn't away for work, and how I followed him to The Castle Inn that he said he was going to and he wasn't there. Jon walks into the living room and sits down, I follow.

'For Christ's sake, I'm not having an affair. Not in the way that you think.' His voice has softened.

I look at him confused. 'Not how I think? What then?'

He takes a breath. 'I still love my wife...

Marie. I've always loved her and will never stop loving her. Her sudden death didn't just stop my feelings for her.'

My mind is trying to race ahead to see what he's trying to get at.

He continues. 'That hotel I stayed at was where Marie and I spent our anniversary. I was there for our anniversary, to be close to her, to absorb the memories. To just be there; to feel her with me. I didn't go to that pub for food with Alan because I was out for dinner on my own, at a place where I'd taken Marie on our first date. I could visualise her sitting opposite me, with her shy smile and her laughter. I can't let her go.'

Jon can see that I'm struggling with what to say.

'Yes, I lied, but you wouldn't understand. It's personal to me.' He's searching my face for some kind of understanding.

'I might've done. I'm not blind to the fact that Marie will always be a part of you. You should talk to me about how you're feeling.'

'That works both ways, doesn't it? You couldn't come to me about how you were feeling so you just develop some obsession with... some murderer and his wife?' His voice is rising again.

'It might not even have anything to do with them; the police can't find a connection—'

'Yet,' he snaps, standing up. 'I'm getting back to my daughter.'

I take his arm to hold him back, 'Do you even

love me at all?'

'You brought some life, comfort and security back into Felicity. I love you for that.'

That didn't answer my question. He removes my arm and walks away. I want to go with him, but I can't summon the energy to try. I don't feel welcome to, so I just let him go. I hear the sound of a woman's voice as he leaves through the front door. Seconds later, I'm face to face with my best friend.

I buckle at the sight of Mala, and she throws her arms around me to hold me up. She allows me to cry against her shoulder until there's nothing left to shed. She strokes my hair and whispers, 'It'll be okay' in my ear.

'Girl, you need a coffee,' she says, more brightly.

She leaves me slumped on the sofa, to mull over Jon's words. I can't see any way back from this. He'll never forgive me, and I don't believe he's ever loved me. People thought he was marrying me too soon after Marie died, not that anyone ever said that – not to me anyway – but I could sense it. The only true unconditional love that I have ever experienced is through Felicity, and now she is in the hands of monsters.

Mala returns with the coffee, and I gladly take it. My throat is so dry and sore from all of the talking and the crying.

'I couldn't believe what I was seeing when I saw Felicity's face splashed on the news,'

Mala says gently. 'I know you're probably sick of talking, but you said Jason threatened your family, so if he's behind it, the guys at work can cause him some shit, you know... rip his balls off, cause him some pain, that kinda thing.'

I try and smile at Mala's offer of violence, but I have to confess, it's going to come out now anyway. 'Jason never assaulted me.'

My friend's eyes widen, as once more I find myself telling everything.

'Holy Moly. I want to be mad at you for not confiding in me. Damn, girl, you were convincing.'

'Please don't. I can't take it—'

Mala embraces me again. 'What's done is done. It's now important we focus on Felicity, right?'

I nod.

'So, it still could be Jason's fella and this Carla behind it? Crazy to think they were blackmailing you to try to keep Jason inside... his own loved ones.'

'The man that's been threatening me knew everything. He knew what I had and hadn't done before I could tell him, so someone on the inside was feeding back to him. I can only think it was Jason himself when he was phoning home. Telling them everything without realising.'

Mala takes a glug of her coffee, looking thoughtful. 'Do you want me to come with you to see Phil. You'll have to explain—'

I shuffle away from my friend as a sudden

previous thought strikes me. 'How well do you know Phil? I mean, really?'

'You've lost me?'

'Well, if Jason wasn't letting out the info then someone was—'

'Whoa, hold up right there, sister. Are you seriously saying Phil is in with a gang who goes around kidnapping young girls?'

I jump up and start pacing the floor, 'Wouldn't you suspect everyone, if you were in my shoes?'

'Not Phil, I wouldn't. C'mon, you're being ridiculous.'

'I'm not ridiculous, you're blind. You're so smitten, you can't see what he's really like, what he might be capable of.'

Mala gets up and goes to answer me back, but she takes a deep breath and says calmly, 'You're in shock. You need to go join Jon at the hospital. Give Harper my love.' She doesn't look me in the eye as she speaks. She then lets herself out.

'Damn it.' I throw my coffee mug against the wall and watch the contents splatter everywhere.

Mala's right, though. I can't sit here going out of my mind. I'm going to the hospital whether I'm welcome or not.

CHAPTER FIFTY-ONE
Harper

Harper awoke, reality filling her thoughts once more. She was grateful for the medication to help her sleep. It helped her to shut out the agonising thoughts, just for a while. The reality is that it's morning and her little sister has been missing the whole night.

'Ah, you're awake,' the doctor says, smiling, entering the room accompanied by one of the nurses.

The nurse sets to carrying out Harper's observations.

The doctor asks her how she's feeling, and all Harper can do is shrug her shoulders. 'Well, the good news is that you can go home this morning. Your obs are normal; we're no longer concerned about the severity of your concussion. You can rest up at home with some painkillers.'

Harper doesn't know how to feel about going home. It doesn't feel right, not without her sister there. The nurse must sense Harper's apprehension and gently takes her hand.

'Are my parents coming?' Harper croaks.

'I've spoken with your dad already and he's on his way as we speak. The police have also asked if they can speak with you again, but I've suggested that they contact your dad once you're home.'

'You're such a brave young lady,' the nurse soothes. 'You need to be at home for your sister, ready and waiting to welcome her home. She'll be found. Be strong for her.'

Harper nods, tearing up.

'We'll leave you to get yourself up and dressed. Your dad will be here any minute,' the doctor says.

They both give her a reassuring smile before heading out of the room.

Harper gingerly pulls her nightdress off, her ribs still sore. She can't shake the uneasy feeling about going home, seeing her dad so broken. Memories flood in from her mother's death, the pain, the grief. She'd never seen her dad cry before and not since, not until last night. He had broken down at her bedside, beside himself with worry. Then Kate turned up and Harper could feel an atmosphere between them. Something was wrong. She felt nauseated at the thought, that it was her – that they blame her for abandoning Felicity. She believes that her dad and Kate must hate her and that they wish it was Felicity coming home and not her.

Moments after she finishes getting ready, Kate hurries in.

'Hey love, let's get you out of here. How are you feeling?'

'Where's dad?'

'He was coming but the detective turned

up, wanting to discuss putting together a reconstruction and an appeal. He couldn't turn him away.'

'We have to do everything we can,' Harper says, searching her stepmum's face, hoping not to see any blame towards her.

Kate pulls her in for a tight hug, forgetting once more about Harper's broken ribs.

'Ooh, I'm sorry.' Kate lets go as Harper winces. 'We'll do everything.' She looks at her with pure determination. 'Oh, and I have a surprise for you. C'mon let's get you discharged.'

Fortunately, the process doesn't take long and Harper is soon being led along the hospital corridors. The buzz of passing nurses and the general public makes Harper feel giddy. She lowers her head, convinced that everyone is staring at her. They get to the main doors, and it takes Harper just a second to see him. She runs and jumps into the arms of her best friend, Callum.

'I grabbed him on the way,' Kate says.

Harper sobs into his shoulder, then realises how much pain she's in and lets him go.

'Jeez, look at you,' Callum says, looking at the dressing still covering Harper's cheek. 'I'm so relieved you're okay, Harps. I can't believe all this.'

'I'm so happy you're here. I really need you.' Harper ignores the pain and hugs him again.

'C'mon you two. Let's walk up to the car. Sorry

it's at the other end. It's the closest I could get,' Kate says.

They stroll quietly in the morning sun. Harper could sense Callum was feeling a bit awkward. What do you say when your sister has been kidnapped? She doesn't blame him; she hasn't got the right words either. It's hard to express the guilt, terror and hopelessness she feels.

'Shit,' Kate says, as they reach the car. She pats her shoulders down, 'I must've left my handbag in your room... Yes, I put it down then... Damn it, my brain at the moment.'

'Do you want me to run and get it?' Callum offers.

Kate's eyes well up as she looks back across the car park. 'No, you wait here with Harper. I'll be as quick as I can. Will you be okay?'

Harper nods and leans against the car bonnet, watching as her stepmom hurries away.

'I'm not surprised her head's all over the place,' Callum says.

'This is the worst kind of nightmare. I need my sister back.' Harper hugs herself, fighting back the tears.

'Her face is all over the internet. We'll find her. Oh, you'll never guess... I bumped into Lexi Keggans last night. She was only asking after you, asking if you were OK and that you have her respect.'

'It takes this hell to gain that bitch's respect? She can shove her respect up her—'

Two figures step into view, halting Harper in her tracks. She looks up, speechless.

'Hello Harper,' Carla says, grinning.

'Hello again,' Gregg also says.

Harper feels any colour left in her face drain away. 'I don't think I should be talking to you,' she says hesitantly.

'You should've thought about that before snooping around my house and into my business,' Carla says.

Gregg closes in on Callum and flashes a blade, pointing it at his stomach.

'What the—?' Callum whimpers, his eyes wide.

Harper gasps.

'Don't scream,' Carla says calmly. 'You're coming with us. Get into our car quietly and your boyfriend won't have his intestines removed.'

Gregg points the knife even closer to Callum's stomach.

'Why are you doing this?' Harper's voice breaks, catching the fear in her throat.

'You want to be reunited with your sister, don't you?' Carla grins wickedly.

'The little toerag won't eat or drink,' Gregg sneers.

'We're running out of time,' Carla snaps. 'Walk calmly with us to the car right now. Don't cause a scene. Got that?'

Harper looks desperately at Callum. He looks like he's going to cry, his eyes confused.

'Okay,' Harper agrees.

Callum shakes his head, 'No.'

Gregg puts his arm around Callum's shoulder and pulls him in close.

'Okay, it's okay,' Harper insists. 'Cal, let's just do what they say.'

They walk past two rows of cars, then stop at the black Mazda parked on the end.

'Get in,' Gregg says, unlocking the doors.

Harper looks pleadingly at Callum who still has a knife discreetly pointing at him. 'Leave him alone,' she musters.

'Get in now,' Carla growls.

Harper slides into the back seat, followed by Callum. Carla slams the door shut. She heads round to the passenger side and gets in. Gregg jumps in the driver's seat, starts the engine and pulls away.

'Ah, young love,' Carla mocks, looking in the rear-view mirror. 'Brave lad, your boyfriend. And you saved his skin... precious.' She addresses Harper.

'He's not my boyfriend,' Harper says breathlessly. 'So leave him alone, let him go.' As they speed away Harper pulls at the door handle.

'That won't work again,' Gregg laughs.

Carla opens the glove box and removes a gun, raising it enough for them to see it. 'Sit back, relax, enjoy the ride,' She turns round to face Harper. 'Not your boyfriend, huh? Is it the whole best friend thing but you want more scenario?'

Harper slumps back in her seat.

'Pretty thing like you? Well except for your mashed-up face right now. Oh, or is he gay.' Carla raises her arched eyebrows at Callum.

'Shut up,' Harper shouts. She hangs her head and hugs herself tight, to hide her tears.

Callum shuffles closer to Harper, linking her arm.

Carla laughs. 'I've been in your shoes. Being in love with your gay best friend is a bitch.'

'What you on about?' Gregg scoffs. 'You don't know what love is.' He waits a beat, 'Hang on... Andrew, that dweeb you live with? Him? Jason's Mr?'

'Just concentrate on the road,' Carla snaps.

'Now the penny freaking drops,' Gregg sneers. 'You don't wanna keep old Jase in prison because he killed Michael, you wanna keep Andrew all to yourself. Whilst the dog's inside the cat—'

'You wouldn't understand a thing. Shut the hell up and drive.'

Gregg chuckles and turns the radio on. Harper wipes her nose on her sleeve and keeps her hair in front of her face. Kate was right about Carla all along, she sniffles to herself. She feels so stupid for ever stepping foot near that house on Nelder Street. Why couldn't she have just trusted her stepmum and stayed out of things? This is all her fault and now her best friend has been dragged into it. She prays that they are really taking them to join her sister. At least they will be back together; she'll be so scared.

She vows never to leave her again. But Harper feels overwhelmingly sick at the thought of what might come next – what Carla's plans are for them. Carla and Gregg have shown their faces. They know their kidnappers. It dawns on Harper that they have no intention of letting them go, ever.

CHAPTER FIFTY-TWO

I'm back at the car, breathless and disorientated. I can't see Harper and Callum. The hospital car park is full, and there are people coming and going, but the place may as well be void of everything. My mouth instantly dries out and pins and needles rush through my fingers. I turn this way and that way and there's no sign of them. Now I have my bag, I fumble for my phone. There's a text message–

We have them.

I throw my hand to my mouth and stifle a cry. This is real. They've come back for Harper and they've taken Callum too. They were here, watching, waiting. They took them. My fingers struggle to hit the right keys on my phone, they're shaking so much. Do I call the police or Jon first? *How do I tell Jon?* I was bringing his daughter home. She was coming home to safety. Jon had mellowed with me a little last night, accepting that I didn't intend any of this, that he could imagine how scared I was at being blackmailed. It's impossible to think straight sometimes, isn't it, when you're under so much pressure, so much fear? It's hard to think rationally. He started to see that. The important thing was to keep united and strong to bring

Felicity home. But now this is going to kill him.

I punch in the numbers 999. 'Hello, Police…'

CHAPTER FIFTY-THREE
Gregg

Gregg points the gun at Harper and Callum and orders them up the stairs.

Charlie Coleman shouts after them. 'Put the lad in the room to the left of the girls.'

Gregg bites his tongue. It's not like his sister hasn't told him enough times already. He follows close behind the teens, who are clutching each other. At the top of the stairs, Gregg roughly pushes Callum away and orders him into his room. It's almost tragic, he thinks, as he sees the boy give the girl one last desperate look. Gregg shoves him in and bolts the door.

'Ready to see your sis?' Gregg smirks.

He unbolts Felicity's room, and Harper rushes straight in as soon as she claps eyes on her little sister who's curled up on the bed. Harper throws her arms around the young girl and they both burst into tears.

'I told you I'd always come back for you. Are you hurt? Are you okay?' Harper says, wiping away fat tears.

Gregg watches them. 'Should've got me tissues ready,' he mocks.

'How could you?' Harper braves, 'She's only seven. Why are you doing this to us?'

'Money, sweetheart.'

Harper carries on hugging and stroking the hair of the girl, who's visibly shaking.

'I've got you now. I won't leave you again,' Harper whispers in her sister's ear.

'Don't say a lot, does she?' Gregg mocks, looking scared as the teen glares at him.

And then a small voice croaks up. 'Harper, she lied to me.' the seven-year-old says, looking into the face of her big sister.

'Well, well, it speaks,' Gregg scoffs.

Harper keeps her back to Gregg and focuses on her sister. 'Who, Fizzy? Tell me.'

The little girl says in barely a whisper: 'Kate lied to me. She said the bad man won't come for me if I never speak to anyone. I didn't talk, I didn't, but the bad man came anyway.'

Gregg steps closer to them; his interest peaks.

'It's okay. Tell me what bad man Kate was on about. I don't understand,' Harper asks gently through her tears.

'The bogeyman killed Mummy. It's my fault. She wanted me to share my sweets with her and I said if she took my sweets, the bogeyman would get her, like in that cartoon I used to watch. She pinched my sweetie and then that robber came and knocked her down and she died.'

'No, no, Felicity. Listen, that was not your fault. You were just three years old. Is that what you've been thinking all this time? Blaming yourself? What do you mean. Kate lied?'

'I told Kate my bad secret and she said I was right not to talk to anyone else because my words do make bad things happen and the bad man will come get me or Daddy or you. She said she was the only person in the whole wide world who could keep me safe, so only to talk to her. So why did the bad man come?'

Gregg mocks a horrified expression, points to his chest and mouths, 'Me?' But the girls weren't looking at him.

'Kate actually told you that?' Harper gasps. 'When did you tell Kate your bad secret?'

Felicity takes a big breath and carries on talking in her small voice. 'When she and Daddy started dating. I could speak to Kate because she smelt like mummy. She wears her favourite perfume.'

'Reach for the Stars,' Harper interjects.

'I felt scared that I'd talked to Kate. I couldn't help it; she smelt like Mummy. I told her I thought she was going to die because I spoke to her and that's when I told her why. She said I was doing the right thing. I did something wrong, didn't I? The bad man got us.' The young girl scurries under the bed covers, throwing the duvet over her head.

Harper tries to peel the duvet back, 'No. Kate should never have told you that. None of that is true; none of this is your fault. Talking doesn't summon the bogeyman. Kate has lied to you and I'm going to make her pay for this.'

'Well, hate to leave this happy reunion, but I've got things to do,' Gregg chirps up.

He puffs out some air and shakes his head at that revelation and leaves the room, bolting the door behind him. He jogs downstairs and finds Carla alone in the kitchen.

'Well, I know why that kid is screwed up in the head,' he says.

Carla shoots him an irritated look. 'Whatever, arrangements are made for tonight.'

'What exactly? Don't you think we oughta think about how we're gonna cover up the fact those kids have seen our faces?'

'It's taken care of; the three of them are being shipped out tonight.'

'Shipped out?'

'I've sold them. Where they're ending up, I doubt they'll be free to squeal.'

'Like, as in trafficking? Are we trafficking now? Jesus Christ, Riley. Are you losing your mind?'

'Those kids are too hot to handle now, and I'm not risking my career. I clawed my way to the top and I'm not losing everything. This way I can keep my head down for a bit before starting again.'

'I said you should never have gone after these kids. Why are you so damn stubborn?'

'That Midwinter woman pissed me off, okay? Turning up at my house out the blue snooping, then bumbling around like an idiot in that prison. Fuck her.'

'Trafficking though? This is heavy shit you're piling up.'

Carla flashes Gregg an icy stare. 'Wind your neck in and don't think about standing in my way. The last guy that did is rotting underground. You've no idea what I'm capable of.'

Gregg thinks that Carla is feeling the pressure as he watches her pace around the kitchen. He mulls over what she's said. 'Who've you put underground?' He rubs his chin and collects his thoughts, piecing things together in his mind's eye. 'You fucking bitch. It was Michael, wasn't it? It's like that dweeb Jason said, isn't it? He stabbed him once but you sneaked in and finished him off, didn't you? You didn't want to just keep Jason locked up inside, you actually put him there. Saw your chance to get him out the picture so you could shack up with Andrew. Is this what all this has been about? Seriously? So how's that working out for you? Still gay is he?'

Carla lunges at him and he feels a burning slice into his thigh. She's slashed him with a blade that he didn't see coming. Gregg stumbles back and grabs at the wound to stem the bleeding.

'Remind you of when we were kids? Dead leg Gregg,' Carla sneers.

'You actually killed Mikey? You are so many shades of fucked up, you know that?' He throws himself at her, grabbing her wrist holding the knife. She kicks him with her pointed heel in his shin. With his other hand, he grabs her by the throat, the blood from his hand smearing around her skin. She gets another kick to his shin in, but the rage he feels numbs the blows. He thrusts his knee up, impacting into her stomach. She recoils, but his grip around her throat remains solid. With his other hand around her wrist, he smashes it against the wall until she drops the knife. He stoops to grab it. She launches herself at him with all her strength but she's met with the blade. He plunges it into her stomach; she staggers back. She looks at him, eyes wide. All he can see is hate, and he plunges the knife in again. 'That one's for Mikey.'

Blood dribbles from the corner of her mouth before her legs buckle and she collapses to the floor. Gregg looks up with a start as Charlie and Brian burst into the room. They stop, stunned for a second as they take in the scene before them. Gregg makes eye contact, then they all spot the gun on the table. Gregg is closer; he ignores the searing pain in his leg and lunges towards the table, snatching up the gun a second before Charlie gets there. He fires two shots in quick succession, putting a hole in both Coleman and Brian. Coleman groans so he puts another bullet through his skull.

Gregg kneels at his sister's body, she's gurgling. Not quite dead. 'Well sis, nothing like family to screw your life up, hey?' He swipes the knife back up and slices it into her heart. He sits back on his bottom and wipes his brow, taking in a moment's peace. *Nothing like a bit of peace and quiet.* The pain in his leg is reminding him of the gash in it. He hobbles over to the kitchen drawers and starts rummaging until he finds a dressing that he's able to patch over the wound.

Gregg searches each of the bodies and takes their mobile phones, then heads upstairs. He bursts open Callum's door and waves the gun at him, telling him to move. Callum follows him to the girls' room. Gregg slams open the bolts and practically kicks his way into the room. Both girls scuttle back at the sight of him. He's aware he's covered in blood. Callum rushes to join the girls, throwing protective arms around them both. Gregg opens the door wide and steps to the side.

'Go,' he says, gesturing for them to leave.

They look at each other hesitantly.

'Get outta here. Go,' he repeats.

Callum hesitantly leads the way; the three of them huddle close. As Harper passes Gregg, he stops her, grabbing her arm.

'Take these,' he growls, handing her three mobile phones. 'Hand these to the cops. They'll find everything they need on them... and take this too.' He hands her his own mobile phone. 'You might want to run somewhere other than home. Take it from me, kid. I ain't no saint. I'm a monster, pond life, scum, even the bogeyman. Call me what you want. But your stepmum... she's something else. You want another revelation? She handed you right over to me on a plate. You'll find the messages between us on this phone; I've taken the lock off. You'll see the details: the time, the place, how she'd leave you unattended so we could make our move. You, boy, wasn't planned, but we had to go with it.'

'She wouldn't,' Harper croaks.

'I've just said it to my sister who's had a knife through her heart in more than one way. Nothing like family to screw your life over. Go, scram.'

Callum pulls at Harper's arm. She is holding Felicity's hand tightly. They leave the room.

Gregg shouts after them. 'Turn right at the bottom of stairs and out the front door. Don't go in the kitchen.'

He listens for the front door to shut. They're gone.

CHAPTER FIFTY-FOUR
Harper

'Nearly home, loves.' The old lady twists round and smiles at Harper, Callum and Felicity huddled in the back seat. 'Kenneth, slow down dear. These children have been through enough; let's get them home in one piece.'

The old man driving eases his foot from the accelerator. 'Your faces have been all over the news and the internet. I'll have to have your autographs.' He chuckles.

'Really Kenneth, how can you joke?' The old lady turns again to the back seat. 'He doesn't mean it. What a relief you're all okay.'

'It's okay,' Harper says. 'Thank you for stopping for us.'

'It's not like we had a choice, you jumping in the middle of the road like that,' Kenneth laughs.

'He doesn't mean it. You don't mean it, do you Kenneth? Ignore him, my loves.'

Harper smiles at the lady.

'Just look at his phone,' Callum says to Harper.

She had been toying with it since they'd been picked up. With one arm around her little sister, she turns the phone on. Once it flashes to life, she presses the messages icon. And there it is in black and white. Tears full of hurt fill her eyes.

'How could she do that to us? I never trusted her and could never put my finger on it. But she loved me. She doted on Felicity. How could she be so cruel? What we thought was love was nothing but abuse.' Harper shows Callum the messages.

'Jesus,' Callum gasps.

And there it said it all, just as Gregg had said. Kate had plotted with them to hand her over, without question or anything. Just like that. Gregg had made a threat but Kate responded with *Just have her.* Kate goes on to give instructions. The hurt Harper feels manifests as real pain in her chest and stomach.

'Oh loves,' the old lady says. 'I don't know all that's gone on, but you get the help you need. Sounds like you need looking after.'

'Sure you don't want to go to the police station first, kids?' Kenneth asks.

'No, we need our dad,' Harper says, choking up.

Moments later they are pulling up onto the Midwinters' driveway. Harper sees her dad straight away in the window and he's out the house in a flash. Harper and Felicity scramble out of the car and their dad throws his arms around them, sobbing uncontrollably. When he catches a breath, he looks up at the elderly couple.

Kenneth hands him a phone number he's scribbled down. 'If you need us for anything. We just found them on the road, scared witless.'

'We'll leave you to it. You need your family time,' the old lady says.

Jon briskly shakes both the couple's hands and thanks them profusely for bringing them home.

'Let's get you inside, girls,' Jon says to his daughters. 'Tell me everything, I've been worried sick. Callum, come in. Your parents - we'll need to call them.'

'Where's Kate?' Harper asks.

'She'll be back shortly. The police have been in and out. She's at the station answering all their questions, doing everything to find you.'

'Dad... We need to talk. Felicity has some things to tell you,' Harper says, squeezing her sister's hand.

Jon hands Callum a phone and urges him to call his mum. They head to the kitchen. Harper pulls up a chair close to her sister and their dad sits opposite.

'Go on, Felicity, I promise it will be okay. Tell Dad everything you told me. You can do this.'

Felicity starts to speak in her small voice. Harper has never seen such a mixture of expressions on her dad's face. He obviously hasn't slept. He's pale, with dark circles under his eyes. He's been crying a lot, but he looks mesmerised by his little girl who is looking him in the face and speaking to him. Something that so many take for granted. He's full of love yet anger as Felicity's secret unravels. He chokes up and moves around to hold his little girl.

'How did I not pick up on any of this?' he croaks. 'In no way are you to blame for Mummy dying. In no way is it your fault you were kidnapped. Kate has told you the worst lies and I'm going to keep her away from you from now on, okay?'

'Dad, there's more,' Harper says. She is about to finish telling her dad about Kate conspiring with Gregg and Carla and showing him the texts when Kate bursts into the room.

'I thought I could hear your voices,' she gasps, and rushes straight to Felicity. She tries to embrace her but she squirms away and Jon barges in between them.

'Stay away from my sister!' Harper screams at her stepmum.

Kate looks taken aback, the colour draining from her face.

'Did you have Harper kidnapped?' Jon yells, 'Have you been terrorising my little girl for the past two years to keep quiet or bad men will get her?'

Kate looks like she's trying to speak.

'Don't deny it,' Harper shouts.

'You're mistaken, I, I... no, you're wrong. Don't listen to her, Jon. She's always hated me.' Kate stabs her finger towards Harper.

'You're staying away from my daughters. Get out now.' Jon roughly grabs Kate's arm and attempts to march her from the kitchen. She resists. As they pass the kitchen counter she swipes a knife from the stand.

Harper dashes forwards when she sees it, but

Kate was fast. She plunges the knife into Jon's shoulder. He falls back in surprise, releasing his hold on her. Felicity screams.

Harper grabs a chair and raises it in defence at Kate who is now pointing the knife at her. Jon straightens up clutching his wound with one hand and raising the other.

'Don't hurt her, Kate. Put the knife down.'

'None of you have ever loved me for me,' Kate growls.

In one sudden movement, Callum charges in, rugby tackling Kate to the floor. Harper throws the chair down and stamps on Kate's arm, which is trying to wave the knife at Callum. Kate is screaming like a caged animal and Jon joins in the effort to restrain her.

Harper calls over to her little sister. 'Can you get the phone? Hurry.'

Felicity hops from her chair and brings the house phone back to the kitchen, but she doesn't hand it to anyone. She dials 999 and asks for the police.

Harper couldn't be prouder. From being too terrified to speak to anyone since her mum's death, her little sister has done more talking in a way that she should never have to do. The police are bursting in within minutes - they were on their way back to the house anyway. They move swiftly, getting Kate off the floor and into handcuffs.

'The paramedics will be here any minute,' PC

Stokes says. He sits Jon down, pressing a towel against his knife wound to stem the bleeding.

'Get her the hell out of my house,' Jon says forcefully.

Kate is led away under caution.

Harper hugs her sister. 'That was so brave of you,' she tells her. 'Here's a big sister promise to you. There are bad men and there are bad women, and I will never let any of them near you again. We'll prove to that nasty man, Gregg, that our family is strong, and we won't screw each other over. He's wrong. Do you trust me?'

Felicity smiles, nods, and hugs her. 'Are you okay, Daddy?' she asks, looking at Jon.

Harper and her dad cast a knowing look at each other. They both feel overwhelming pride for Felicity.

'Yes, it stings a bit. I'll be right as rain,' he reassures her.

Harper bends a little to listen closer to her sister, who's tugging on her arm to tell her something else.

'I don't think I want a dog called Kylie anymore,' she says.

CHAPTER FIFTY-FIVE
Gregg

Gregg whistles along to some tune on the car radio that he doesn't know. He feels a kind of release, a weight lifted, so he whistles with the windows down and the breeze in his face. He's ignoring the blood seeping through the dressing on his thigh. Six hours or so until he reaches Scotland, then he'll drive some more and keep on going until it's just him and the mountains. Starting a new life is never going to be an option for him now, he knows it. He's not just a kidnapper now, but a killer, and his DNA is every- stinking -where. There are witnesses, and those kids will have handed his phone over to the police by now. He knows he's screwed, but he'll keep driving and whistling. He'll reach the mountains, pure isolation and peace, take in the scenery, then face what's coming. That's if he doesn't drive himself off one of those mountain cliffs. He smiles to himself. He hasn't yet decided.

CHAPTER FIFTY-SIX

'Sorry to keep you again, Mrs Midwinter, but you're creating a lot more paperwork for me. The accusations against you are stacking up.'

I'm numb now to Detective Matthews's smug expression. I'm not even going to argue with him. There's no point. I've lost.

'You'll have a solicitor with you shortly. We have evidence that you conspired with Carla and Gregg Riley, to kidnap your stepdaughter, Harper. That's a serious charge. Do you have anything to say to that?'

I shake my head.

Detective Matthews looks unimpressed, 'Are you admitting that you handed Harper over to a criminal gang, knowing that she'd be gang-raped and beaten?'

I stare at him for a moment. He'll never understand the anger I felt, the betrayal that consumes me. Why even try? I felt sick when the realisation sank in that Harper had been taken, when I saw she wasn't in the hospital car park – that it had actually happened. Adrenaline surged through me, and I did question myself. What had I done? But that girl had always hated me. She thought I was having an affair, for Christ's sake. *Me*. She set out to destroy me and her father. She hated me that much. She interfered and she had to pay. I tried to love her, I really did, but it was never good enough, I was never good enough for her. She abandoned Fizzy; it was only right she went back to them to suffer.

'Yes,' I simply say.

He draws a deep breath, 'You are also accused of child cruelty. Emotionally blackmailing your stepdaughter, Felicity Midwinter; keeping her under your control by tormenting her not to speak to anyone but yourself.' Matthews raises his eyebrows at me.

I think back to the first day I met Fizzy, this little sweet girl sitting next to me on our bench at the park. She asks me about the book I'm reading then she tells me I smell like her mummy. Jon jogged over, looking flustered, and it was love at first sight. I got used to being important to Fizzy as time went on. I wanted to bottle that special feeling of being needed and loved. Jon told me that I was a gift, something precious. I'd never felt that way before and I couldn't lose it, I just couldn't. I didn't try hard to keep Fizz's selective mutism from improving. It was easy. She was a terrified little girl.

I didn't want it all to end like this. I'd lost my grip; I know that. Feeling cherished and special hung by a thread. Fizzy was blurting out more words here and there, Harper had it in for me, no matter what, and I couldn't compete with Jon's dead wife. He was still thinking about that rotting corpse more than me. I shift in my chair at the thought of them all at home now, hugging and talking, relieved I'm no longer there. It's too much. I slam my hands down on the table and feel my shoulders shudder under the weight of my tears.

I wipe my eyes and look at Matthews with his icy stare. 'You wouldn't understand how she made me feel. She was my little silent Midwinter. Just mine.'

The End

LETTER FROM THE AUTHOR

Dear Reader,

Thank you for choosing to read The Silent Midwinter. It is my debut psychological thriller and it means a great deal to me that you gave it a chance. If you enjoyed the book, please consider leaving a review, it gives independent authors a huge boost.

Every effort has been made to ensure this book is in good shape, however some typos can slip through the net. If any are spotted and it slows down the enjoyment of the book for you, then please get in touch and amendments can be made. I am active on social media, just search for Jamie-Lee Brooke Author on Facebook, Instagram and Twitter for all of my news and updates.

Many thanks for reading!

ACKNOWLEDGEMENTS

I have so many people to thank that it makes me feel eternally grateful that I had so much support in putting this book together. I want to say thank you to my wonderful proof reader, Anna Wallace, who I learnt a great deal from and a big thank you to Dee Groocock of Stellar Reads for her editing skills. Also thanks goes out to Kate Eveleigh for additional input. Special thanks also goes to Zoe O'Farrell of Zooloo's book tours for championing me along and organising an outstanding book tour for me.

Next I come to my amazing group of beta readers who's early insight helped me to shape the final story. Big thank you to Sarah Leck, Deb Fellows, Kate Middleton, Sarah Federici, Vanessa Morgan, Carla Buckley and Phil Price.

Extra special thanks goes to my author buddies who not only read an early draft of the book but have also consistently been my biggest supporters, cheerleaders and my rocks. So huge thanks to Carla Kovach, Phil Price, Julia Sutton and Abigail Osborne.

A final thank you goes to all of the wonderful readers, bloggers and reviewers for their enthusiasm and support.

BOOKS BY THIS AUTHOR

Blind House

Fame is about to get deadly in this terrifying, fresh take on a haunted house thriller.

Set in an idyllic Cotswolds village, rookie paranormal investigator, Megan Forrest, is roped into investigating the strange goings-on at the home of Hollywood actor, Ross Huston.

Ross and his wife Deborah are convinced that their Victorian mansion is being haunted by the mentally ill patients who resided there in the late nineteenth century.

Patients who were brutally treated and murdered at the hands of a cruel doctor.

As Megan investigates ghosts from the past, two women from the present go missing- women who were last seen at the Huston's property. Who was the doctor and how is everything connected?

When Megan finds herself swept up in a dangerous game, she can't escape.

Who was the Doctor?
One thing she knows for sure, is that there is something watching her...

Printed in Great Britain
by Amazon